NOTHING SACRED

DAVID THORNE

CORVUS

First published in Great Britain in 2015 by Corvus,
an imprint of Atlantic Books Ltd.
This paperback edition published in Great Britain in 2015 by
Corvus, an imprint of Atlantic Books Ltd.

10 9 8 7 6 5 4 3 2 1

A CIP catalogue record for this book is available from
the British Library.

Paperback ISBN: 978 1 78239 365 8
E-book ISBN: 978 1 78239 364 1

Printed and bound by Novoprint S.A, Barcelona

Corvus
An imprint of Atlantic Books Ltd
Ormond House
26–27 Boswell Street
London
WC1N 3JZ

www.corvus-books.co.uk

NOTHING SACRED

David Thorne has worked as a writer for the last 15 years, originally in advertising, then in television and radio comedy. He has written material for many comedians, including Jimmy Carr, Alan Carr, David Mitchell and Bob Mortimer. He was a major contributor to the BAFTA-winning *Armstrong and Miller Show*, and has worked on shows including *Facejacker*, *Harry and Paul* and *Alan Carr: Chatty Man*. *Nothing Sacred* is his second novel in the Daniel Connell series.

NOTHING SACRED

1

GABE AND I are coming back from the coast, Gabe driving too fast through flat country under a low blank grey sky, heading for the arterial road that will take us home. Gabe is telling me once again about the size of the shark he pulled out of the North Sea three hours ago, the shark writhing and bucking, Gabe managing to control it in both arms on the rocking deck long enough to give a proud predatory grin to the photographer, which was me. I let him boast as the road rushes past, branches slapping the wing mirror next to me as he cheats blind bends; it is good to see him happy, living in the moment, relishing a battle that he can still fight.

We have been out on the boat of Harry Rafferty, a man who I have known for years, ever since I was a child. Our fathers had been friends, both of them part-time villains and full-time drinkers; we had been their neglected sons. Together we spent hours half-heartedly kicking a football around weed-ridden pub car parks, waiting for our fathers to emerge, desultorily participating in the fiction that this was normal, that this was what all children did on Saturday nights; that we were in no way different.

For a while Harry went the same way as his father, running with a neighbourhood crew and nearly going down for the firebombing of a local nightclub in which a young woman was terribly burned. But, like me, he eventually managed to escape the gravitational pull of his suburban Essex upbringing and connections, moving to the coast where he now runs an apparently legitimate charter fishing business.

He has one of the fastest boats coming off the Thames Estuary, with twin 400 horsepower diesels which he did not waste time pointing out; he told us that they were for reaching the fishing grounds faster, no point fucking about getting to where the sharks were.

'More time for the punters to get their lines wet,' he said.

'That right?' I said. Harry wore a battered cotton skipper's cap and a sweatshirt that read *My Boat, My Rules* and a smile that was far harder to read.

'Why else, Danny?'

'Never taken it to Spain? Over to Holland?'

'Why'd I do that?' As he said this his eyes crinkled and I could not help but smile back, Gabe chuckling behind me. The man is a rascal. I do not believe for one moment that his boat has never taken on illicit cargo, that it stays in harbour every night there is no moon. But his history is, to some extent, my history and I cannot moralise, even if I am a lawyer by trade. What he does is his business, not mine.

'So, what are we fishing for?' Gabe asked him.

'Smooth hounds, tope, skate. Bass on lighter tackle. Be a good day out. Trust me.'

'Think we'll catch anything?' I said.

'Your mate, definitely. What I remember of you, Danny son, you couldn't catch fucking clap.'

Going on a fishing trip had been my idea, a way to reconnect with Gabe, my best friend but a man who has not been the same since he was invalided out of Afghanistan, a captain of the Royal Tank Regiment who would never command a platoon again. Some men never find their calling in life; for Gabe, being in the army was the only thing he ever wanted to do and, once in it, I believe that he loved it ardently and unquestioningly. To lose it has been his undoing, a grief he cannot come to terms with.

'Fishing?'

'Be fun. Day out.'

He frowned, like fun was a dirty word, frivolous, nothing that he would willingly entertain. He looked at me, then shrugged. 'Sure, all right. Fishing. Whatever, Danny.'

But it was not long after Harry had opened up the engines and the boat was bouncing over grey waves like a pebble thrown by some delinquent giant that Gabe was smiling into the spray, holding tight to the guardrail as we left the Thames Estuary and headed out into the North Sea. Adrenalin is adrenalin, even if it is not being supplied by the British Army, and when he got his first bite, his reel shrieking as a big fish took thirty metres of line on a vicious run, I do not doubt that he was having fun.

It was the last cast of the day that landed Gabe his shark; even Harry, who cultivated a careful air of seen-it-all weariness, could not help but let out an agitated *'Fuck me'* as he watched the dark outline of the shark arrowing beneath the boat. What Gabe lacks in my blunt strength he makes up for in determination; even fishing off the one leg he didn't leave in Afghanistan, there was no doubt about the eventual winner of the fight. I do not imagine that Gabe has ever given up on anything in his life. And as he held the shark in his arms, I knew with a relieved elation that he was not a lost cause, that he still held the capacity for joy.

He laughed as he struggled to hold the big fish and Harry told him to fuck off, how he'd caught one twice the size off the coast of Ireland, at least twice the size. Then I took his photograph and things, for that one instant, were blameless and entirely good.

Now we are back in his car and Gabe is mocking me for the fish I did manage to catch: several runt-like smooth hounds, like miniature sharks, and a skate which, as Harry told me, broke all kinds of records; unfortunately the wrong kinds. But it is good to see Gabe laugh, good to see him take pleasure in an ordinary day, and I do not mind his ridicule. Anything is better than the cloud he has been under for so many months. My phone rings and I check the number. It is a client, one of my only clients, and I cannot afford to not give him my full professional attention. But I am out of the office and the man calling is Aatif, a Pakistani national whose visa application I am trying to push through. I do not feel like pointing out to him that having an unexplained Somali entrance stamp on his passport is always going to set alarm bells ringing, particularly when there is no exit stamp, and that his application is, essentially, dead in the water. I swear softly, cancel his call.

Gabe looks across at me, amused. 'Work?'

'Some guy, wants a visa to stay in the UK. Got a dodgy Somali stamp on his passport.'

Gabe nods. 'Home Office aren't having any of it.'

'They think everyone's an insurgent. Everything's got to be spotless or there's no chance.'

Gabe doesn't answer. His leg was blown off below the knee by an IED as he led his company on patrol through an area infamous for sheltering insurgents, many of who came from across the border from Pakistan. I speak quickly, fill the silence.

'Anyway, looks like he'll be on his way back home soon.'

'That what you're doing now? Visas?'

'Got to make money somehow.'

'Christ, Danny, you used to be better than that.'

'It's a living.'

Gabe raises an eyebrow. 'If you say so.'

But I have to admit, Gabe has a point. This kind of work is a world away from the cases I used to take on, back when I worked at one of the City's most respected firms. Still, I cannot help but resent his contempt for the work that I am now doing; at least I am working. Since Gabe left the army he has done, as far as I can tell, nothing at all. Yet he has just bought himself a new car, is having renovations done to the house his parents left him that I could never afford. I wonder what he is living on, where the money is coming from.

I know what Gabe is capable of, and I know that he has a need for adrenalin. One of the reasons that he loved the army so much, I believe, is the buzz that killing, or the possibility of killing, gave him. It is a hard thing to accept of a friend that I grew up with, but he has become something harder and far less civilised than he once was. Now he has money and no visible means of support. Not something noteworthy in Essex, where the origin of people's money is so often murky, the subject of rumour and speculation; but worrying in Gabe, who has always been straight up, honest. What is he involved in? I know that I need to confront him about it, get to the truth; but confronting Gabe about anything is not an act I take lightly.

Gabe shifts in his seat and winces. After a cold day on a boat, fighting a shark, I imagine that his leg must be troubling him and feel a brief stab of guilt for expecting him to cope without consequences.

'How's the leg?'

'Still missing in action,' says Gabe, eyes front, his tone closing down the discussion before it has even begun. Still, I cannot help myself; I have been excluded from this part of Gabe's life for too long.

'Just...'

Gabe turns to face me, his cold clear eyes locked on mine, evaluating, challenging, their blue as icy as an Arctic wolf's. 'Yes, Danny?'

'Just worry. You know. About—'

'Hell's this wanker doing?' says Gabe, interrupting, looking in his rear-view mirror. I turn in the passenger seat, see the rear window filled with the grille of a Range Rover, huge and black. It is so close that I cannot see the windscreen above, or who is driving. Gabe speeds up, a surly snarl coming from the exhaust, the Range Rover quickly receding. This car he has bought clearly has a big engine. It cannot have been cheap.

'You were saying,' says Gabe, nothing but challenge in his voice, daring me to keep going. But Gabe knows me as well as I know myself; I have never backed away from a challenge, regardless of who throws it down.

'Nice car,' I say. 'Cost much?'

'Fair bit,' says Gabe. His voice is tight, clipped. Now we are into it. No going back.

'Getting that work done on your house.'

'Noticed that?'

'Wish I could afford work like that.'

'Yes? Maybe you stopped messing about with visas, got some decent cases.'

This is no good; I do not want this conversation to descend into bickering, or worse. I am talking to Gabe because I care, not because I am after a pissing competition.

'Listen, Gabe, I just wonder where you're getting the money.'

'You what?'

I take a breath, watch the road in front, choose my words. 'You've got no job. Your army pension's what, ten per cent of fuck all? And you're spending it like water. Where's it coming from?'

Gabe smiles, a baring of his teeth. 'Oh yeah, now I get it, Danny. Someone you know gets hold of some cash, you think they're, what? On the rob? Selling drugs? No, women? Fuck you. I'm not your old man.'

That is not fair and I can feel my pulse quickening, a dangerous sign. I know all too well where my temper can lead.

We are approaching a bend, the road broadening, and Gabe looks over at me, his eyes fractionally wider than usual so that I can see almost the entire iris, pale blue ringed with a blue slightly darker, their wideness the only sign that he is angry. He opens his mouth to speak and I sense rather than see a dark shadow fall over the car. There is a violent jolt and Gabe struggles with the steering wheel. I think he has it under control when there is another huge impact from behind and the world is a blur past the windscreen, my head whipped back as the car spins around. Gabe is still trying to get control but it is as if we have been picked up, spun by some unseen force. We stop suddenly, another impact, this time the trunk of a tree slamming against Gabe's side of the car. Leaves cover the windows, darkness. I am completely disorientated. I do not know where we are, what has happened. The car is suddenly silent. I look across at Gabe who is turning the key in the ignition because the car has stalled. He looks intent, methodical, glances up into the rear-view mirror as he puts the car in gear. I look ahead again and see a man in a balaclava pointing a pistol at us, legs apart, gun held in two hands. The balaclava is black, everything he is wearing is black, he has black gloves on. I look across at Gabe, who is watching the man without expression, and then my door opens and a hand reaches across, unclips my seat belt and pulls me out with an arm around my neck. I am too confused to fight back, and as I am pulled back. I choke and my vision begins to dim but I can see a man smash Gabe's window and Gabe take his hands from the steering wheel in a gesture of surrender which, for some reason, makes me unutterably sad.

I am face down on dirt and I turn my head to see Gabe lying next to me. His face is towards me and I can look directly into his eyes. There is a foot on my back. I see a hand put a gun to Gabe's head and feel a pressure on the side of mine, just above my ear. Gabe's eyes do not react; I can read nothing in them. No fear or anger or confusion. They seem calm. I hear a metallic sound from the gun against my head, a slight jolt. The hand holding the gun against Gabe's head pulls back the slide and it makes the same sound. Gabe blinks at it. There is a momentary silence.

'Ready?' says a voice.

'Let's do it.'

'Sweet dreams.'

The hand holding the gun against the side of Gabe's head pulls the trigger. He blinks again but there is only a click. For the first time Gabe's eyes react. He looks surprised. The gun against my head makes another click as I feel it jump against my skin. The foot lifts off my back. I hear footsteps walk away, a car door slam, another.

I think that everyone has gone when a voice directly above us says: 'Last chance. That's the message. We won't ask again.'

I hear his footsteps walk off, then an engine start up and a car pull away. Gabe and I just lie there for five, ten seconds, not moving, as if there is somebody still standing above us and if we look he will kill us. Perhaps there is. But eventually Gabe shakes his head against the dirt and pushes himself up with both hands onto his good knee and then onto one foot, the prosthetic foot following. He is as clumsy and awkward as a new-born foal getting to its feet for the first time. I turn over and sit up, hands around my knees.

'Well,' says Gabe.

'Yeah,' I say. I cannot say anything else. I have no idea what just happened.

'Just to be sure,' Gabe said. 'We are still alive, right?'

We are in Gabe's kitchen, sitting opposite one another with a bottle of Scotch in between, drunk down to the top of the label. It is all he has to offer, though right now it is exactly what I need.

I have been in this kitchen so many times in my life, from a young teenager upwards, and still I miss the presence of Gabe's mother fussing about us, offering us cake, biscuits, the smell, and the feeling of warmth and care. But she has been dead five years now, Gabe's father following soon after.

'Feeling better?' he asks.

'Blinding,' I say. The Scotch is doing its work, a warm tingle from my heart through to my arms and legs, up the back of my neck into my head. Already what happened is losing its menace. I survived it, I am alive, thus it cannot have been so serious. Except that, of course, it was. Gabe is gazing at me with professional concern and I know that I have to put my hands up, confess what I know. I owe it to him.

'Gabe...' I hesitate.

Gabe picks up the bottle, carefully pours us both a top-up, nods me to go on. How is it that his hands are not shaking?

'What just happened.' I smile, comes out more of a culpable grimace. 'Listen, it was me they were warning off. Shouldn't have been you there. Involved. I'm sorry.'

'After you, were they?'

'I'm into something. Something pretty big.'

Gabe nods slowly. Frowns. 'Anything to do with the military?'

'Military? No, nothing like that. Something... It's complicated.'

Gabe holds up his drink, looks at me through the glass. 'That was a military manoeuvre. The way they took us off the road. Couldn't have been anyone else.'

'Gabe, this thing I'm involved in... It's serious.'

'Not saying it isn't. Just saying. They were military. Or ex-military. One of the two.'

I shrug, take a drink. 'Maybe they're hiring out. I don't know. Listen, Gabe, I'm sorry.'

Gabe puts his glass down on the table, rests on his elbows, fixes me with his eyes. 'Danny, you're not the only one with troubles. I'll give you a hundred to one those jokers were after me.'

I am about to take a drink, stop, frown. 'Yeah? Why?'

'Seems we've both got problems.'

'It'd have to be a pretty fucking big one for them to do that. I mean, shit, Gabe, those guns.'

Gabe nods seriously, looks down at the table, back at me. 'Pretty fucking big.'

'So what is it?'

Gabe shakes his head, smiles, takes a drink. 'No, go on, Dan. You first. From the beginning.'

2

AT ONE STAGE in my life Victoria Lowrie had been a vision of beauty so rare that it was as if she possessed magical powers. Often, men would not even dare to look at her, and everything came so easily to her that she treated life like a game that she could never lose at. I remembered once she told me that she had spent a week in Marbella and had never bought a single drink; that she could not remember the last time anybody had said no to her. Back then, I imagined that she was charmed, that there were perhaps only a handful of women like her in the world. But we believe many things when we are young, when we have not yet learned that there is nothing inviolate, nothing which life cannot beat down and destroy.

As I looked at her across my desk and wished that I kept a box of tissues on it, it was hard to imagine she could be the same person. I had no claims on beauty or elegance; people, friends of mine, said that in a suit I looked like I belonged outside the door of a nightclub. But compared to Vick I was not doing badly. She looked ten years older than her true age: her face puffed and mottled and strained and,

13

if I was to be honest, unlovely; her once sumptuous blonde hair dirty and limp. But given what had just happened to her, I could not be surprised. She had had a difficult life but nothing, I suspected, that approached this.

'All right,' I said. 'Okay, listen, take it easy. Start at the beginning. Slowly.'

She looked at me, her face collapsed in absolute despair, her misshapen mouth moist and sagging and trembling, and nodded and sobbed again. I sat there trying not to look uncomfortable and waited for her to finish. These moments were what boxes of tissues were for.

'It's... Oh, Danny, it's going to sound so stupid.'

'Doesn't matter,' I said. 'From the beginning.'

'I don't even know... Oh, Jesus, you'll think I'm mental.'

'Just tell me.'

'You know how I used to be... But I ain't like that any more, I ain't. Really. So whatever you think of me, of what I was like...' She leaned forward, made sure that I was looking directly at her, into her eyes. 'I ain't like that any more.'

Vick was, if not my first girlfriend, then the first girlfriend I had who gave me such an intensity of feeling that I believed I was in love. In truth, that feeling may just as well have been jealousy to the point of insanity. I never for one second thought that I was in her league, and spent our entire relationship waiting for her to realise this, find someone better. I did not truly know what kept us going for the year or so we survived; there was nothing good going on between us.

It is said that the ideal relationship is one in which both people complement each other and bring out their positive qualities. With Vick, she brought out nothing in me but jealousy and anger. For her part, she treated me like a lunatic plaything, winding me up and pointing me in any direction she chose, generally with regrettable consequences. Vick was a heavy drinker; understandably, I supposed, given that she never had to pay for them. But when she drank she also became spiteful, like a bored child who wants to know how far she can push things. Talking to other men, inventing outrages, bringing them to me. Me, drunk and as insecure as any twenty-year-old out with a heart-stoppingly beautiful woman would be.

We split up after she claimed a man had offered her two hundred pounds and a gram of coke for a blowjob in a nightclub toilet. After I had been pulled off him, it turned out that he was a flight attendant so camp that for the first few minutes of talking to him I thought he was putting me on. Vick thought it was hilarious, shrieking with laughter as the poor man dabbed aggrievedly at his split lip, asking what the fuck I'd hit him for. Even the barman handing out the napkins could not help but snigger. The guy I'd hit, though, did not see the funny side and threatened to call the police. I'd had to spend all the money I had buying him cocktails before he was mollified. That was enough for me, for us.

But that was then, and I could see no trace of the spoilt, carefree girl of twenty years ago in Vick today. None at all.

'It started with little things,' she said. 'Things that weren't right. Silly things, really.'

'Like?'

'Like...' She took a deep breath, dabbed at her eyes with what was left of her tissue, a sodden ball peeping out of her fist. 'Like furniture moving about.'

'Furniture.'

'Yeah, probably only a couple of times.'

'Like what? How had it moved?'

'Like the sofa's on the other side of the room, that was one time. I've come downstairs...' She paused. 'Come downstairs, and the sofa's...' Her voice rose, a keening wail. 'It's on the other side of the *room*.'

'All right, okay. Calm. What else?'

She took a couple of shaky breaths, composed herself, shut her eyes. 'The other time, the dining room table...' But it was too much and she broke into a sob. 'It's upside down.' Now she sobbed uncontrollably. 'Why's it upside down?'

I tried to look concerned, leaned forward, picked up a pen, made a note. This was not what I trained as a lawyer for.

'Not the kids?'

'They're three and five. Lifting a table?'

'And nobody had broken in?'

'No.' She sniffed, exhaled deeply. 'See, that's the thing. I'm one of them people – you'll laugh 'cos I never was, but nowadays, it's the chain on the door, double-check all the locks. And nothing was unlocked, damaged, nothing like that. And...' She stopped and closed her eyes, thinking back to something she did not want to say.

'What? Vick?'

'On my bedroom floor, in the morning, was this bird. A crow. I stepped on it. When I got out of bed.'

'A crow?'

'On its back. I stepped on it, Danny. How'd it get there?'

I imagined its stiff claws, dull gleaming eyes; imagined its sleek brittle feel as it gave underfoot, its broken-backed untidy posture. Could not help but feel a cold echo of the terror Vick must have felt.

'You tell the police?'

'Course I did. They come over, had a poke round. You know what they're like, couldn't have given a toss. One of them's trying not to laugh, little wanker.'

'What do you think it was?'

Vick's eyes widened and she shrugged. 'I dunno. How do things move around on their own? How do birds get in my bedroom? You tell me.'

'I'm a lawyer,' I said. 'It's not really my thing.'

'I didn't imagine it.' Her voice was rising; she was close to losing it, at the ragged edge of what she could stand.

I held my hands up. 'Hey, Vick. It's okay. Listen, take five, yes? I'll get you a coffee.'

My office was one room and a corridor, on a busy street between a betting shop and an estate agents specialising in renting shitholes out to people who could not afford any better; just another shabby street in the ugly, tawdry brick and concrete sprawl of Essex commuter towns. Coffee was made in the corridor, on a small table. I filled the kettle up with mineral water of a strange brand that I bought from the Turkish shop opposite. This was where I made my living; where I had landed.

Four years ago I had an office in a leading law firm, my own secretary who made me coffee, and I could drink it looking out over the City. My last big case had been a piece of dispute resolution worth upwards of forty million pounds, on behalf of one of the country's biggest construction firms; a West End hotel had been built using materials that would have been outlawed in Honduras, never mind Knightsbridge, and it had been my job to mitigate the losses. Now I was making coffee for a ghost from my past who was asking me to look into a case that not only was worth no money, but was not even within my remit. Furniture that moved by itself, dead birds materialising out of nowhere: it was no business of mine. But for the fact that we had history, I would have shown her the door already. I wondered how I could let her down gently.

'What's Ryan have to say about it?' I asked her.

'Doesn't have a clue.'

'He still got keys to the house?'

'No. He weren't even around second time it happened, was away.'

'Might be trying to get at you.' Her ex-husband was the obvious culprit for something like this, still harbouring pain and anger, looking for ways to get her back. He knew her. Knew how to push her buttons.

But Vick shook her head. 'He ain't like that. And he weren't there. Even if he was, he ain't got a key.'

'Okay. So.' I breathed in. What was I getting involved

in? 'Your furniture's moving around. This dead bird. What happens next?'

Vick picked up her mug, took a trial sip. Hot. 'Next, might be a week later, I'm getting ready to go upstairs for bed, kids are already sleeping, and that's the last thing I remember. I wake up next day on the lawn. Outside. How'd I get there?'

'On the lawn?'

'Had to get little Ollie to let me in. Danny, the chain was still on the door. How'd I get out the house?'

'Can't remember anything?'

'Nothing.'

For the first time I saw fear in her eyes, as well as despair. 'And you weren't...?'

'No, Danny, fucking hell, no. I weren't. Honest.'

Perhaps it was a consequence of all of those free drinks that Vick had enjoyed, but by her early twenties she had become a full-blown alcoholic, with a reputation around town and a bitter hardness developed to counteract the whispers. Her father was also an alcoholic who had long ago lost everything and lived on the charity of his friends or, if not, rough on the streets. So perhaps, too, she had a genetic predisposition to alcohol addiction. Whatever, drink was her downfall. After we split up she had become a model, at first with a promising future but later, as the drink took hold, she moved into the glamour side of the industry, sub-Page Three top-shelf titillation, before she became effectively unemployable.

But I had to give Vick credit: unlike her father, she'd managed to turn things around. She left modelling, married

19

a soldier in the Royal Engineers and now, single again, was working as a teacher's assistant at a local college. She had been sober for years, eking out an unglamorous living a million miles away from where she had once been, the golden girl with the world at her feet. She smiled frailly at me from across the desk, huddled with two hands over her coffee, and I felt a sudden wave of affection for her. We were not so dissimilar, she and I.

One day in my blue-chip, gilt-edged City law firm, I had threatened to break the spine of a senior partner after he had humiliated my secretary, had meted out sexual abuse simply because he could because he was the one in the eight-hundred-pound suit and not her. I believed at the time that I was justified, still believe it now; but word soon got around that I was more thug than gentleman, not the right kind of person for a profession as respectable as the law. My days at the top table were over.

Now we were both in my office, drinking coffee from chipped mugs, two hard-luck stories with only ourselves to blame. Vick sighed, took another swallow of my dreadful coffee, and continued.

'So anyway, that's happened and I'm thinking... I dunno what I'm thinking. I'm thinking something ain't right.'

She was telling me. Furniture moving, now she's tele-porting through walls. 'Vick, this just sounds...'

'I know. I told you. Mental.'

'Strange.'

'Yeah, but then, Danny, what happened this week...'

This was what Vick's story had been leading up to,

what had caused her to sob without shame or control for so long. It was hard to watch a woman who had lost everything that meant anything to her, hard to witness her grief and confusion.

'My kids, Ollie and little Gwynn, my *kids*, Danny... I get up in the morning and they've got these bruises, these fucking *bruises*, all over them. My babies. On their arms, their legs, Ollie's eye. Bruises all over them, and like, I dunno, like marks, like lines, like they've been tied up or something.' She put her head in her hands, shook her head into them.

'You didn't hear anything?'

'No,' she said, muffled through her palms.

'All night.'

She looked up, defiant. 'I'm a mother, Danny. I hear everything. Everything. And I didn't hear nothing.'

'What did they say?'

'Didn't say nothing. I asked them, they didn't know. Just... Come out of nowhere.'

My expression must have given away my scepticism because I saw a spark of anger in her eyes briefly get the better of her grief. 'What?'

'Vick. They didn't say anything? How does that work?'

'Not you and all, Danny.'

'Okay,' I said. 'Okay, Vick. So then what?'

'Then I take them to the doctor and he phones up social services and they fucking take them away.'

Despite Vick's history, despite all that I knew about her, I believed what she told me; believed that she had nothing to do with what happened to her children. Nobody was that good an actor. But this did not change the fact that there was very little I could do for her. I was a lawyer but I had no experience in family cases; I would not know where to begin.

Then I looked over at her, her eyes fixed on me like a child's after they have asked their parents for a Christmas present they know is beyond their means. I thought back on our years, our shared history, and I knew that I could not simply walk away from her. Besides, it was not as if I was weighed down by my caseload. I had time on my hands.

'Listen, Vick, I'll do what I can.'

'I just want to see them, Danny. They won't let me see them. Four days I ain't seen them. Imagine...' She choked back a sob. 'Imagine what they're thinking. Wondering where I am. Who's looking after them?' This last said with a sharp desperation.

'I know it must be hard.'

Vick shook her head at the floor, shoulders slumped. 'I didn't do anything, Danny. I didn't do anything.' And then, quietly, heartbreakingly, a despairing murmur, 'What are they having to eat?'

I stepped from around my desk, squatted next to her, put a hand on her shoulder and felt her warmth for the first time in decades. Took a deep breath, wondering what I was getting myself into.

Said: 'I'll do what I can.'

3

MARIA WAS SITTING looking at me with a satisfied expression on her face; she had just leaned across my kitchen table and hit me on the top of my head with the spoon from her coffee, hard, and it was more painful than I would have imagined, although I tried not to show it. Her expression proved her intent: she had meant to hurt me. This was a new experience for me. I was not used to being hit without retaliating.

'Hell was that for?'

'Everybody celebrates their birthday, you big ape. Unless they're psychopaths.'

'I don't.'

Maria looked at me critically, head to one side. She crossed her eyes stupidly, though it made her no less beautiful. 'Psycho.'

'Childish.'

She got up from the table, picked up her mug, went to the sink. 'Come on, Daniel Connell. I've booked.'

'I don't do birthdays.'

Maria had her back to me and she put both hands on the edge of the sink and sighed. I felt bad but it was true:

I could not remember the last time I had done something to celebrate. When I was eight or nine my father left me alone for the weekend of my birthday, went to Brighton or Blackpool or some other garish coastal town for forty-eight hours of drinking and fighting, putting the fear of God into the locals. I remembered eating cold beans in the blue light thrown out by the TV, wondering what lay beyond its weak illumination, certain that some malign presence lurked in the corner of the living room. I did not leave the relative safety of the sofa for hours, shivering because I would not dare fetch a blanket. When my father returned in the early hours of Monday I was still there. He claimed that he had asked a friend to stop in, check on me. He never mentioned my birthday. And I had never paid it any heed since.

Maria, though, was not a lady who willingly took no for an answer.

'If you don't come,' she said, turning from the sink, a vegetable knife in her hand, 'I'll cut your throat as you sleep.'

I could not think of a decent answer to that.

Earlier, Maria had given me a card and a watch, looked on with trepidation as I unwrapped the paper, opened the padded leather box, tried it on. I had not expected anything, was for a moment stuck for anything to say. What do people say?

'Thanks,' said Maria, breaking the silence, eyebrows raised, nodding encouragement. 'That's traditional.'

'Thanks,' I said.

'Like it?'

'I love it,' I said, and although it sounded simple and trite it was true. This was enough, just this, to be here with Maria right now.

'How'd you know it was my birthday?'

'Looked in your passport.'

'How did you find that?'

'With difficulty. Had to look everywhere. Who keeps it in the kitchen?'

I had no answer to that either, but smiled at Maria's easy assumption that she could look where she liked in my home, do as she pleased. I did not know anybody, had never known anybody, who treated me with such nonchalance, showed such casual disregard for boundaries. I put the card on the mantelpiece in my living room, where I had to admit it looked a little lonely.

'Wow, Mr Popular,' said Maria. 'Not even one from Gabe?'

'Not a card person, Gabe.'

'No,' she said. 'No, you may have a point there. How is he, anyway?'

'Honestly? No idea.'

It was a good question, and one I wished that I could answer. For a man who'd had, for the last twenty years, a clear mission, I worried that Gabe was left bereft now, marooned in civilian life entirely without direction or goal. Since he had been released from Selly Oak hospital, his ragged leg wound patched up and healed and his prosthetic limb fitted, he had spent most of his time at home, alone. He was used to army routine, surrounded by his men, giving and following orders. Now he had no job, no income, nothing to lend him pride or dignity. I knew that it could not be easy.

But recently, in the sporadic times that I had seen him, I had noticed a change in him; an air of purpose, a contained stillness he used to wear like an aura when he came home on leave, still in uniform, fresh from Bosnia or Iraq or Sierra Leone. I had not asked him what he had going on, did not consider it my business. Yet I could not help but worry, and I hoped that whatever he was now involved in, it was not destructive. Turning trained killers loose in society without job or role after decades of fighting could have, I knew, dangerous consequences. I promised myself that I would visit him, check on him, do it soon.

Although we were in April, it was cold outside; we seemed locked in an eternal winter, spring attempting an entrance and then quickly retreating as if the flat frozen land was not ready, the low sullen skies unwilling to open up and let the blue in. Still, Maria, like any good Essex girl, did not wear a coat; she might have been a respectable primary school teacher but when she was going out, she was doing it right. She was wearing a short skirt, heels and a top that was, I suspected, created with clubbers in the Balearics in mind; her long dark hair was down, curling over her shoulders, and she looked fantastic.

'Not cold?'

'Idiot. Course I am. Can you walk faster?'

Maria had booked at a Mexican restaurant around the corner from my home, its authenticity only slightly marred by the fact that it was staffed almost exclusively by Eastern Europeans. But it was close and the food was good, the atmosphere friendly, and besides, I was out with Maria. I did not greatly care about anything else.

'So, what's going on?' said Maria as we sat, a waiter pushing in her chair, Maria thanking him with a smile that I was willing to bet had made his night.

'Going on?' I picked up a menu. 'Nothing much.'

'Something's up. Work?'

'No.'

Maria pushed my menu down, looked at me sternly. 'You lie. Come on, Daniel. You can talk to me. It's kind of the point of this, you know? Of us.'

Us. The matter-of-fact way she used the word, as if it was natural that we were together rather than it being some lucky accident of fate I would never have believed had I not been sitting here, right now, opposite her. I could not accustom myself to it: us, we, a couple.

But perhaps she was right, it would help to talk through it with her; perhaps that was the point. So I told her about Vick, about what she had said to me in my office. Watching Maria's face as I told the story was a lesson in the powers of empathy, her expression changing from intrigue to shock to horrified pity as Vick's children were taken away from her. After I had finished, she sighed, shook her head.

'What she must be going through.'

'Yeah.'

'Sounds… I don't know what it sounds like. Gives me the creeps. Her, alone in that house.'

27

'Never seen anyone so desperate.'

'With all that happened. Things moving around, the way she woke up outside. Then the kids. What next?'

I had not thought of it like that, put down my glass. 'How d'you mean?'

'Well, like it's escalating, isn't it? Getting worse.'

'You think?'

Maria took a long sip of wine, thought about what I had told her, her eyes unfocused as she put herself in the place of Vick, tried to feel what she must be feeling. She shook herself out of it.

'What are you going to do?'

'Don't know. Speak to social services. Apply pressure.' I shrugged. 'Christ knows.'

The truth was, I did not know where to begin with Vick's story, did not have the first idea what horror had violated her life. I was not superstitious but what was happening to her sounded like it had more in common with the supernatural realm than the legal.

For a respectable primary school teacher, Maria could put away a lot of tequila; after we had left the restaurant, she insisted that we did not call it a night, that we went on to a bar. She pointed one out across the dark street, *Karma* glowing in purple neon. We were arm in arm and she tugged me along.

'Not that one.'

'Too classy?'

'Really, Maria, not that one.'

'Oh.' She heard my tone, looked at me suspiciously, put on a deep voice. 'Got a beef?'

'Something like that. Let's try somewhere else.'

'Really?'

'Really.'

The bar was owned by a local gangster called Vincent Halliday, a man who I had not seen or spoken to for months but with whom I had a history. To walk into his place would be a crazy provocation. There was no way I was going through those doors, not tonight. Aggravations, resentments, old scores; it sometimes seemed to me that my Essex home was built on these, as much as on hastily concreted marshland.

'Okay, I won't ask. Let's try that… what's it called? The new place.'

I must have looked unwilling, because Maria gave me another tug. 'Come on. What's the worst that can happen?'

I was coming back from the men's, where four or five kids of school-leaving age had been crammed into a cubicle, giggling over their first lines of coke, swearing and snorting. The bar was dark, and the music was loud and there was an atmosphere of dormant aggression; the clientele was too young and too drunk and still had too much to prove, and I was too old to be in a place like this. Maria was at the bar and a man, no more than twenty-four or -five with a white t-shirt, fake tan and whitened teeth, was talking to her, laughing and leaning in too close to her ear as he shared whatever he imagined passed for wit. Maria noticed me as I approached, rolled her eyes at me, pulled away from him.

'It's all right, Daniel, this gentleman was just leaving,' she said.

The man might have been young but he was taller than me. He looked me up and down, apparently unimpressed by what he saw.

'This yours, is it?' he said to Maria. I could only assume he was talking about me. He did not smile; clearly he saved his good humour for the ladies.

'So go on then,' I said. 'Leave.'

He had gym muscles under his t-shirt, his triceps unnaturally pronounced. Behind him I noticed two other men taking an interest: his friends, back-up, one of who had the neck, shoulders and acne of a serial steroid user.

'Think she prefers me,' the man said, putting an arm around Maria's shoulders. He was drunk and I suspect more besides, but this was too much, way too much. Before I could do anything, though, Maria shook his arm off, turned to him.

'Don't make me call your mother,' she said with nothing but contempt in her voice. She turned to me, said firmly, 'We're going, Daniel.'

'Jog on then,' said the man, making a show of dismissing us. He turned back to his friends, muttered, 'Slag anyway.'

Maria walked away but I did not follow, not immediately. My upbringing and, I had come to accept, my innate character made me incapable of ignoring such a disgraceful insult; I could not, like Maria, excuse the man's casual disdain. I stood there and he must have felt my presence because he turned back around, said, 'What?'

I put my left hand around his throat, worked my thumb into the space behind his jaw, underneath his ear. His eyes widened in shock at my strength. He put both hands on my forearm to push my hand away and for the first time realised my mass, what he had got himself involved with. It was almost as if I was squeezing the man out of the boy, his eyes looking around for help, for somebody to stop what the nasty man was doing. But his friends suddenly did not want to know. I looked over and they would not meet my eye, the steroid user peering intently at the ice cubes in what remained of his drink, prodding them carefully.

I did not say anything, did not need to. It was not often that I was grateful for the face I was born with, hard and forbidding as it was, but in situations like these it could be a useful deterrent. I saw pain and regret and fear in his eyes, and sensed tears weren't far behind. There, I thought. See what happens?

I let go and the man took a shaky breath and looked down at the floor, tried to pretend he wasn't there. I turned to leave and saw Maria watching me from three metres away, on the edge of a semicircle that had been created by people backing away from what was going on at the bar, from what I might have done. I'd thought that she had left, had not meant her to see this. I shrugged, hands out, palms up: what could I do? She did not react, just turned around and headed for the door. But I had seen her face and the look on it had been anger, and something else which was more like disgust.

Any given Friday night saw any number of couples walking along streets in my neighbourhood, one walking fast, the other trying to keep up, hands busy, explaining, apologising. Tonight, I was the one doing the explaining; Maria was not having any of it.

'You hear what he called you?' I said.

'*He started it*,' said Maria, contemptuously.

'Well,' I said, an attempt to sound moral, 'he did.'

'You were old enough to be his father.'

'So? He thought you were old enough to be his girlfriend.'

'*Danny*.' She stopped, turned; she was infuriated. 'Jesus.'

'What?'

She looked at my face, examined it as if searching for something, some imperfection. 'Do I need to be scared of you?'

'Of me?' I was surprised, shocked. 'No, Maria. No. I'll always protect you.'

'Not exactly what I asked,' said Maria, frowning.

'Listen,' I said, but I did not know what to say next, struggled to think of the right words, wondered how I had got things so wrong. Seeing my confusion seemed to touch something in Maria because her tight face relaxed, something gave in her eyes.

'Don't hit people for me, Daniel,' she said. 'I'm a big girl.'

'Okay. All right.' I could not go as far as to say sorry. I wasn't, not really. Regardless of what Maria said, he'd had it coming. 'Anyway, I didn't hit him. Just...' What had I done? I shrugged. 'Squeezed a bit.'

'Squeezed,' said Maria sceptically, but her anger had gone and despite herself she smiled at my half-hearted justification, then laughed at what I suspected was my hapless expression, a warm, generous despairing chuckle.

Cars hissed past us, a chill drizzly rain sparking coldly through headlights. Maria shook her head at me then leaned over and kissed my cheek, took my hand and turned and led me, gently but with a purpose that I dared not question, back from where we had come, through the dark and the drunks and the dramas, back to the quiet street where I lived.

4

NEXT MORNING I woke up to find Maria gone and panicked for some seconds, imagining that she had left me, that what she had seen last night had caused her to change her mind about us. But then I heard her clattering about in the kitchen and soon after her feet on the stairs. She appeared in the doorway with a cup of coffee for me, wincing at her headache, blaming me, us, the world.

I arrived at my office to find a message from Vick on my answering machine, asking for any progress. She sounded, if anything, more desperate than she had when she visited my office. I wondered if she had had any sleep in the last few days. There was also a message from the social worker in charge of Vick's case who said her name was Ms Armstrong, giving me a time to visit; clearly social workers started their days earlier than lawyers.

Looking about my office I realised that I did not have a great deal else to do: no pressing cases, nobody to chase, no clients to report back to. Just a meeting with a social worker about a case I did not want and could not influence. Force of habit had brought me in to work; I ought to have stayed in bed.

Ms Armstrong was middle-aged and white but had her hair piled on top of her head African style, wrapped in a brightly coloured cloth. She was enormous and wore a blue velvety dress that draped over her large breasts nearly to the ground, giving her the shape of a massive bell. Yet despite her bulk she had a brisk energy. She gave my hand a couple of tugs without smiling before turning with a curt 'Follow me', out of the reception and along a linoleum-squared corridor. I had to hurry to keep up with her.

'Thank you for seeing me,' I said to her back, a statement she did not bother to reply to. There were large windows along the corridor and through them I could see a large play area, like a children's nursery, but the children in it ranged in age from two or three to early teens. Some were playing, some writing and drawing at tables, some watching a television attached to one of the walls, which was showing a cartoon I did not recognise. The walls in the play area were painted red and purple and pink, but despite the gaiety of the walls, the children did not seem happy, going through their activities in a desultory way as if through duty rather than pleasure. I wondered if Vick's children, Ollie and Gwynn, were in there; wondered if they had any idea what was happening to them.

We turned a corner, leaving the children behind, and Ms Armstrong opened a door, showed me into a small office. There was a desk, a chair and shelves along one wall with books and box files on them, a window at the end. With both of us in the small room there was little space to manoeuvre and I had to press myself against the shelves to let Ms Armstrong pass me to get to her desk.

'Coffee, tea?' she said, nodding at a waist-high cupboard next to me that had a kettle on it, two dirty mugs, a jar of coffee. It made the facilities in my office corridor seem luxurious.

'Thanks, no,' I said.

She lowered herself into her chair with a sound of exertion, pointed a hand at the chair in front of the desk.

'Thank you for seeing me,' I said again as I sat down, in case Ms Armstrong had not heard me the first time.

She nodded quickly, a little irritably. 'I have to say I do not know what you hope to achieve,' she said, as if I was wasting both of our precious time, as if my presence was an unwanted distraction, which, I imagined, it certainly was. 'There is very little for a lawyer to do at this stage.'

'My client has had no contact with her children for three days,' I said. 'I'm sure you can understand her distress.'

There was a lever-arch file on Ms Armstrong's desk and she opened it, read aloud. 'Multiple contusions, evidence of ligatures consistent with restraint.' She looked at me. 'I'm sure you can understand the children's distress.'

'My client contends that she knows nothing about how these occurred,' I said. I was aware of how pompous I sounded, the typical superior lawyer lording it with elaborate diction. Ms Armstrong exuded an air of decency, of organised goodness; I did not wish to be confrontational. I softened my approach. 'Really, she is frantic.'

Ms Armstrong closed the file and rested both elbows on her desk, wrapped one hand over another, rested her chin on them. It was an oddly masculine gesture, one that made me feel that she was not somebody to be messed with. She looked at me, took a breath.

'It takes as much time as it takes, Mr Connell,' she said. 'I am afraid that these children are now in the system. The system cannot be hurried.' She smiled, something rueful in her expression. 'I am waiting for the psychiatric report. After that we can arrange contact. You might reassure your client that her children are being well looked after and that she need not worry.'

'She does worry.'

'Yes. Well.'

'She worries that they are suffering irreparable psychological harm. Which would be, ultimately, your responsibility.'

Ms Armstrong nodded to herself, turned, looked out of her window briefly, turned back to me. Her demeanour had changed and I realised that I had made a mistake, that I had been wrong to issue an oblique threat; she did not deserve it, and I had lost any goodwill she might have held.

'Mr Connell, those children have already suffered harm. Given the choice between a week's bewilderment here, or returning them home to serious physical abuse, I am happy with where they are.'

I had to admit, put like that, her position was difficult to argue with.

'Mr Connell,' Ms Armstrong said. 'How well do you know your client?'

'Well enough,' I said, wrong-footed by her sudden question.

'You know something of her history?'

'A little.'

'She has a history of alcoholism. Were you aware of that?'

'Yes.'

'Were you also aware that after waking up outside her house, the police found an empty bottle of vodka in her garden?'

I was not. I did not reply.

'Mr Connell. Alcoholics lie. It's what they do; it's the way that they negotiate their way through life. Lie to themselves, lie to their loved ones, their children. They even lie to their lawyers.' This last said with some scorn.

'She is sober,' I said. It even sounded feeble to me.

'Her father was an alcoholic, too. These patterns are repeated, Mr Connell. Time and again. Cycles of abuse.'

As far as I knew, Vick had never been abused by her father. But then, it was never anything we had discussed. Our relationship had been strictly good time; we had taken care not to stray into dangerous emotional territory. I did not know what to say to Ms Armstrong, felt as if she had all of the ammunition in this exchange.

'When will she be able to see her children?'

Ms Armstrong sighed. 'A day, a couple of days. It shouldn't be long.'

I was achieving nothing. I moved to leave but Ms Armstrong held up a hand.

'What puzzles me,' she said, 'is the father. The children should be with him, but he doesn't want to know. Won't even visit them.' She looked at me, frowned. 'Mrs Lowrie tells me that he is a good parent, that he dotes on them. That's what doesn't make sense. What is the situation there?'

Leaving Ms Armstrong, I again had to pass the room full of children. They seemed to be moving in slow motion, lethargic, stuck as they were in this institutional limbo, taken away from their families but their future not yet decided. I thought about my own childhood, my neglectful father; often in my life I had wondered why he had not given up on me, thrown me into care. I now believed that the reason he had suffered me all those years was due to guilt about what he had done to my mother, of what became of her and his part in it; as if keeping me on was his own, prolonged act of atonement.

I wondered, too, about what Ms Armstrong had told me, about Vick and her drinking. When Vick had been in my office she had been sober, I was sure of that. I knew what she was like when she had been drinking, how she behaved. But did that mean she was clean? Like Ms Armstrong said, alcoholics lied. And suffered from blackouts, during which they could move furniture, wake up outdoors. Yet I could not see Vick injuring her children; her grief and horror at what had happened had been sincere, her confusion total. Though if I was honest, there was now more than a shade of doubt in my mind about her story.

But she was an old friend, and past ties are past ties. I could not give up on her yet. Not before I had visited her ex-husband and found out just why he had washed his hands of his own children when they needed him most.

5

MS ARMSTRONG MAY have had a point, regarding cycles of abuse, the father's misdeeds being inevitably re-enacted by the daughter. Perhaps Vick was drinking again, subjecting her children to violence; perhaps her family history meant it was practically preordained. I did not know. But what I did know was that, in cases of family abuse and violence, the perpetrator was more often than not a family member. And if it wasn't Vick, then the next suspect in line was Ryan. A model parent does not leave his children to be taken into care; he does not wash his hands of them. His behaviour did not seem right, seemed suspect. I owed it to Vick to find him, speak to him, see if I could not make some sense of what had happened to Vick and her children.

Vick had given me Ryan's most recent address and I drove there after visiting Ms Armstrong. It was becoming dark and he was living above a shop selling white goods whose brand names I did not recognise, light from the forlorn showroom bright against the gloom of the early evening, throwing a dull shine onto the dirty pavement. The shop was on a busy road and I had to park some streets away, walk back. There was a peeling blue painted door next to the shop and I pressed a metal buzzer, listened for an answer through the grille. But either it was not working or whoever lived inside held no fear of strangers because it buzzed me in without asking my name or business. Inside the door was a pile of junk mail like autumn leaves and I stepped through them and up a dark staircase; I could feel my pupils widening in the half-light. A door opened at the top and I could see a figure silhouetted, long hair, a woman.

'Yes?'

'Looking for Ryan,' I said. 'Ryan Lowrie.'

'Ain't here.'

'Know where he is?' I was reaching the top of the staircase and I could see that the woman was wearing a dressing gown so short that I instinctively averted my eyes.

'Ain't seen him.'

The woman had permed hair and her roots needed attention. Her hair was two colours: blonde at the ends, brown halfway up. She wore no make-up and looked as if she had just woken, although it was almost night.

'You ain't coming in,' she said.

I stopped near the top of the stairs, two steps below her so that I was the shorter of us. I looked up at her.

'Know where he might be?'

'Search me. You his friend?'

'Kind of.'

'Didn't think he had any.'

'Everyone's got friends.'

42

She snorted like I had made a joke. 'I'm getting ready for work. He ain't here.'

'Must be somewhere.'

'Everyone's somewhere,' she said, ridicule in her voice. She looked down at me and sighed. 'Best bet's the bookies,' she said, then laughed. 'Best bet,' she said, amused by her unintentional joke.

'He's gambling?'

'Ain't doing much of anything else,' she said. 'Far's I can tell. He works, he gambles.'

I thanked her and turned on the staircase, headed back down. I stopped, turned back to her. 'Your intercom not working?'

'Yeah. Why?'

'Might want to use it. Can't trust everyone.'

The woman laughed softly, although backlit by the door I could not see her expression. 'Go on, Saint whoever-you-are,' she said. 'Piss off. I've got to go to work.'

She closed the door and I could no longer see anything, blind on the stairway.

I had seen Ryan around, knew him by sight but had never spoken to him. But of course you cannot live in my neighbourhood without hearing things, and I knew a little about him, his history. At one time he had been an inveterate and well-known gambler and, at least latterly, not a successful one; I remembered stories of trouble with local bookies, of warnings, murmurs that he was earmarked for a fall. But that was years ago, when he was still a young man; he had straightened himself out since then, joined the army, made something of himself.

I wondered whether his history of compulsion, and his success in beating that addiction, was what had made him such a steadying influence for Vick. Nobody before had been able to handle her, but he had helped her clean up. I had been invited to their wedding but had not gone; I was not somebody who enjoyed revisiting his past and I had no fond memories of my time with Vick. Still, I had been happy to hear that she had met somebody and that her life was getting back on track. Why, then, was it now so completely derailed? Was it down to Ryan?

Where I lived it sometimes felt that bookies were the only industry keeping the shopping streets a viable economic proposal, although how long-term prosperity could be secured through exploiting the poor and desperate was a strategy I had difficulty understanding. Every third shop had odds in the window, images of horses, footballers, the seductive promise of a glamorous win. I visited three bookies, asked bored young women behind the counters whether they had seen Ryan. One of them did not know who I was talking about. The other two did, but hadn't seen him that day, although they told me that he had been in frequently over the last weeks. Something in their expressions, a softening of their professional indifference, suggested that his was a hard-luck story that touched even their seen-it-all souls.

The fourth was a shabby, carpet-tiled outfit, empty except for a black man asleep on a hard chair underneath a screen that was switched off, and an older white man pushing a vacuum cleaner. He turned it off when I walked in, said, 'Closed.'

I nodded. 'Just looking for someone.'

He looked at the man asleep on the chair. He was snoring. 'Unless you're after Chambers, you're out of luck.'

'Know Ryan Lowrie?'

'Ryan Lowrie,' he said, peering up at the polystyrene-tiled ceiling as if looking for the answer there. He looked at me. He wore thick gold-rimmed glasses, which made his eyes seem huge. Looked like he'd been wearing them since the seventies. 'Don't know.'

'I think you do,' I said. 'Just want to talk to him.'

'And you ain't the only one,' he said. 'Leave me out.'

'I'm a friend,' I said. 'Friend of his wife, Victoria.'

'Yeah?' He wiped a watery eye with a finger, pushing his glasses to one side. He looked back at me, this time with more scrutiny. 'He's married?'

'Was.'

'Things they don't tell you,' he said. 'Why d'you want him?'

'To do with his children,' I said. 'Can't say any more. I'm a lawyer.'

'That right? Don't look like one. No offence.'

'None taken. You seen him?'

'He was in earlier. Hit a good run.'

The man on the chair, Chambers, snored so loudly that he woke himself up. He sat up, looked around him. The man I was speaking to lifted his hand to him, said, 'Home time, my friend.'

Chambers patted the pockets of his leather jacket, re-assured himself that whatever was important to him was still there, got up, unsteadily left. We watched him leave, watched the glass door bang close behind him.

'My clientele,' the man said softly. He did not say anything else, just stood there, one hand on his vacuum cleaner.

'Ryan Lowrie,' I said.

'Yes,' he said, blinking his way back to the here and now. 'What about him?'

'Looking for him.'

'You said. And like I said, he was in earlier. Won big.' He paused, reconsidered. 'Well, won.'

'Know where he is now?'

For the first time the man showed some animation. He took his glasses off, rubbed them on his diamond-checked sweater. 'How the hell'd I know that?'

Fine. I'd had enough; seen the inside of enough bookies, tasted enough of Ryan Lowrie's tawdry life. I'd told Vick I'd help, but everybody has a limit. I nodded, turned to go, put a hand on the aluminium handle of the glass door.

'I'd hope he'd spend it wisely,' the man said to my back. 'Pay some people back. What he owes.'

I turned and the man pinched the bridge of his nose, a sad gesture. 'But people like Ryan...' He sniffed. 'It was me, I'd be trying the casino.'

I have never been to Monte Carlo but once with my previous lawyers' firm we had flown by private jet to Le Touquet, a well-to-do holiday resort in northern France and a weekend destination of choice for high-rolling Parisians. The casinos there had been everything I had expected and more: hushed, dark, swaddled in rich velvet, served by noiseless waiters and ministered by female croupiers in black dresses and gorgeous diamonds provided nightly by the management. One of the managing partners of my firm had lost £10,000 on one spin of the roulette wheel, laughed, bought everybody Champagne. Easy come, easy go.

My local casino had little in common with those places. Two huge Eastern European men gave me the once-over before unhooking a scruffy velvet rope and letting me into a black-painted lobby where a middle-aged woman in a nylon shirt asked me for ten pounds just to get in. I handed it over and pushed through double doors that shared a wire-reinforced glass circle.

Whoever claims that casinos are places of glamour and excitement should visit the Four Aces. I followed luridly carpeted steps down onto the floor of the casino, lights up too bright, I assumed so that the management could better keep an eye on the clientele who were, at first glance, anything but high-rolling. Middle-aged men in coats and plastic shoes played one-armed bandits mechanically, like technicians operating machines at the end of a sixteen-hour shift. Past them, croupiers and gamblers put down cards and raked in chips at tables as if they were in a hurry; a hurry to get to the end of a hand, to get the bad news over with. There was an undercurrent of desperation, an absence of joy: people were here not out of choice but compulsion or the lack of any other plausible means of making money.

I did not see Ryan on the casino floor but at the other side of the room was another flight of stairs leading up to a mezzanine. I passed blue baize tables, the smell of sweat and dismal drone of conversation, and walked up. At the top were more tables but here the lights were lower and it was quieter. There was a bar along one wall with backlit optics and a barman who looked up when I appeared. The players were better dressed and played with an intentness which suggested that up here there was more at stake than disappointment.

I went to the bar and ordered a gin and tonic and when it arrived I looked over the tables and the players. I recognised a couple of faces, one an acquaintance of my father's who had done time for importing drugs, I could no longer remember what or how. On a table to my left, next to the balcony overlooking the main floor, I could see Ryan. He was playing poker and there was a stack of chips next to his elbow. There were four other players at the table, facing a pretty croupier who was too good for this place and looked like she knew it. Ryan's stack was higher than theirs. Clearly, the luck he'd enjoyed earlier had continued to the poker table.

Now I had found him I could only wait for him to get bored or run out of money. From what I knew of compulsive gamblers, I'd better hope he ran out of money soon, or I could be waiting a long time.

'You want another?' the barman asked me, arms resting over the bar, both of us watching the action, or what there was of it.

'No,' I said. 'That Ryan Lowrie?'

'Might be,' he said, cagey. 'Why d'you want him?'

Why did everybody ask that? 'Personal.'

'That's him,' the barman said. 'But...'

'Yes?'

'Nothing,' the barman said and turned around, arranged bottles. I sat in silence and drank, watched Ryan push a stack of chips across the table, watched the croupier rake more chips back to him. His luck had not run out yet, or his money. I signalled the barman over.

'Do coffee?'

The barman did not answer, just smiled at the absurdity of my question. 'You know him?' he asked me, nodding over at Ryan.

'Kind of.'

'Listen...' He hesitated.

'Yes?'

'Just, he's damaged goods. Stay clear. 'Specially in here.'

'Owe money?'

The barman nodded. 'In here, it's not what you might call... It ain't exactly Vegas, know what I mean?'

'No.'

'Put it like this. Ain't the management running this place. Not really.'

'Right,' I said, but then his face closed up and he turned away, went back to arranging bottles on the backlit ledge behind the bar. I looked around. At the top of the stairs two men had arrived. They did not look British: too dark, stubble too thick, black leather jackets and jeans, trainers, fashion sense of the Eastern Bloc. They looked around and saw Ryan, walked towards him.

'Friends of yours?' I said to the barman.

He turned back to me, half smiled, something apologetic. He did not want to get involved. He was probably making the minimum wage; I could hardly blame him. One of the men walked to Ryan's table, bent down to him, said something in his ear. Ryan listened, nodded slowly. He slid a chip over to the croupier, said something. She smiled back nervously. Ryan stood up and the man picked up his chips, had to use two hands. Ryan walked towards me, didn't notice me. At the table, the man leaned over, said something to the croupier. She picked up the chip Ryan had slid to her. Put it in the man's hands. He turned to follow Ryan. The table watched him go. I had seen enough. I downed my drink and headed back down the stairs, didn't look back.

I had parked behind the casino and by the time I had got to my car and pulled around in front of the building, Ryan was coming down the front steps, the two dark-haired men each side of him. I stopped, left the engine running. Got out, walked around the car onto the pavement.

'Get in,' I said to Ryan.

He looked at me, took a second to register who I was. Frowned, confused.

'Danny?'

'Who are you?' one of the men asked. He was in his early thirties, short, solid.

I did not answer. 'Get in,' I said again to Ryan.

Ryan moved to go and the other man put his hand on Ryan's arm.

'Let him go,' I said.

Both men looked at me. Both were smaller than me but their attitude and eyes were all purpose and aggression. I did not know where they were from. But wherever it was, I accepted as a given that they had seen more than me. Done more. Done worse, far worse.

But ultimately that was mere hoodoo. The fact was that I was bigger than them. We were on a busy street. Some things were worth it. Looking at Ryan, his bowed head and cheap jacket, I could not imagine that he was. Not to these men. The man holding Ryan let go and I backed up around my car, stood at the door.

'Get in,' I said one more time. Ryan opened the door, slipped swiftly inside like a scolded schoolboy. I lowered myself in, closed the door. Hit the locks and pulled away. In my rear-view mirror, the two men watched me until I turned a corner and disappeared.

I pulled up in the car park of a pub and killed the engine. Ryan had not said a word since I had driven away from the casino. Just looked out of the window, occasionally said something to himself in a whisper I could not hear. I had now been looking for him for hours. He was an absent father, a failed husband, a compulsive gambler. It may not have been fair, but looking at him I could feel nothing but contempt.

'Who were they?' I said.

'People I owe money to.'

'Gambling?'

Ryan laughed, didn't smile. 'D'you think?'

'What were they, Albanian?'

'How'd I know? Who cares?'

'Ryan? I just saved you from a beating or worse. You want to tell me what's going on?'

He took a breath, put a fist against the car window. Turned to me. 'What, four nights ago? I burn out at poker, lose it all. This woman next to me, gorgeous, says, "You want to borrow some chips?" Like, she's beautiful and she's letting me gamble. You know?'

'Uh-huh.'

'So I borrow the chips. Four hundred. Lost it like that. Next thing I know one of those guys, tells me I need to pay back double the next day. Double that the next. You can see where that's going.'

I could see. Ryan Lowrie, caught by the oldest trick in the casino. But I had not come to talk about his problems. He was in trouble; that was his worry. If it had only happened four nights ago, it wasn't anything to do with what had been going on with Vick. And she was why I was here. Ryan picked at a nail, sighed.

'So,' I said. 'You want to tell me about it?'

Ryan looked at me and there was defiance in his eyes. 'About what?'

'What's going on. With Vick, her kids. Your kids.'

'Search me,' he said.

I had an urge to bounce his head off the dash. 'You know they're in care, right?'

Ryan closed his eyes, nodded. The light of the car park was yellow and his face looked sickly.

'So go on,' I said. 'Why? Why didn't you take them in?'

'Please. My flat? You seen it?'

'Know what it's like there? Where they are?'

Again Ryan closed his eyes, for some moments. He shook his head, fast, decisive. 'Safer where they are.'

'What's that supposed to mean?'

Ryan reached out a hand, put it on the dash as if to steady himself, though we were going nowhere. 'Seen me. Life I've got. What kind of security can I give them?'

I watched him in frustration. 'Look at me,' I said.

Ryan turned to face me. He was breathing hard, though from anger or some other emotion I could not tell.

'Did you do it?' I said.

'What?'

'Sneak in, move the furniture? Play with her mind?' His face had turned blank. I thought of Vick, could not help but twist the knife, get a rise. 'Couldn't bear to think of her on her own, maybe got a new man?'

Ryan pulled at the door handle. 'I'm leaving.'

I reached over, pulled his hand away. 'Answer me.'

'Let me out.'

'What I can't understand is, how could you do that? To your own children?'

'You think I did that? You think I could do that? Fuck you.'

I could feel my anger rising, at this man, this weak man. Yet at the same time I could not imagine him doing

53

it, could not imagine him waging some psychological war against Vick. There was something about him, something resigned. This was the man who beat addiction, joined the army, proved a match for Vick?

'Just tell me what's going on,' I said.

'You...' he started, but didn't finish. He opened his door and put a foot out, turned. 'Please,' he said. 'Leave me alone. Leave us alone.'

I took a card out, handed it to him. 'Ryan, I'm here to help. You need anything, you call me.'

He looked at my card I was holding out, thought about it, reluctantly took it. He got out of my car, closed the door, walked away into the night. I watched him go, wondered what more I could have said to him. But I had had enough. It was late and he was not worth it.

6

WE WERE ON court, Gabe and I, and I had just sent down a serve which must have been nudging a hundred and twenty miles an hour, a flat nasty hissing bomb, which made for my opponent's body and which was on him before I'd finished my follow-through, before he could blink. All he could do was fend it off; he shook his head, walked to the net as I changed sides to serve to his partner.

'Serve,' said Gabe.

I nodded, acknowledged him but did not reply. I was in the groove and did not want to break my concentration. I bounced the ball, tossed it up and hit over it, putting on a vicious amount of topspin. The ball jumped as it hit the other side of the court, so high that the guy receiving had to hit his return above his head, a nothing shot, looping and soft and which Gabe, at the net, put away with an ease that bordered on contempt. Our opponents looked at each other and smiled, and I had to give them credit; they were at least losing gracefully.

'Game,' said Gabe, 'change ends,' and limped to the other side of the court. He may have been playing off one leg, and he may not have been able to chase balls out wide, but at the net and on his serve he was a better competitor than most able-bodied club players, and had become as good a volleyer as any I had come up against. He picked up a towel as he passed the net, rubbed his neck, looked at me and winked. I smiled and inside my chest felt a brief blossoming of euphoria at being here, with my best friend, handing out yet another emphatic beating.

Our opponents were two young lads who, I thought with a trace of nostalgia, could almost have been Gabe and me twenty years ago, one lean and agile, the other thick-set and silent and imposing. I guessed they were in their late teens and they came with a reputation, up-and-comers from a tennis club on the coast who had been their club champions and managed a respectable fifth in the county doubles.

They had walked onto court and taken one look at us, an amputee and a bulky bruiser better suited to a boxing ring, and exchanged glances that were so transparently readable they might as well have walked up to us and told us that we had no chance, that the match was already won. But Gabe and I had been playing together for over two decades now and although we were not as mobile as we once were, we could read another player's moves before he had even considered what shot he was going to hit.

Gabe served the first game and we narrowly won it; not by such a margin that our opponents felt a moment of doubt about the final outcome, but winning the first game has its own psychological significance. Gabe hit a beautiful volley to break them in their first service game, and then I stepped up and served so accurately, so viciously and so mercilessly that by the end of that third game their resolve was shot, their pride ruined and their minds set on trying, at least, to keep the score line respectable. I felt sympathy for them; I had been in their position enough times as a young man. But tennis is a cruel game and I decided that this would be a valuable lesson for them: never underestimate your opponents.

Now Gabe was serving for the match, slicing a serve out wide to the deuce court, which, although not fast, pulled the lean player well out into the tramlines. He was returning nowhere but cross-court, so I stepped over to cover the centre of the net and, when his return came, punched it backhand behind his big partner into the open court. Outthought and, ultimately, outplayed; sometimes tennis felt almost too easy, a re-enactment of a million previous points stored deep in some atavistic muscle memory. There is something to be said for age.

'Played,' said the lean guy, shaking my hand at the net. Despite the fact that they had just been beaten six–three, six–one, there was a smile in his eyes. He seemed a fine young man. I held my hand out to his surly partner who had said perhaps five words since arriving, expecting nothing, but he slapped his big hand into mine and, to my surprise, laughed generously.

'Fucking hell,' he said. 'That's what being murdered feels like.'

'You played well,' said Gabe.

'Bollocks,' he said. 'You two took us apart.' He took Gabe's hand. 'Fucking awesome.'

'Buy you a drink?' I said.

He gave me a mock hard-man stare. 'Be the least you could do.'

The big guy was an apprentice electrician and the younger man working to go to university where he hoped to study architecture. They had been playing together for five years, and Gabe and I had to go some way to persuade them to keep playing together for another.

'Never been beaten like that before,' the lean guy, whose name was Jonny, said as I handed him a bottle. 'Thanks. For the beer.'

'You do play well,' Gabe said. 'Don't get down.'

'Know how many times we've been beaten?' I said.

The big guy, Jake, made a show of counting on his fingers, looked up at me like he had the answer. 'Never?'

'Unbelievable tennis,' said Jonny. He paused, said to Gabe, 'What happened to your leg?'

I was surprised and at the same time impressed. Very few people would ask that question of anybody, too stymied by embarrassment; even fewer would ask it of Gabe, a man who is as approachable as an aerosol on a fire.

'Lost it,' said Gabe shortly, turning his head and taking a drink to prevent any further questions. The young guy nodded, mortified, and there was an awkward silence. Christ's sake, Gabe, I thought. Lighten up.

The clubhouse was full of people; it was a Saturday and there were squads on, children playing and parents looking on, other members milling around waiting for the courts to clear to get a game. I nodded hello to George, one of the oldest members and one of the first to have spotted my talent. He winked back.

'So,' Jake asked, breaking the silence, 'got any advice?'

'Practice,' I said. 'Never stop.'

'Like you two need it.'

'You reckon,' I said. 'Know what I'm going to be doing for the next two hours? Feeding volleys.' Pointed at Gabe. 'To this.'

In many ways, Branfield Road Lawn Tennis Club had been my salvation, a place of solace from my home, a place that offered praise and goodwill rather than misery and neglect. I had been accepted and encouraged by people here who were more generous and less judgmental than any I had met before in my life, and I owed them a debt of gratitude that I could never fully repay.

I could not count the number of times Gabe and I had passed afternoons together honing different aspects of our game, critically dismantling each other's ground strokes, serves and volleys before together rebuilding them into more effective, elegant weapons. These memories were, from all of my childhood and youth, the purest and most precious that I held.

Now I was lacing ground strokes towards the net where Gabe was hitting forehand volleys and backhand volleys and drop shots with an almost robotic disdain, pivoting and jumping with his prosthetic leg, exploiting it rather than letting it handicap him. I wondered if he would be able to apply this lesson – that the loss of his leg did not mean the end of ambition – to the rest of his life.

'Bit more depth on the backhand,' I said. 'Too much back-spin.'

'You feel sorry for those guys?'

'A bit. Do them good.'

Gabe hit a backhand, crisper, flat and fast and an inch from the baseline.

'Better.'

'Remember those finals we got beaten?'

'Yep.' I did not even have to ask which finals. As young men Gabe and I had won our fair share of competitions, but one year came up against two boys who seemed to share a connection that was almost telepathic. Technically we were on the same level, but tactically they might as well have been a different species.

'Did us good,' I said.

'Eventually.'

'I think I'm over it.'

'I'm getting there,' said Gabe. 'One day at a time.'

A man had been watching us play for the last couple of minutes; the club was now empty and he was hanging around the edge of the court, looking through the wire fence. He was behind Gabe and Gabe had not noticed him. Now the man was pushing open the wire door, walking onto the court. He was not wearing tennis gear, had on a black nylon jacket, jeans, white trainers. He was young, mid- to late-twenties, short hair. He walked onto our court with an assurance that felt somehow insolent, like every step he took was a challenge.

'Help you?' I said.

Gabe turned and looked at the man and stopped, still. From his reaction I guessed that he must know him. The man picked up a tennis ball and this small act, of holding a tennis ball that belonged to me, seemed like a calculated provocation. He smiled.

'All right, Gabe?' he said.

'What do you want?' said Gabe. I could see that he was gripping his racket tight, his knuckles white. There was a change in the air like the onset of a thunderstorm, a subtle heaviness in the atmosphere. Something was going down of which I had no idea.

'Want? Nothing,' said the man. 'Had a match?'

Gabe did not reply.

'You win?'

Gabe just stood there, not backing away, not approaching, a standoff. He did not say anything.

'We've not heard from you,' the man said. 'Wanted to check in.'

Still nothing from Gabe. I wondered how long he could keep silent. There was something surreal about the scene, a stranger talking, nobody answering, here on a quiet tennis court. The man had something of Gabe about him, an assured yet undemonstrative air of capability. He did not appear aware of any tension.

61

'Wanted to let you know,' he said, 'that we know where you are. If we need you.'

This was too much for me. Gabe may have been able to suffer this man's brash intrusion, but my blood had always run hotter.

'If you don't drop that ball and get off this court—' I began, but Gabe waved his tennis racket to silence me.

'Who are you with now?' said Gabe. 'Left the company?'

The man smiled. 'Out, on to better things.' He rubbed his forefinger against his thumb. 'And don't want anybody fucking it up.'

Gabe nodded. 'You've got five seconds to walk off this court or my partner and I carry you.'

'Touchy,' the man said.

'One,' said Gabe.

The man held up his hands in a gesture of surrender, my tennis ball still in one hand.

'Two,' said Gabe.

The man backed up to the edge of the tennis court, stopped in the steel frame.

'Three,' said Gabe.

The man threw my tennis ball to the ground, derisively, pointed a finger at Gabe.

'Goodbye,' said Gabe, turning his back to him. The man sauntered out of the tennis club, through the two tall bushes at its entrance, an exaggerated swagger to his walk. I watched him go, made sure he was gone, turned to Gabe.

'Friend of yours?' I said to him. He did not answer, but then I had not expected him to.

Later, I was at home in my kitchen with Maria. I had just had a shower and had a glow that only a decisive victory at tennis could give me. Maria also played tennis, had played for the county, and watched me with a knowing amusement.

'I hope you didn't beat them too badly,' she said.

'They'll be crying themselves to sleep,' I said.

'So sad, the extent of the delusion.'

Gabe and I had wrapped things up after the man left. Gabe was no longer in the mood to play and he would not answer my questions: a good day ending in an atmosphere of suspicion and discord. I did not understand what had happened on the tennis court, what had passed between Gabe and the man. This was a story I had no part in.

Still, I could not help but worry. Gabe was into something and he was deliberately keeping me out of it; I could only imagine that it was something illegal, something that I would not condone. Gabe's skills were, essentially, twofold: leading men, and killing them. The former had many legitimate applications in civilian life; the other I did not want to think about.

But I was at home with Maria and I shook off these thoughts. She had cooked and the kitchen was warm and she had opened a bottle of Rioja, poured me a glass.

'Sit,' she said, turning to take something from the oven.

'What is it?'

'Tagine,' she said, placing it on the table and prodding it as you would a family pet that may be dead. 'Supposed to be.'

But I did not care. The simple act of somebody putting food down in front of me, going to the trouble to prepare it for me, was near enough to a miracle that I had to close my eyes for some seconds, compose myself.

Perhaps it was the emotional toll of the last few days, I do not know, but I looked Maria candidly in the eyes and said, 'I don't deserve you. All this.'

Her eyes were so wide that I could see almost the whole iris, green with flecks of grey; her gaze was so forthright and uninhibited that it seemed as if she was showing me all she was, leaving nothing hidden. She reached her hand out to my cheek, stroked it. Said: 'You haven't tried it yet.'

7

THAT NIGHT WHILE I slept peacefully next to Maria in a
bed that felt cut adrift from the world of ordinary concerns,
a blaze started in Vick's home. A lit gas fire in the living
room ignited drying clothes, and within minutes black
smoke from burning material, net curtains and cheap
furniture was covering the ceiling like the roiling clouds of
a medieval vision of the apocalypse, pushing at the edges
of the room before stealing out, into the hall and up the
stairs, silent and stealthy as a team of killers. Vick did not
have her bedroom door closed and soon she was inhaling
the tarry chemical smoke in her sleep, its strange smell
and harsh taste invading her dreams so that she believed
she was confined within her own version of hell.

A neighbour, a Polish man who everybody called Peter
and who worked a night shift repairing rolling stock for the
railway, was passing and saw flames, Vick's curtains falling
in bright embers from around her living room window.
He pounded on the door and, knowing that Vick had children, called the fire service before kicking in the door and
running upstairs, throwing open doors and screaming as

loudly as he could in Polish words that Vick did not understand.

By this time she had inhaled so many toxic fumes that she felt as if she had been drugged and could not tell her legs to straighten. She still felt trapped in some hellish netherworld and that the man in her room was a demon of some kind. He lifted her up, put her over his shoulder and clattered down the stairs through smoke so thick that he could not see his feet or hands, felt as if he had to pass through another dimension before he could get to the front door.

The fire service arrived and put out the fire before it destroyed the house, leaving her front garden a ruin of mud and footprints and black water-filled puddles, the smell of roads being laid, hot pitch and burning. Vick spent the night in hospital with a mask over her mouth, which forced clean pure air into her damaged lungs. The sedative the doctors injected into her arms gave her the first dreamless sleep she'd had in she could not remember how long. When she awoke, a doctor told her two more minutes in that house and she would have been dead.

Now I was sitting at her kitchen table with Vick opposite, an empty glass in front of her, a cigarette unnoticed in her hand. Her hair was dirty and her face still wore traces of smoke, her eyes dark with exhaustion and ingrained soot. It was only eleven in the morning but she was, I could tell, more than half-cut. Probably still sedated, too. She was not watching me; she was looking through open double doors into her ruined living room, where a man wearing a black suit was holding a piece of metal in his hands. The metal was shaped like a Y, each hand holding a branch of the Y so that the stem was pointing away from him. He was pointing it at the walls, which were blackened and inky with sooty edges spreading over the ceiling, gradated as if by a spray can. Her furniture was destroyed, sofa and chairs burned down to their frames, charred springs exposed. The floor was under an inch of water, the patterned carpet underneath it like the dappled bed of a dirty pond.

'Who's that?' I said.

'Quiet,' the man said, as if I had addressed him rather than Vick. He was tiny, maybe five-foot-three, and he had black hair so heavily waxed that it looked lacquered, like glossy tar. He was slim, his face smooth and his hairless hands amazingly small; he looked like a little doll. It would have taken three of him to make one of me. The metal object in his hands twitched as he pointed it into different corners of the room, the water rippling silently as he moved.

'He says there are unquiet spirits,' said Vick. She put her hand on her glass and swayed slightly, as if her glass was stuck to the table, like it was the only stable thing she had to hold onto. I revised my opinion: she was more than half-cut.

'Entities,' hissed the little man. 'We don't call them spirits.' This said as if Vick had used the wrong political terminology, displayed some inexcusable supernatural insensitivity.

Vick and I did not say anything, sat and watched the absurd little man as he put one immaculate black shoe, then another, on one of Vick's ruined armchairs, reached up with his metal object into a corner of the room.

'There are echoes,' he whispered. 'Throughout this room.'

Vick watched him without expression, took an oblivious drag on her cigarette with a shaking hand.

'There is...' The man paused to balance on the charcoaled frame of Vick's armchair. 'Malevolence.'

I could not listen to any more of this. Soon I would either have to laugh at him or hit him.

'What's your name?' I asked as he stepped carefully down from the armchair.

'Salvatore,' he said in an accent that was pure Estuary.

'Bollocks,' I said. 'The name you were born with.'

The little man swallowed and blushed, embarrassed to be put on the spot in front of his client, too gutless to stick up for himself. Given our discrepancy in size, I could not honestly blame him. He was no more substantial than a child.

'Steve,' he said after a few seconds' hesitation.

'You give Steve any money?' I asked Vick, who was still smoking impassively, as if she had no involvement in what was playing out in her own home.

'Fifty,' she said.

'Give it back,' I said to Steve.

'Now hold on—' he started.

'Give it back,' I said, 'and fuck off. Last thing Vick needs is a fraud like you.'

'Fraud,' said Steve. 'Uh-huh. Then explain the bird. The table moving, the demonic injuries. Explain how that fire switched itself on.' He pointed his stick at the gas fire, or what had once been the fire, its black absence.

I could not, and as my silence grew, Steve smiled. I stood up and took a step towards him in the living room. He stepped back, water lapping the heels of his shoes. He took notes out of his trouser pocket, threw them onto the floor, where they floated briefly before sinking into the tarry murk.

'You believe in magic,' I said. 'So do yourself a favour. Disappear.'

'How long you been drinking again?' I asked. I sat back down opposite Vick in the kitchen and passed her a coffee, strong black.

She looked at the clock on her oven, thought for a few seconds. 'About three hours now.'

'Christ sake, Vick,' I said. She would not meet my eyes, stared down at her coffee cup, turned it with her fingernails. I thought about her children, taken away from her, thought about her waking up with a strange man in her room, her home on fire. Could I condemn her for finding comfort in a bottle?

'What did the police say?'

She laughed softly. 'Already think I'm a loony. Told me to be more careful, said not to dry clothes near a fire.'

'Got a point.'

'I didn't, Danny. I wouldn't.'

'Fires don't start by themselves.'

'It wasn't on. I ain't had it on. Can't afford it.' She took a drink of coffee. 'How'd it just turn itself on?'

Again, I could not think of an answer to that. Vick's confusion and fear seemed total, but still. Fires did not start on their own.

'It wasn't magic,' I said. 'Somebody did this.'

'Salvatore,' she said, 'told me this house is bewitched. That it hates me.'

'Salvatore,' I said, 'was talking bollocks.' This raised the ghost of a smile from Vick.

'You can't stay here.'

'Got somebody picking me up. Stay with them.'

'Vick... There's got to be an explanation.'

'If it ain't magic, then I must be mad. Am I mad?'

Seeing one of Vick's tears fall onto the flat surface of her coffee was, I thought, one of the saddest things I had ever witnessed. I left her to weep silently over the steam from her mug, her shoulders gently shaking, for her children she could no longer see, and her life she could no longer fathom.

'I think I must be mad,' she said eventually. She looked up at me. 'Aren't I?'

I was not prepared for this; I had come round to see Vick to tell her about my visit to the social worker, to reassure her as best I could. I had not known about the fire, had not expected to be sitting in her kitchen, trying to comfort a woman who had lost her husband, her children, her home, and who had very nearly lost her life only hours before. I believe that she was still under the effects of her sedation; drink alone could not have given her the otherworldly calm she seemed to possess, as if her emotions were working too far beneath the surface to trouble her exterior. Still, I did not know what I could do, or say. Steve the psychic would probably have done a better job.

She nodded and quietly drank her coffee as I told her about Ms Armstrong, told her that her children were in safe hands, that she would have them back soon, that I hoped she would have them back soon. The truth was, I had little to tell her, very little to reassure her with.

Perhaps it was the mention of her children, but she suddenly sat up straighter and looked at me, said, 'Photos.' With an unsteady panic she opened a dresser in the living room and took out photograph albums, made a sound like the coo of a bird when she realised that they were not damaged, that she had not had that taken away from her.

'You never met Ollie and Gwynn, did you?' The way Vick said their names, lingering on them as if savouring their taste – love showed itself in the quietest ways.

'No,' I said.

'Here,' she said, sitting down next to me at the kitchen table. She put the albums down, picked the top one and put it between us. With Vick next to me, the album open between us, I felt a strange intimacy, as if we were a couple revisiting the highlights of our history together. I wondered how aware she was of the ruins of her home around her; how much of her realised the full horror of her surroundings and situation. She seemed far from rational.

'That's Ollie,' she said, pointing to a shot of a little boy knee-deep in the muddy brown water of the Thames estuary, a spade in his hand and a wide smile on his face. 'And there's the two of them,' holding dripping ice creams and squinting into the sun. On the opposite page of the album was a picture of the two children wrapped in the arms of Ryan.

'Vick,' I said, 'what's the story with Ryan? What happened?'

Vick shrugged. 'After the kids, he didn't want it.' She looked above her at the ceiling for some moments, drifted away into her past. 'He loved to be with me, bought me flowers, so many flowers. Looked after me, did anything for me.'

She leaned forward, picked up a pack of cigarettes, a lighter, lit one. She inhaled, swallowed the smoke with a sad gasp. She looked at her coffee as if seeing it for the first time, lifted it and drank.

'Vick? Asking about Ryan.'

'When I met him I was a mess. He sorted me out. But then, soon's we had the kids, it all changed. I lived for them, and he weren't so... necessary. Least that's what he thought. Changed everything.'

'You know he's gambling again?' I said.

She didn't. She paused, cigarette frozen just before her lips. 'You sure?'

'Saw him the other night. Betting more than he owns.'

She inhaled, exhaled with a frustrated sigh. 'Might explain why he ain't been answering his phone.' She stubbed her cigarette out, screwed it into the ashtray violently. 'Oh, Ryan.'

'You still haven't seen him?'

She shook her head sadly. 'I've left messages, been round.

Nothing. Can't get hold of him. Like he don't want to know.'
She reached for another cigarette. 'Looks like it's just me.'
She looked at me, and lit up in her eyes was desperation
and something else, beseeching, as she flicked her lighter.
'And you.'

I left Vick's house in the late afternoon. As I left her at her
front door, she had looked at me with red eyes and wrapped
herself tighter in her top, said, 'I hate this place, Danny.
It fucking terrifies me.' She'd looked behind her, into her
blackened hall. 'Whatever it is, it's wicked.'

Her friend had arrived, was upstairs packing clothes for
Vick, everything she'd need. But still, leaving her framed in
her dark doorway, I could not help but wonder at what would
happen to her once she had sobered up and the drugs had
worn off. When she had to coldly examine the full horror of
what had befallen her, and what little the future held.

I had nothing else to do that afternoon, no clients or cases
that needed attention, and I drove out east into the flat
Essex country with the dying sun behind me, the skeletal
branches of trees muted in the gathering gloom, dark birds
flapping aimlessly over sleeping fields. The sky seemed vast
and indifferent, and I felt small and insignificant underneath its weight.

Heading away from the lights and dramas of my town felt
almost as if I was travelling back in time, passing red-brick
and clapboard cottages built so long ago that they seemed
part of the landscape, formed in some forgotten past. I had
heard that there were villages in the farthest reaches of

Essex that still blocked up their doors with crossed broomsticks to ward off witches, people who claimed to have seen their forms crossing the night skies, fluttering blackly over ancient village greens. I thought back to Vick, left in a house she believed harboured malevolent spirits; was the best advice I could give her to cross broomsticks over her front door?

But I was not a superstitious man, and I did not doubt that somebody had done this to her, that somebody had tried to kill her. I did not know who or why, did not know how I could help her, but I knew that I could not cut her loose or give up on her. I turned my car around and headed back to civilisation, and the only family I still had. If I needed any reminder that life was, in essence, base, prosaic and entirely bereft of mystery, an evening with my father would supply it.

My father ate food as if it was still alive on his fork and it was only through determined and aggressive biting and chewing that it could be subdued and killed; he attacked his plate of dinner as if it was a threat, like it was personal. As Maria and I watched him, his huge tattooed forearms on the table, massive shoulders hunched over his plate, I could not help but think that this was the way he approached life in general: angry, violent and nasty. He chewed agitatedly and I could see the muscles in his jaws working, bulging under his skin, making a cracking sound with every bite down.

Maria smiled winsomely but I could see in the fixedness of her smile that she was unsettled by my father's presence, by his animal intensity, the subliminal rage he carried about with him. He had no business around a dining table; he held his knife like a weapon.

'More wine, Francis?' she said.

My father, who everybody else in the world knew as Frankie, nodded, still chewing, took a huge swallow of meat, which made his throat visibly swell. 'This, Maria, my darling, is fucking blinding.'

Maria was one of the kindest, most generous and decent people I had ever met. It was true when I told her that I did not believe I deserved her, could not think of anybody who would. My father, on the other hand, was an embittered and uneducated bully who found pleasure in other people's misfortune, who enjoyed inflicting pain and violence. I had never heard him laugh sincerely, had rarely seen him smile. I had seen people cross streets to avoid him.

Now, though, he was doing his best to be polite, listening to what Maria was saying, nodding at his plate, agreeing, grunting responses. I had never seen him behave in such a civilised fashion, was astonished. Maria had my father wrapped around her little finger.

I had not wanted Maria to invite my father to dinner, had tried to talk her out of it; the thought of his presence in my home felt like a violation, as if some of his cruelty might rub off, taint it. I told her what he had done to my mother, the life of humiliation, fear and misery he had consigned her to; gave her details of his constant neglect, the hurt he had subjected me to. But she had not listened, insisted that it was important, that family mattered. Maria's father, a kind Spanish man who spent thirty years cutting local men's hair, had recently died and she visited her mother every other day, cooked for her. I had seen them together and they spoke to each other with love and respect and an ease that made them seem more like sisters than mother and daughter. I suspected that Maria simply could not conceive of the levels of dysfunction and resentment that underpinned the relationship I had with my father; though an evening spent with him would, I thought, likely give her an indication.

'So he's handcuffed to this midget, I should say the midget's handcuffed to him, and the midget's rotten, pissed out of his head, can't stay awake, all he wants to do is sleep, but the geezer, he keeps slapping him on his head, *wake up, I've paid you so fucking* – 'scuse me, my darling – *wake up*. And this midget, he's getting proper fucking angry, proper aggravated.'

Maria nodded quickly, as if to hurry my father along, get this story finished with. My father took Maria's nod for interest, enthusiasm for the details he was recounting. He took a deep breath, shook his head in malicious delight.

'So the midget's gone to sleep again and the geezer's slapped him on the head, and that's it, the midget's had enough and next thing he's picked up a bottle, *smash*, he's broken it on the table and he's stabbing the geezer, *bang bang bang*, course the geezer's handcuffed to this fucking midget and he can't get away, he's screaming, the midget, he's fucking crazy, the geezer's mates are trying to get the bottle off him, oh, it's fucking chaos.' My father laughed, a hacking bark, shook his head again.

'But Francis, that's terrible,' said Maria, an expression on her face as if she had just caught the odour of something revolting. 'Just horrible.'

'Fucking chaos,' my father said again. 'Oh dear, oh dear.'

That was, apparently, my father's favourite story, of a stag party he had met in a beer garden the summer before. They had been to the match, paid £300 to hire a dwarf for the day, who they had then made helplessly drunk by spiking his drinks. Perhaps it was the most palatable anecdote my father had in his repertoire; it would not surprise me.

'Did you ever take Daniel to the football?' asked Maria, grateful for an excuse to change the subject.

My father turned to look at me, a furtive glance, looked back at Maria. His demeanour had changed instantly, from delighted to a surly guilt. 'Can't say I did, no.'

'But what was he like, Francis? As a boy?' Maria was probing and I wanted to warn her off, change the subject, but she was looking intently at my father and would not meet my eye, would not let go.

My father was chewing and he thought as he chewed, the silence only broken by the pop of his jaw. He swallowed, took a drink of wine, said eventually, 'Quiet.'

'Really.' There was a forced brightness in Maria's voice I recognised and knew was there to mask her true feelings, which I guessed were shock and revulsion. So that was it. I had been quiet. Eighteen years spent under his roof and that was the best he could come up with.

'Took him snooker once,' my father said, as if even he had realised the meagreness of his response to Maria's question. I frowned, thought back, dimly remembered a dingy snooker hall, bright baize under the lights, my father pointing out the rudiments of the game until he lost his patience and went to the bar to sulk. I had played on my own, picking off the odd red, colour, waiting for him to be drunk enough to take me home.

My father held up his fork, examined what he had skewered, said in an offhand way, 'He was shit.'

I brought my wallet with me to the doorstep, ready for the inevitable question, but this time my father did not even ask, just took my wallet from me, took out two, three, four notes, grunted what might have been a thanks.

'Nice girl,' he said.

'Yeah,' I said.

Maria had not kissed my father when he left, had instead shaken his hand, an act that told its own story. I guessed that he would not be invited back in a hurry.

'Right, well.'

'See you.'

'Yeah.' My father half turned to go, stopped, as if there was something he wished to say to me. Since I had found out about my mother, and his part in her tragic story, I had felt that there was something he wanted to say to me, perhaps confess. But I did not expect him to ever find the moral courage and I was right, at least tonight. He turned without another word and walked away down the street, hands in his jacket pockets, hunched against whatever insult the world was preparing to throw his way. Some people were beyond help.

8

WHILE I HAD been enduring my father's company, Gabe had been at home alone, drinking a beer, channel-surfing, glad to have his prosthetic leg off; stretched out on the sofa he was as content as he could be outside of a warzone. He crushed his beer can, laughing derisively at the war film he was watching, when a bullet drilled through his living room window, shattering it and passing his ear with a zip like a mosquito heard in the dark.

Regardless of the beer he'd had and the unlikeliness of a shooting in his leafy neighbourhood, he rolled off the sofa, reattached his leg and crawled to the wall next to the shattered window. Outside a car was idling, red-tinged exhaust fumes rising thickly into the night through the car's brake lights. Another shot came in, chipped wood off his window frame. Gabe ducked back, saw another bullet bore through the brick of his front wall, then tumble with a lazy subsonic buzz through his front room.

Gabe dragged himself underneath the window, took a look from the other side. A car pulled away from the kerb, slowly, as if to taunt him, show its impunity.

But almost two decades in the army had taught Gabe to keep his head under fire. Nor was he a man who could allow such insolence to go unanswered. Without a second's reflection, he got to his feet, picked up his keys, left his house, started his car and headed off in pursuit.

Gabe caught up with the car along Main Road, came up behind it doing seventy, headlights on full. His beams picked out heads, two in front, two back. One turned, saw Gabe approach. The car picked up speed and by the time they hit Gallows Corner roundabout they were pushing ninety, both cars up on two wheels. Gabe saw headlights through his side window, other drivers taking evasive action, slamming to a halt to avoid them as they barrelled through. The car in front nearly lost it exiting the roundabout, the back end spinning out, only recovered by colliding with a stationary van that bounced it back on course in a shower of sparks.

They hit the A12 and Gabe got up close behind the car, so close he could see the colour of the men's hair in his headlights, see the amazed expression on one of the men's face as he looked behind him. He got close enough to nudge the other car's bumper, saw the same man point a gun at him, no more than two metres away. Up ahead the lights were red, a busy intersection. Cars were streaming across and Gabe eased off. The men in front veered left, looking for a gap. They got halfway through before they were broadsided by a flatbed truck. The car lifted into the air, spun, steam pluming from its grille. Gabe pulled up, opened his door. All cars on the intersection had stopped. There was no movement from the destroyed car. He approached it, passed a car, saw a puzzled child's face pressed to the window. A bullet hit the front tyre of the car, a hiss of air escaping.

Civilian casualties, another thing Gabe had witnessed in the army. He backed off, back to his car, waited. Slowly the two front doors of the destroyed car opened, two men got out. Both with guns. One covered Gabe while another tried both rear doors, got one open. There must have been twenty, thirty cars watching, their beams picking out the men. None of the cars moving, as if they were at a chaotic drive-in watching the main feature. The man who had opened the rear door helped another man out. All three regrouped in front of their car, facing Gabe. By now he had retreated behind his car, protected by its length.

One man was still in the car. Didn't seem to concern the three standing in front. One stayed where he was. The two others ran to another car. They held their guns to both front windows, passenger and driver's, elbows raised high, guns pointing down. Mouths open, shouting urgent, unequivocal orders. The doors opened and a man and woman stepped out. The man had his hands up. The woman was in a short dress, flapping her hands, stepped backwards, went down on a stiletto heel. Both men got in and the man by the wrecked car ran over, got into the back. They backed up, gunned the engine, peeled away, snort of exhaust and rear lights disappearing into the night.

But a shootout at a major intersection, though traumatic for most present, was a relatively trivial event for Gabe.

He got back into his car, negotiated his way through the stationary cars, and headed back in pursuit.

The car the men had stolen was fast and it took Gabe over three minutes to catch up. He saw them from a distance, hit 130 to get close. He tailgated them, looking for a way past, but they jinked across lanes, blocking him. He came alongside and they veered into him, sound of metal on metal, a shudder going through his car, tyres looking for grip. He braked, tucked back behind. The car in front took a sudden left, its back again sliding out. Gabe did not have time to follow, overshot their exit. He slammed on the handbrake, overcooked it and put his car in a spin. Got it headed back the way he'd come. Wrong way on a dual carriageway. Drove the two hundred metres back to the exit the men had taken, turned into it, lit up by the headlights of an approaching lorry, heard its horn Doppler past his rear bumper.

But by the time Gabe had found the car it was abandoned, three doors still open and lights still on. It was in an industrial estate, parked in front of a megastore selling cut-price furniture. Gabe stopped, opened his door, leaned on its frame, then hit it, again and again and again.

The police had come for him three hours later; his car had been picked up by eleven cameras during his pursuit, his plate run in seconds. He had called me two hours later, and I had arrived at the station at a little after five in the morning.

Sergeant Hicklin stopped the tape machine, sat back in his chair, smiled widely. I had to smother a smile back. My relationship with the police had never been a comfortable one; my father had instilled an abiding suspicion of them, and more recently I had been a victim of police corruption that a missing finger made hard to forget. Hicklin was old school and a man I respected, even trusted. Regardless, he was getting nothing from me.

'Right, Mr McBride,' he said. 'Off the record now. Stop pissing me about. You know exactly who they were.'

'My client has already told you, on the record,' I said. 'A full and detailed account. So how about you stop pissing about and either charge him, for what I have no idea, or let him go.'

'For speeding, careless driving, dangerous driving, for...' Sergeant Hicklin seemed to run out of words. 'Take your pick.'

'If you were going to do it, you'd have done it,' I said. 'We both know that.'

Sergeant Hicklin sighed, looked upwards as if there he might find some help. We were in an interview room, Hicklin one side of a desk, me and Gabe the other. Gabe was slouched in his chair; he seemed bored, uninterested now he'd finished his account. A uniformed policeman stood in the corner. He was young and was following it all with his eyes. Hicklin sighed again, yawned.

'Want to hear the rest?' Hicklin said.

'There's a rest?' I said.

'Oh, there's a rest.'

The man left in the car at the intersection was in hospital with a broken femur and various internal complications,

Sergeant Hicklin told us. He wasn't talking, although that was mostly because so far he'd refused to regain consciousness. Now that the interview was over, Sergeant Hicklin was not so officious. There was something in his eyes, a light that I could not help but enjoy.

The other three abandoned their vehicle and made off on foot, running through the streets behind the A12. They came out under the white glare of road lights on a main road and saw a McDonald's drive-through where a couple in a car were picking up burgers. The men surrounded the car, opened the doors and when the driver put up a fight, they hit him repeatedly with the butt of a handgun while his girlfriend screamed, one hand still clenched on the bag holding her burgers, which, she said, there wasn't any way she was giving to them. Car, yes. Burgers, no chance.

Hicklin laughed softly as he recounted this detail, raised an eyebrow, invited a response. I looked at Gabe and shook my head. Hicklin knew what he was doing, was looking for Gabe to say something, give himself away now the pressure was off. But I was Gabe's lawyer, and that wasn't about to happen.

'So,' I said, 'we're free to go.'

'I know where you live,' Hicklin said. 'When I need you.'

I nodded at Gabe, who stood up, smiled at Hicklin, but did not say anything.

'Please,' Hicklin said, putting out a hand. The uniformed policeman opened the door and led us to the front desk where Gabe signed for his possessions and we walked out together into the dark morning.

'Want to tell me,' I said gently, 'what the hell all that was about?'

We were in my car and so far Gabe had said nothing; he had his head against the window and might as well have been asleep.

'Not really,' he said. 'If I'm honest.'

'I'm your lawyer,' I said. 'No, forget that. I'm your friend.'

'Listen, Danny. Thanks for coming down. But that's all I needed. This... Just leave it.'

'You had a gun, right?'

'Danny...'

'Just tell me. What would you have done? If you'd found them?'

Gabe sighed. 'I didn't though, did I? So please. Leave it.'

'I know when someone's into something,' I say. 'New car, money, a bullet through your window. This isn't you.'

'You've no idea.'

'You can't expect me not to care.'

'I expect you to respect my wishes.'

There. Done. The Gabe effect. No sentiment, no emotion. As I drove I wondered if, at heart, he had always been like that, or whether the army had instilled this core of granite. I guessed it didn't matter. The result was the same; there was no point reasoning with the man. I did not doubt that he knew who had shot out his front window; had no doubt that it was linked to his money, to the man at the tennis court, to his new-found sense of purpose. Once again I wondered about what it could be, but could only fear the worst; that Gabe, once so honest and decent, was putting his military experience to bad use. I looked across at him, his lean face, his closed eyes, and could not help but notice the way he arranged his legs, the cost of his injury even when in repose. Could I blame him for whatever it was he was doing? Would I be any different, given the same circumstances?

We arrived at his house and Gabe pulled himself up and out, stood up slowly. He leaned into the car, said, 'Thanks, Danny. I owe you one.'

I nodded, didn't say anything. Drove away, leaving him alone outside his house, sky beginning to lighten behind him. What else could I do?

9

FOR THE NEXT few days a cold wind blew and with it, nothing new. Through my office windows I watched people walk past, harassed women resentfully shoving buggies, jostling, laughing children avoiding school and, later, tired returning office workers, eyes shuttered and jaws set against the wind, jackets held resentfully closed at the neck. I did not hear any more from Vick and, in truth, I was glad. It does me little credit, but I did not know what further part I could play in her story and I tried to persuade myself that no news was probably good news, that I had done all that I could, that there was nothing more I could offer her.

I spent the days catching up on casework and fending calls from Hicklin, who called to tell me that he was not happy with Gabe's statement, that the man in hospital had still not regained consciousness, and that if he died, Gabe could be liable for manslaughter at best. I listened to him patiently, told him that unless he had anything more, he should stop wasting my time. Told him that Gabe had a window missing, that a bullet had been dug out of his living room wall. That he had over fifty witnesses who saw a flatbed truck total the injured man's car, while Gabe was stopped twenty metres away. I rearranged pens as I listened to him, squared piles of paper. Stifled yawns.

My casework was no more rewarding. I dutifully chased Aatif's visa application, desultorily contested speeding tickets, worked on the eviction of a tenant who had been running an unlicensed tattoo parlour from a three-bed semi owned by a client. The man was not only facing eviction but several other criminal proceedings, related to three cases of septicaemia and one complaint brought by an aggrieved lady who had had a dolphin tattooed across her back. She had intended the dolphin to be spiritual but felt that it looked more like a salmon or pike and was seeking recompense for physical and emotional trauma. I had seen the photos of the tattoo in dispute and could not help but sympathise.

But the work was trivial and my heart not in it. After two days of this monotony, I began to crave something more. At times like these I would call Gabe, arrange a match, take my boredom and frustration out on court. But the wind was too strong and between us there was something else, some turbulence that I did not understand and could not seem to broach.

I went to the gym, lifted weights until my shoulders ached and the muscles along the backs of my arms and calves trembled and spasmed. However hard I pushed myself, though, at the back of my mind I could not shake the horror of Vick's situation, of how close she had come to death. I could not help but think of Ryan, wonder what his role in it all was; what, if anything, it had to do with his gambling. Whether I cared to admit it or not, Vick's story, the thought of her children in the custody of an indifferent authority, had got under my skin. It was not something I could work out, nor was it something I could sweat out.

That night I drove to my house and Maria was there waiting for me. In my life I had never before had the luxury of somebody who thought for me, considered my feelings, who negotiated my moods so that I did not have to. But Maria had noticed that I was not myself, had sensed my dissatisfaction. As I walked through the door she gently prevented me from taking off my coat, shook me roughly by my chin and asked me if I had any money on me.

'Why?'

'Tonight, my miserable little friend, we are out.'

Maria had a technique for picking a winning greyhound, watching them as they paraded before the race and putting everything on any dog she saw relieving itself. If no dog did, she sat the race out. If two urinated, she went both ways. So far she had won over £150 and her technique was looking sound; Gabe and I had stopped mocking her for it, were beginning to consider getting in on the action. The man on the table next to ours already had, handing ten £50 notes to the girl who took the bets, peeling them off a stack of notes six inches high. She came back with his winnings wearing a nervous look and I doubted whether she had ever held that much money in her life before.

We were in the restaurant overlooking the track, watching through huge glass windows high up. The track was lit by floodlights, and the spectators and trainers and bookies on the ground looked like actors on a stage set, the night sky black above them. Although it was a week-night, the dogs always had an atmosphere of carnival, the drink and spectacle of the greyhounds and possibility of winning money creating a feeling of disconnection from the mundane world of rules beyond the stadium. Even Gabe seemed relaxed, enjoying himself, arms spread out on the banquette as he watched the racing below. Whatever he'd got himself into, he was doing a good job of putting it aside this evening.

The next runners were being shown off beneath us, each dog wearing a differently patterned jacket, which corre-sponded to the odds for each dog flashed up on TV screens in the restaurant. Maria was watching them intently and I watched her, looked at her grave eyes and slightly parted lips, and sitting next to her I felt as if no man was ever luckier.

'There he goes,' said Gabe as one of the dogs relieved itself.

'She,' said Maria. 'She's a bitch.'

'Sixty to one and she hasn't won a race all season,' said Gabe sceptically.

'Such little faith,' said Maria. The girl who took the bets was at our table and Maria handed her £50, got a slip of paper with her bet on. Gabe shook his head at the girl and I gave her ten, told her to put it on the favourite.

'Square,' said Maria.

'Just going by the form.'

'No imagination,' she said. 'My dog will prevail.'

'Prevail,' I said. 'It's an interesting word.'

'It's what will happen.'

The dogs were walked back to the starting cages, which had been wheeled across the track, and the noise in the restaurant subsided slightly as we waited for the start of the race. The mechanised rabbit was flying around the track on the opposite side to the dogs, getting closer and closer, and as it passed the starting cages they sprang open and the dogs came running out, bunching into a group on the inside of the track, a blur of colours and legs and dipping heads. The restaurant exploded into noise and an overweight man in an untucked shirt and red tie stood up and repeatedly screamed, *'Go on the six doggie.'* The starting cages were wheeled away and the dogs flashed beneath us for their first lap; they were so fast I could not tell which dog was in the lead. Maria was gripping the edge of our table and leaning forward towards the windows. The dogs were now on the far side of the track and I could see that Maria's dog was at the front and that mine was nowhere. They came around the final bend and Maria's dog was well ahead. It won by three lengths and as it crossed the line, Maria screamed in happiness and clapped her hands. She turned to me, her eyes glowing with emphatic triumph, and she grabbed my cheeks with each hand in delight, gave them a shake.

'Christ sake,' said Gabe.

'I win,' said Maria and she stuck her tongue out at Gabe, who looked at her in feigned disgust.

The man on the table next to us got up and walked towards us, said 'Sorry' to me and, without asking her permission, kissed Maria on the cheek.

'Fuck me,' he said. 'That bitch just bought me a fucking Merc.'

But my feeling of goodwill was not to last long. I had been trying to ignore them, trying to concentrate on the evening and Maria and Gabe and the good time we were supposed to be having. But two men had been watching us from the bar and by the sixth race I could no longer tolerate it; their gaze was a direct provocation and I could no more ignore it than I could fly. Gabe had noticed them too and he looked at me, raised an eyebrow, and I shook my head. I could handle this myself.

'Getting a vodka,' I said. 'Anybody want anything?'

'Go on then,' said Maria. 'Got to spend all this cash on something.' She peeled a note off her stack and tucked it under my belt. 'Off you go.'

I got up and walked to the bar, my eyes locked on the two men. They could see that I was coming but did not look concerned; they were smiling, entirely at ease. I caught the eye of the barman, ordered two vodka and tonics. After he had taken my order, I turned to the two men.

'You after a bunk up?'

'Do what?' said one of the men.

'Way you've been looking at me. You must fancy me. Right?'

93

The men laughed without amusement. 'Wanted a word,' the taller man said.

The barman put my drinks on the bar and I handed him money. 'So go on,' I said. 'What do you want?'

I waited for my change and looked at them. The taller man was wearing a t-shirt and his arms were unnaturally long, which made them look slender, but his wrists were thick and his arms were covered with light hair and sinewy with muscle. He had a hard, long face and blue eyes. The short man was barely five foot and had a slightly deformed face; his eyes were large and wide apart and his head was almost round with sparse red hair on top. Together they made a slightly disturbing pair.

'This your card?' said the taller man. He held my business card between his first and second finger.

I broke eye contact, took my change from the barman, looked back. 'Where'd you get that?'

The man ignored me. The short man smiled and it made him look briefly imbecilic.

'Ry-an Low-rie,' he said in a singsong voice, high like a girl's.

The taller man tore my card in half. 'Stay away from him.'

I picked up one of the glasses, took a drink. 'What makes you think you can tell me what to do?'

The small man sniggered, a child's giggle. 'You don't want to get involved.'

'Oh?'

'Like Magnus says,' the taller man said, 'walk away.'

I nodded, took a moment. 'You're Magnus?' I said to the strange-looking man. Turned to the taller man. 'And you are?'

He just smiled, shook his head.

'Well, Magnus and Whatever-the-fuck-your-name-is,' I said. 'Here's the thing. My clients are my business. Clear?'

Magnus and his partner smiled at each other. 'That your girlfriend?' said Magnus, looking over to Maria, who was saying something to Gabe, laughing.

The other man whistled, low. 'Looks clean. Bet she isn't.'

I squeezed my glass so hard I was surprised it didn't shatter. I tried to master my temper, closed my eyes briefly. Opened them, looked at them.

'Mention her again and I'll make you eat this glass,' I said.

The man smiled. 'You cannot imagine the shit you are getting into. Do you realise who you're dealing with?'

'Have a good evening,' I said to them. 'We're finished.'

I turned and walked away from them. As I got nearer to our table Maria looked up and smiled and my expression must have been bleak because her smile faltered, and it was everything I could do to summon up an expression that approached human, that contained any warmth at all.

Maria decided to sit out the last race. She had won enough for the evening and she was aware of the atmosphere I carried back with me from the bar, knew that something had happened to change the mood. Gabe gave me a questioning look and again I shook my head at him: now was not the time. But I am what I am and my intrinsic nature was incapable of accepting what had just transpired between those two men and me; I could not let such aggression go unanswered. When I saw Magnus through the windows below me, shaking hands with a trackside bookie and heading for the exit, the other man next to him, I stood up and excused myself, told Maria I had to go back to the office, asked Gabe to take her home. Without waiting for an answer I headed out of the restaurant. I hustled down a stairwell, hurried towards the turnstiles that led out to the car park. My heart pumped with a sudden release of adrenalin, my vision was dark and narrow. It was a feeling I knew well and that, if I was honest, part of me loved like a junkie loves the needle.

I reached the car park in time to see Magnus and the other man climb into a car – BMW, dark colour I could not make out in the orange haze of the car park. I got into my car, waited for them to drive past, reversed out and followed.

10

THE MEN DROVE out of town, and I followed them around the concrete ring road and back out onto the A127, recognising the shape of their rear lights again whenever I lost sight of them for a second. It had started to rain and it billowed like fine curtains across the road, lit up by high yellow streetlights. They did not travel far, took a left up a rural road, followed it around bends and pulled up a long gravel drive. The gateway was bordered by high hedges and I could not see what was beyond.

I parked twenty metres further and got out, ran up the gravel drive, the wind so strong I could feel it trying to push me off course. The two men were getting out of their car maybe eighty metres in front of me. I sprinted, the sound of my feet on the gravel drowned by the groan and shiver of trees that bordered the drive.

The two men were walking towards a large house, the taller man in front, the strange, short man called Magnus some metres behind, looking at his phone, the screen bright in the darkness. I punched down into the back of his head and he fell in front of me and I stumbled on his leg, trod on his ankle and felt it give way. The man in front had not heard anything and was opening the door to the house. I came up behind him and he did not hear me. I put a palm against the side of his head, put everything behind it, slammed his head into the frame of the door. I saw his legs give but he did not go over. I held him by the back of his coat, pushed him into the house. The hallway was lit by a single lamp. He recovered his balance, half turned to me. I put both hands into his chest, shoved him into a white-painted door. He hit it with his back and the impact burst it open and he staggered through. I followed quickly before he got time to recover, before I lost my advantage. He was a big man; if he got the chance, he'd do me damage.

The room was a kitchen, big and brightly lit. Huge glass doors opposite, black from the night outside. The floor was light, shiny, tiled. In the middle of the kitchen was a large island. Next to it was a man feeding a baby. The baby was in a high chair. The man was my height, early fifties. He had a deep tan and grey hair and was wearing a white shirt, dark trousers. He was holding a plastic spoon and it was frozen in mid-air as he looked at me. I felt as if I had stumbled into a play, a bad dream where I was on stage but did not know the lines. The man did not seem surprised to see me.

The man from the dogs was backed against a counter, both hands behind him supporting his weight, shaking his head stupidly. The man feeding the baby backed up to the edge of the room, calm, against the dark window. The baby started making noises, unhappy. I did not move. I did not know what to do. There should not be a baby here. Nobody said anything for one, two, three seconds.

'How many of you are there?' the man said. His eyes showed no curiosity.

I frowned, took a moment. 'What?'

'How many?'

'No,' I said. 'Just me.'

He blinked slowly. His eyes were very blue. 'Just you.'

'I'm sorry,' the man I had attacked started. Blood leaked from a wound in his head like parted lips. The man in the white shirt held up a hand, did not look at him.

'Do you know where you are?' he said to me.

I shook my head. 'No.'

The baby started to cry, crotchety coughs and gulps. He looked at it indifferently, looked back at me. Neither of us said anything. The man was good looking. The hand holding the spoon was steady. Under the bright lights I could see that his knuckles were scarred, showing white against the tan. The spoon in his hand snapped. He did not react, continued to look at me, beige baby food now on the back of his perfectly bronzed hand.

Something caught his attention and he looked past me, down at the doorway. I turned, looked down and saw Magnus. He was on his front, pulling himself through the door, hands looking for purchase on the tiled floor. He left blood on its pale surface as he dragged himself, slipped. He twisted his strange head up at me and grinned, gaps in his teeth dark with blood. One of his legs was limp like a doll's, the other toeing the floor, looking for grip.

'Called Carl,' he said to the man, although he continued to look up at me. 'Coming. With Jamie.'

The man in the shirt nodded. He looked disgusted, like he did not want this thing in his home. Magnus did not seem right in here, this pristine place; a grotesque intrusion, a hideous string puppet unsuccessfully brought to life. He spat blood onto the tiles, giggled.

'Carl and *Ja*-mie,' he sang.

'What do you want?' the man said to me.

I stepped forward. Without looking he moved left, opened a drawer, took out a gun. He did not point it at me, rested it on the counter next to him. I stopped.

'Asked you a question.'

'This man,' I nodded at Magnus, 'threatened me. Threatened my girlfriend.'

'That right?' he said. Beams of light played against his back through the glass doors. His hair was lit up, gold haloed, shirt edges transparent white. I heard a car, the engine, gravel crunch. The lights disappeared, sound of doors slamming. I knew that I was in a bad place. The man in the shirt showed no emotion. Had not done. The baby protested, a bad-tempered hiccuppy *ah-ah-ah*. The man kept looking at me. He breathed heavily and although he seemed calm, I sensed a rage there, some fury his chest could barely contain.

'Came into my house,' he said.

Behind me I heard running feet and a man burst into the kitchen. He stepped over Magnus, who chuckled into the tiles, looked down at him, saw me too late. I hit him under the armpit, felt bulk and then the hard fence-work of ribs against my knuckles. He staggered up against the counter and then I was hit, impact in my head and my neck twisted. I did not know where it had come from, but when I opened my eyes I was looking up at the spotlights in the ceiling and there was another man there, above me, face dark under the lights. Hands on his knees, face so close to mine, blocking out the light. I could smell him, cigarettes.

'Take him across the way,' I heard a voice say, like in a dream, from another place. It was the man, the man who had been feeding the baby. He had scarred knuckles; I remembered that. The tiles were cool against my cheek. I so much wanted to get up, but they seemed so cool.

The meaty *thunk* of a spade. Driven into damp firm earth. Again. Again. Grunts of exertion. A voice. Between impacts: *You. Brought it. Back. Here.* Silence, breathing. A whimper, something spat out. Scuff of shoes on concrete. Hacking at a root, anger: *Back.* Hack. *Here.* The earth giving. Sounds softer now, wetness. Another whimper, mewl of a wounded animal.

Tried to open my eyes. Dark, distant light through an open door. Legs, shapes, shoulders moving in silhouette. The sound not a spade but the impact of blows, fists on damaged flesh. My head heavy. Pain pulsing like my brain had been pierced. Urge to vomit, bright liquid turbulence above my stomach, below my throat. Shapes moving. A gathering. Dark shapes looking down at a dark mound. Opened my eyes wider and the pulsing grew. Like my eyelids contained my pain. Closed them again, relief. Something was happening. Something terrible was happening.

A new voice. A man's, reasoning: *Ain't that enough?* The first voice: *I say when it's enough.* Again that sound. Spade's edge in damp earth. Again. Again. Again. Again.

My cheek stinging. Aftermath of a slap. The man in the white shirt squatting down next to me. Nothing in his eyes.

'Know who I am?'

My head hurt and I thought I might vomit. I leaned to my left but the feeling passed. I looked back at the man. His eyes were very blue.

'No.'

'I'm Alex Blake. Mean anything to you?'

I nodded.

'Say again?'

'Yes,' I said.

I knew the name. Who didn't? If I had known this was the Blakes' home, I would not have come near. Would have left well alone. Never go near the Blakes. Keep an ocean between you. Past Alex Blake I saw the dark heap of the man I followed here, the man who threatened me. He was not moving. The wreckage of his face was turned to me, against the ground, a soft-boiled eye leaking bloody yolk. A car was parked next to us. A garage? Anything could happen here. Anything.

Blake looked at me, incurious. Evaluating. A problem, nothing more. Although he was close I felt an impossible distance between us, a gulf in humanity. This was not a man you could plead with. He would pull the trigger on a weeping mother.

The two men were still here. What were their names? Carl and Jamie. Not moving. Waiting.

'So,' Blake said. 'Who are you?'

'Daniel Connell.'

'Who knows you're here?'

I did not reply. My head. The pain.

He nodded. 'Right. You were following Liam and Magnus.'

Liam. That was his name. I wondered if he was still alive.

'Got a phone?'

'Yes.'

'Take it out.'

There was nothing I could do. I put my hand in my pocket, fumbled, pulled it out. Handed it to him. He thumbed the screen, nodded to himself. He passed it to one of the men. The man I had hit.

'Made no calls, no messages,' Blake said. 'Nobody knows you're here.'

I did not say anything.

'You didn't want to get involved,' he said.

'I have no idea what is going on. He' – I nodded at where Liam lay, at what was left of him – 'he threatened me.'

'You said. And?'

I said nothing. For the first time he seemed impatient. He wiped an eye with flat fingers. He wore a large gold watch. It slipped on his wrist. His knuckles were covered in dark dried blood, cracking, crumbling.

'I can't have you come here, walk in like that. Let you tell people, let it be known.'

I tried to nod, show some understanding. Show no fear. The pain shook my body. Again I felt the urge to vomit.

Blake stood up. Behind him, one of the men, the man I had not hit, opened the boot of the car. It opened slowly. It was dark inside.

'No,' I said. 'There's no need...' I did not finish. I would not plead. Not to these men. They were going to put me in there. I did not want to be put in there. In this garage, with these three men, I might as well have been in Syria, Saudi, some underground bunker where blameless men disappear daily. Where rules we accept as given do not exist.

A door to my left opened, showing the night, and a man walked in. He was wearing a camouflage jacket and a woollen hat. He glanced at me, across at Liam, did not react. He waited for Blake to speak, disciplined, at attention.

'Yes?'

'Got customs outside. Parked on the road. Eyes on us.'

Blake tightened his eyes slightly, a subtle tell of emotion. He stood up, looked across at Liam, down at me. 'Saw him arrive.' Not a question. Nobody replied, waited for him to continue. He sighed.

'Check Liam, make sure he's alive. And get rid of him,' nodding at me. 'I've fucking had enough.'

Carl and Jamie were big men, late forties or early fifties, heads shaved and bearing the nicked eyebrows and damaged ears of old-school muscle. They walked me away from the building where Liam was lying, a large metal-sided barn behind the main house. There were more buildings next to it, and more men standing under lights, hard men breathing smoke. Somebody arrived in a lorry, climbed down, gazed at me without interest. Perhaps I had still not fully come back from my netherworld of unconsciousness, but I could not help but see the men as cruel and wicked souls carrying out some unknown, infernal operation; could not help but feel the evil of this place.

We passed the house and headed down Blake's drive, back to familiar surroundings, to normality. As we walked I felt some of my strength return. Carl or Jamie had a hand on my shoulder and I shook it off, turned to them, gave them the stare. The one I had hit smiled. Carl.

'Any idea how lucky you are?'

'Just to be clear,' Jamie said. 'He comes across you again, he'll take you, and that little piece of yours, to a place he's got on the coast. Spend a weekend on her while you watch, bury you both so deep it'll take a fucking earthquake before anyone sees you again. Clear?'

I did not answer. Away from Blake and his awful presence I felt less fear. These men I was used to. These men I had met before, met their kind. I had never met anybody like Alex Blake.

'You might want to think about leaving Essex,' said Jamie.

'Not going to happen,' I said.

'Personally,' said Carl, 'I can't see a future for you.'

'He pay you to have an opinion?' I said.

We reached my car. It was very dark. We stopped and Carl said, 'You hit me. Want to make this easy?'

He pushed me against my car, my back against the driver's door. Even through my jacket I could feel the cold of the metal. I looked at them both, moonlight picking out the stubble on their heads, the scars. Weighed them up, weighed my chances. Slim. Fuck it. I just wanted to go home.

'Be my guest,' I said.

He nodded, hit me in the stomach, underneath the ribcage. Short take back but the impact was huge, his fist travelling up into my lungs, shoulder forced into my chest, his face next to mine. Must have been a boxer, ex-boxer, timing like that. I exhaled as if vomiting, an uncontrolled whoosh, felt my legs buckle. Carl stepped back and I nearly fell. Jamie pushed me back against my car, gripped my jacket at the shoulder, held me up.

'All right?'

I breathed, nodded, and he let go. They turned away and walked back up to Alex Blake's home. From my knees looking upwards it looked like a citadel, looming above me out of the dark. I could not get away quickly enough.

11

AFTER THREE GLASSES of Scotch, I still could not imagine
that I would ever get close to sleep; when I closed my eyes
I saw the half-remembered image of Liam, a bloodied
bundle, his face like raw meat. A man who would make an
example of someone who worked for him, punish him for
an error of judgement in such a way. I drank and it was
only by looking at the cold, still, prosaic reality of my living
room that I could believe I was alive, that I had got away
so lightly from Alex Blake.

But the body can take only so much, and although the
edge of sleep had seemed far away, at some point I dropped
off it completely. I woke on my sofa with the fourth glass
untouched and a pale, indifferent sun leaking into the
room. My eyes felt as if they had been abraded by sand-
paper and my ribs ached from where Carl had hit me. I sat
up, tried to rub the itch out of my eyes, thought about what
had happened, what my next move would be.

What I should do was call Vick, tell her I was sorry but
that there was nothing more I could do, or was willing to do,
to help her – she was on her own. This was not my business,

yet it had brought the threat of violence to my door, to Maria. I had no dog in this fight. Time to walk away. But before I could do that, there was somebody I needed to see.

Today addiction is accepted as a disease rather than a moral defect or failing, treated with understanding rather than punishment. But Ryan Lowrie, in the grip of an uncontrollable compulsion or not, had given my card to men who used violence and intimidation as a way of life, as a means of business. I could not simply forget that. He owed me an apology, and an explanation.

There was no answer when I pressed the buzzer to Ryan's flat and, if I was honest, that was no bad thing. If I had found Ryan I know that I would have had difficulty controlling my temper. I was still shaken from the events of the night before and was looking for somebody to blame, to unload my fear onto. Ryan, small and slight and culpable, was the ideal candidate. I did not have Vick's number with me, could not ask her where he was working, and anyway, making an example of Ryan at his place of work would have been a step too far. If I wanted to get hold of Ryan, there was only one sure way.

The woman at the first bookies did not even ask me why I wanted Ryan, whether he was in any trouble; she just took the offered twenty and my card, told me she'd call me if he turned up but, given the way he'd been losing recently, she wasn't holding her breath.

At the next, a girl barely out of school was at the counter and she hesitated when I asked her to give me a call if she saw Ryan, looked about her for words of advice although there was nobody there.

'Why?'

'Want to speak to him.'

'Yeah, but, you know. Why?'

'Doesn't matter. Here's another twenty.'

'Ain't the money. Just...' She looked confused, unsure. She shrugged. 'Don't feel comfortable.'

'I'm a lawyer,' I said. I gave her my card. 'It's regarding his children.'

'He's got kids?' She seemed surprised.

'Yes, he's got kids.'

'Okay.' She still did not seem sure but I left her looking at my card, wondering about the mysteries of grown men who could throw their lives away while being responsible for others. As if this was not a situation many of us had long accepted as entirely normal.

My final visit was to the man with the glasses who had pointed me in the direction of the casino. He was no longer vacuuming and Chambers was awake this time, gazing at the screen above him, which showed the odds for a race held at a course I had never heard of.

'You want me to call you.'

'If you could.'

He pushed his glasses down his nose, held my card out at arm's length. 'Known a few lawyers in my time. Didn't trust any of them.'

'He's involved in something. With some bad people.'

'And you might just be one of them.'

I held my palms up. He was too shrewd for me. 'Fair enough.'

He sighed. 'He gambles like my old man used to drink. Dunno what's going on there, but I hate to take his money.' He plucked the twenty from between my fingers. 'I'll give you a call. Ain't nobody else looking out for the poor sod. You ask me, he's a terminal case.'

Gabe was standing outside his house, watching two men replace a pane of glass in one of his front windows. He nodded to me but did not invite me inside even though it was cold and we stood there, watching one of the men apply putty to the pane while the other smoked a cigarette and talked to somebody on his mobile about something that somebody else had done that Saturday night.

'You all right?' Gabe said.

'Yeah. You?'

Gabe nodded, watched the men work. The man on his mobile was laughing and his laugh turned into a cough, which had him doubled over. He wheezed out delighted *Fuck mes* and *You're jokings* to whoever he was speaking to whenever he found the breath.

'Disappeared last night,' he said.

'Had a word with those two from the bar.'

'I figured. Everything okay?'

'Good as gold.'

Gabe and I are speaking carefully, both aware that we are withholding information, that we are being less than honest with one another. But I have come here for answers, and will not let Gabe evade my questions any longer.

'Nobody else shot at you?' I asked.

'Nope.'

'Even if I wasn't your friend, I'm your lawyer. I need to know what's going on.'

'Danny, you don't want to get involved.'

Why was everybody telling me that at the moment? 'Even so,' I said. 'You need to talk to me.'

'That so?'

Gabe did not say any more, let our silence grow. But Gabe was my oldest and best friend and we had been through too much together. He snorted, half laugh half despair, at the vagaries of the world, looked down at his feet, back at me. His eyes were as pale as the winter sky.

'Not going to let this go, are you?'

'No.'

He thought to himself, put his fist to his mouth, index finger against his lips. Seemed to come to a decision. 'All right. Question, since you're the lawyer. Say somebody's been killed. Inquest returns a verdict of, I don't know, accidental death. Right?'

'Right.' Already I did not like the way this was going.

'How could somebody get that inquest reopened?'

'Gabe—' I began, but he held up a hand.

'Just answer the question.'

'How to get an inquest reopened? You'd need new evidence. Something which hadn't been admitted the first time.'

'A witness?'

'If he or she was credible. Gabe, Christ. What's this about?'

He gestured to his window, the men working on it. 'This. It's... complicated.'

'You killed someone?' I said it with a smile but Gabe did not smile back. His eyes did not meet mine, looked to the distance.

'Not exactly,' he said.

'Then what?' I said.

But his face stilled and lost any expression, his eyes impossible to read. He looked past my shoulder and I turned and saw a man, broad with a shaved head.

'Gabe?' I said.

'Yeah, Danny, not now, eh?'

'Who's that?'

'Old friend.' Still his gaze did not meet mine and he called out to the man, 'Gavin.'

The man joined us. 'Gabe.' He turned to me but spoke to Gabe. 'Who's this?'

'Friend of mine,' said Gabe. He did not seem to take offence at the man's question, at being interrogated on his own turf. But I was less able to accept such arrogance, could not help but meet it with my own.

'You got a name?' I said.

He looked at me blankly, turned back to Gabe as if I was a child who had shown some impertinence it was beneath him to acknowledge.

'Bad time?' he said. He might have looked like a slab of Essex muscle but his voice was precise and cultured.

'No,' said Gabe. 'We'll go inside. Dan's just leaving.'

The man gave me an appraising look and walked past

us, towards Gabe's house. Gabe and I did not say anything and this awkwardness was so unfamiliar that I felt a quick wrench of sadness.

'We still fishing Saturday?' I said.

Gabe frowned, thought.

'Fishing. For sharks. Remember?'

'Right. Fishing. Yeah, Danny. I'll see you then.'

He turned and left me standing there on his gravel drive. As I walked back to my car I could hear the cackle of the man who had been on the phone as he told the man fixing the window about Saturday night and how he wouldn't fucking believe what happened, not in a million years.

Maria was at school teaching and did not answer my call. I left a message on her voicemail apologising for last night, told her something had come up and that I'd see her soon, that we'd do something.

I could not concentrate on work, sat at my desk shifting paper and making unnecessary notes, killing time. I wondered about Gabe, thought about his face freezing as the man turned up. He had been about to open up to me, tell me what was going on. But there was always our fishing trip. I had booked a charter boat operated by my old friend Harry Rafferty, and we would be alone, nobody to disturb us. Whatever happened, I would get some answers then.

I was considering closing up for the day when my mobile rang and I looked at it, did not recognise the number, picked it up.

'Daniel Connell.'

'Yeah, John here.' The man spoke in little above a whisper. 'You wanted me to call, if Ryan showed.'

'Yes?' It was the bookie with the glasses.

'Here now. Better be quick though. He's losing money like he knows he can't take it with him.'

I saw Ryan leave the bookies as I drove past, and by the time I had parked he had gone. But I saw him a hundred metres away across a busy ring road and followed him, keeping him in sight, separated by four lanes of traffic. He was wearing a black jacket, black trousers, white shirt. He turned into town, towards the Liberty, a shopping centre of glass and concrete. I called out, saw him turn. I was a long way away and perhaps he did not recognise me. He turned and ran. I watched him go, saw him run into the Liberty. I looked for a gap in cars so that I could follow him.

The Liberty was busy, store windows bright and colourful, the place a sudden relief from the cold grey bleakness outside. There were many people – schoolchildren and old couples and mothers and security – and I could not see Ryan. I pushed through the entrance into the main hall, glass ceiling high above me. A woman was offering massages from a stand in the middle. I looked around. There were so many people. Smell of doughnuts, sound of shop muzak. Caught sight of Ryan, his black jacket, pushing through a door thirty metres away. I jostled through the crowd of people, heard a voice behind me raised in complaint. I pushed through the door, saw a concrete stairwell. Only way was up. I ran up the first flight, saw a door, pushed through it. Cars parked, a woman buckling a child into a buggy. No Ryan. Back out, up another flight, another set of doors. Nothing. Same on the next level. I wondered if I'd missed him. Pushed up the final flight, this time into open air. Top floor, fewer cars. Five or six, parked around the rooftop. Birds black in the sky. Cold wind.

Ryan was watching me from across the rooftop and I put my hands high in the air, called, 'It's Danny. Daniel Connell.'

Ryan did not react and I walked slowly towards him. He was standing with his hands dangling. He looked as forlorn as a lost schoolboy. I felt my anger at him evaporate, replaced by contempt and not a little pity. He was wearing some kind of rent-a-cop outfit like the security guards in the Liberty below us – black trousers and jacket with little epaulettes. He had not changed from whatever he did for a living, protecting stores from shoplifters, chasing laughing kids on skateboards. A long way from the army, I thought. There was something pathetic and small about him: a man with a shitty job and a gambling problem who could not even look after his own children when they needed him most.

'Ran into the Blakes,' I said. 'You gave them my card.'

I had expected some kind of reaction from Ryan. But instead he just gazed past me, the same thousand-yard stare he'd had in the car after the casino. He did not say anything.

'Vick nearly died in a fire the other night,' I said, disdain in my voice. 'Somebody tried to kill her. Know anything about that?'

Slowly he turned his gaze to me, as if reluctant to acknowledge that I existed. He nodded. 'Yeah. Yeah, I know. He told me he'd do it. He laughed.'

This stopped me. I looked at Ryan, his despair; wondered what lay behind it all, what pressure he was really under. People threatening to kill his family, hurting his children, torching his ex-wife's home.

'Hey,' I said softly. I regretted the contempt that I had not bothered to hide from him; felt guilt for assuming his weakness. 'We can do something about this.'

I walked towards him and he backed away, held up a hand. I stopped. He sat slowly on the low wall edging the rooftop, hands on his lap, head bent towards them – an attitude of prayer.

'Ryan,' I said.

'My father taught me to fight my own battles,' he said. 'I'm a father, too. It's down to me.' He swallowed, shoulders hunching. 'Nobody else.'

'Just hold on,' I said. I did not know what else to say. I had so many thoughts in my head.

'This isn't your problem,' he said. 'Do yourself a favour. Keep out of it.'

'Ryan,' I said again.

He sat up, squared his shoulders. Looked me in the eye. For the first time since I had met him, I felt that he was really there. For the first time I sensed a reserve of courage, something small yet fierce and unyielding within him.

'I'll do anything to look after my family,' he said. 'Whatever you think of me.'

'Tell me who's doing this,' I said.

'They tried to kill her. They'll never stop.'

'Is it the Blakes?'

Ryan smiled sadly to himself, shook his head. 'Connor Blake. A name I'll never have to hear again.'

The way he swung his legs over the edge, as if he was on a seafront wall, soft sand just feet the other side, his back to me. He pushed himself off with both hands and I froze, blinked at his sudden absence for I do not know how long. I slowly walked to the edge. Willed myself to look down. Saw a figure approach Ryan who was lying on his side, legs spread like a Sunday morning lie-in, four storeys below me. It was silent and he looked peaceful. At least there was that.

12

WHAT I DID next was, I am honest enough to admit, both legally and morally indefensible. Perhaps it was the lingering threat of Alex Blake; perhaps it was a wish to walk away from Ryan, Vick, their whole dark and forbidding story. Perhaps I should not even attempt to justify what I did. Whatever. Rather than wait for the police to arrive, give them my version of events, help them understand what had driven Ryan over the edge of the fourth floor of a busy car park, I walked away. Headed back to the rooftop door, hurried down the concrete stairwell, walked out of the Liberty to the sound of approaching sirens, and did not look back.

But if I had imagined that leaving the scene of an incident rather than talk with the police would give me a measure of peace, I was wrong. Back home, its stillness and emptiness surrounded me like a reproach, unmitigated by Maria's happy presence. She had forgiven me for leaving her with Gabe the night before but told me that she had better things to do that evening than hang out with me, told me it over the phone with a smile in her voice. We still, at least notionally, lived separately, and she was having girlfriends over at her place, some kind of celebration, though I was not sure what for.

Walking away from Ryan's suicide gave me another dilemma. I had to tell Vick what had happened, could not avoid it. Had to tell her that I had been there but had left the scene. Had to co-opt her into what was, undeniably, a crime. Give her the bad news and at the same time ask her not to tell the police about my role in it. I took a deep breath, called her number. Got a busy signal. Called again and again, busy both times. Tried once more and was put through to voicemail. I sat back, replayed the likely sequence of events: the police call Vick, she calls somebody up, a friend; she heads to the friend's and talks, leaves her phone to ring through, too exhausted to speak to anyone else. I gave up, put my phone down, not without relief. Somebody else was taking care of it. Better them than me.

I turned on my TV, looked for some show to help pass the evening, keep my mind off what I had been through the last forty-eight hours; found a film I had seen before about an abandoned spaceship with some evil nestling deep within. But before the opening titles had ended, I heard a hammering on my door. My lights were on, my car parked outside: too late to pretend to be out. I walked to my door and opened it.

My father was on the doorstep holding a bunch of flowers, and for a moment the vision was so unexpected that I doubted what I was seeing.

'You shouldn't have,' I said.

'Don't be a wanker,' he said. 'Where is she?'

'Not in. Out.'

My father grunted, seemed at a loss about what to do with the flowers in his hands. Eventually he shoved them at me, pushed them into my chest, embarrassed.

'Do something with them then.'

'You want to come in?'

'Thought we were going out.'

I tilted my head, frowned.

'Snooker. Your missus' idea.'

'Right.' Maria had forgotten to tell me. Or perhaps she had not dared. I guessed that this was her attempt to force some kind of reconciliation, build bridges between father and son. There was nothing that I would rather do less than spend an evening alone with my father, after what I had just seen. But at the same time he had information that, for perhaps the first time in my life, might prove useful. I stuck the flowers head down in my kitchen bin, pulled on a jacket and headed on out.

Snooker was a game that required patience, precision, a cool head and the ability to plan two, three shots in the future – an analytical approach. Watching my father miss another red, throwing his cue at the white as if he was bayoneting the enemy, I could think of few games less temperamentally suited to him. Chess, perhaps. His oiled hair glistened under the lights of the table and he was sweating even though it was not warm, pure rage beading his skin. The white hit the red all wrong and the red missed the pocket by a distance, came off three cushions before it stopped.

'Fuck it.'

'Don't hit it so hard.'

'The fuck would you know?'

Instead of answering, I rolled a red into the middle pocket from a tight angle at dead weight. My father did not acknowledge the shot but I could hear him breathe a little heavier, a sign he was becoming agitated.

I settled down over a long blue and, as I lined it up, said to my father, 'Heard of someone called Connor Blake?'

My father did not reply. I took the shot and caught it thick, missed by an inch. I straightened up and looked at him. 'Not one of the Blakes, is he? Those Blakes?'

My father knew most crooked, dodgy, violent and villainous faces in Essex, but you did not need to be an expert on the local underworld to have heard of the Blakes; they were part of local folklore, fairy-tale monsters for adults. Never spoken of, feared, avoided, denied. Yet everybody knew them, what they did. A dark secret reluctantly and shamefully tolerated in our midst.

'The Blakes?' said my father as he chalked his cue, blew on it. 'D'you want to know about them for?'

'They still around?'

My father eyed up a straight red, did not answer. He hit it softly, deliberately, and it dropped into the pocket. 'Yeah,' he said. 'Yeah, they're still around.'

'Haven't heard of them recently. Thought they might have disappeared.'

'Just 'cos you ain't heard of them,' said my father. The cue ball had ended up tight on the cushion and my father did not have the technique to cue smoothly off the side of the table, was jacking his cue up clumsily to hit the top of the white. He got a bad contact and the white barely kissed the blue he'd been aiming for.

'Arsehole.'

'So go on,' I said. 'Connor Blake. You heard of him?'

My father rested the butt of his cue on the floor, held his cue upright like a resting warrior might hold a spear. Away from the table's lights his face was in darkness and I could not read his expression.

'You don't want nothing to do with that,' he said, and I was surprised to hear something like concern in his voice. I was about to ask him why not but he rested his cue against the wall, picked up his drink, downed it in one open-mouthed pour and said, as he headed for the bar, 'Pint?'

With my father gone I had to fight a juvenile urge to nudge my score forward, to see if he would notice. But he almost certainly would have and I wanted a quiet night, a minimum of drama. The lights on the table next to ours came on and a couple of lads sauntered over carrying their tray of snooker balls, young and slightly drunk, laughing loudly. My father came back following them with two pints and set them down on the ledge on the wall next to our table.

'Whose go?'

'Mine.'

He looked at the table suspiciously. 'You move the white?'

'Please.'

There was a shot on to the baulk corner but there was very little room for the red past the brown; I did not want to clip the brown so tried to cheat the pocket but the red stuck in the jaws, leaving it hanging over the pocket, a dolly for my father. He snorted unpleasantly, picked up the chalk. I decided to try again.

'You ever run into him then?'

'Who?'

Getting information out of my father was as difficult as getting a dog to sing. 'Connor Blake,' I said. I appealed to his vanity, his aspirations of being a proper gangster. 'You're in with all that mob, aren't you?'

Whatever my father's misgivings were, he could not help but take the bait, allow himself a moment of glory. 'Course I am.'

'And?'

'Them Blakes, they're what you might say trying to leave all that behind. Move up.'

'Respectable?'

My father shook his head condescendingly, a professor to his naive student. 'Not fucking hardly,' he said. 'Different league, all it is. Try not to get their hands dirty. If you know what I mean.'

I did, at least broadly. At some point villainy became big business and property was bought, businesses were created, top-flight accountants with few scruples were involved and exactly where the profits came from became hard to identify, even for HMRC. Even if the origin of those profits was unspeakable. Gangsters and bankers:

both equally adept at hiding the murk behind the money. At least I now knew why I had been spared. If Blake was being investigated by Customs and Excise, he wouldn't want to have to explain away the dead bodies of local lawyers last seen at his home.

'Why d'you want to know?' said my father.

'Client I've got,' I said. 'Had some bother with them.'

My father turned to me, his back to the snooker table, cue propped in one hand. He rubbed his face with an open palm, smoothed back his oiled hair.

'If your client's got bother with them, son, you've got bother with them. You want to get as far away as you can. Ain't nothing they won't do, nobody they won't touch, respectable or not. Geezer drinks around here, they did his wife. Still he didn't listen. So they did both his sons. That was twenty years ago. Been trying to drink himself to death ever since.'

I thought of Alex Blake, his absence of humanity. 'And Connor Blake?'

'Horrible little fucker,' my father said, turning back to the table. He bent down to his shot. 'Big fucking surprise.' On the table next to us one of the young lads was already cueing his shot and my father was directly behind him. But of course my father had not noticed, and as the lad brought his cue back, he nudged my father's elbow. My father stopped, stood up, turned to the lad who already had a hand up to apologise even though it was not his fault.

'You want to try that again?' said my father.

'Sorry,' said the lad. 'Didn't see you.'

'Want to use your eyes, son,' my father said, giving him the stare. He paused a beat, said, 'What've you got to say?'

The lad had already apologised and I could sense his internal debate, his disinclination to say sorry again fighting his natural urge to avoid confrontation. Just apologise, I thought. It won't hurt.

'Yeah, sorry,' the lad said, enough sullenness in his tone to salve his pride, enough sincerity to mollify my father. My father shook his head at me, bent down to his shot, stopped, stood up. The young lad was still waiting to take his shot. He'd wait for as long as was necessary.

'Listen, Connor Blake, you don't want to get involved. Him or his old man. Whatever it is, walk away. Just walk away.'

He bent down again, hit his shot but hit it too hard, didn't get the stun he wanted, put draw on instead and the white followed the red into the pocket with an impact like a shot.

He stayed down for a moment and I said, 'Yeah but why...' but I had lost him.

He straightened up and turned to the young lad, gripping his cue in both hands, holding it like a barbell, and he said to the young lad who would not meet his eyes, 'Now look what you made me fucking do, you stupid little cunt.'

I got home late and exhausted having talked my father out of physically attacking a boy nearly fifty years his junior for no other crime than being there at the same time as my father happened to be demonstrating his ineptitude at playing snooker. But what my father had told me rang true: whatever Ryan had done to upset the Blakes, nothing had been sacrosanct – his wife, his kids, all made to pay. I thought of Liam, his mistake, allowing me to follow him home and exposing Alex Blake. His punishment, although still terrible, at least now made more sense.

Perhaps Ryan had really had no choice; perhaps suicide had seemed the only way out, the only way he could protect his family from the Blake's pitiless onslaught. I felt a sudden overwhelming feeling of guilt, a sensation like my body was in free fall. I had treated him with disdain, such contempt. My conduct may have driven him over the edge. The feeling of guilt was so strong that for some hours I sat with my head in my hands in my living room, trying to rock away my dreadful culpability, and failing, failing.

13

I HAD RECENTLY bought an abandoned building, which at one point had been a convent, using an unexpected inheritance. I had planning permission to convert it into apartments and was using Andy, an old acquaintance of mine, to carry out the work. I had nothing to contribute to the project, had signed off the architectural plans and told Andy to do it right, take his time, quote me a price and do his best to stick to it. But the next morning I needed something to do so I drove over, parked at the kerb where tall painted wooden boards with *Danger Do Not Enter* signs hid the construction work from the street.

I got out of my car and walked by the tall boards until I came to a door with a security keypad on it. I punched in the code, opened the door and saw men in hard hats, cement being mixed, scaffolding boards over muddy earth. I nodded to a couple of men who I knew by sight and walked into the entrance. As always when I did this, I had to try to suppress the thought of what lay beneath the concrete floor, what was buried there. I had no love for the place, in some senses feared it, but it was mine and it had come to me in

127

strange circumstances. Anyway, looking at the work in full flow around me, it was a little late for second thoughts.

'Danny. You all right?'

Andy was bald, built like a pillar box and one of the most honest and open men I had ever known. He had a daughter at LSE studying Economics who he would talk of with a bewildered yet proud awe.

'Yes, mate. Everything okay?'

'Okay, except for the fact it's bloody freezing. God cancel spring or something?'

'Cold, is it?'

'Funny. Here, electrics are in, on schedule despite acts of God. You want anything particular?'

'Just looking. Seeing you aren't making off with the fire-places.'

Andy laughed. 'First thing I did.'

My mobile rang and I hesitated, did not wish to appear rude, but looking at it I saw that it was Vick's number.

'Sorry, Andy, I have to take this.' I picked up the call. 'Hello?'

'Yeah, you've been calling Vick,' said a woman.

'Yes.'

'You that lawyer?'

'Yes. She hear about Ryan?'

'She heard. Listen, that social worker's been in touch. Says she can visit her kids. Vick wants you there with her.'

'Me?' I did not want this. I did not want to be involved.

'Best you come over here.'

'Where's here?'

The woman gave me her address, told me I couldn't miss it, had a flamingo on the lawn, a plastic one but pink like the real thing. I said goodbye to Andy, thanked him for his work, walked back over the scaffolding boards, through the door and out to my car. And back into Vick's story.

Ms Armstrong still had her hair piled up on top of her head but this time her dress was orange rather than blue, black leggings underneath and sandals on her feet. She carried the same air of goodwill combined with professional distance, which suggested that she had everybody's best intentions at heart but, ultimately, she called the shots and there was no discussion to be had.

'Mrs Lowrie?' she said.

Vick held out her hand and Ms Armstrong took it but did not shake it, instead simply held it for a moment as she looked Vick in the eyes. I wondered how Vick was managing to hold herself together. That she was doing it for her children I did not doubt, but so soon after hearing of Ryan's death, I was amazed she was capable of speech, of thought.

Ms Armstrong nodded, turned and said, 'Follow me,' and again set off so quickly that Vick and I had to hustle after her. We passed the large hangar-like room where children of different ages played and read and waited for whatever fate was being decided for them by adults they had never met.

'They are expecting you,' Ms Armstrong said without turning. 'I need you to understand that you should not give them any assurances regarding when, or if, they are coming back home with you.'

Vick nodded but Ms Armstrong was in front and could not see and she said curtly, 'Mrs Lowrie?'

'Yes,' said Vick. 'All right.'

Ms Armstrong stopped at a door with a card on it that read *Family room* and turned to us.

'I need to be there with you.'

'I want Daniel to be there too.'

'Vick,' I said, but Vick shook her head.

'Please, Dan.'

I shrugged and Ms Armstrong opened the door and stepped aside to let Vick pass. I followed her in, Ms Armstrong behind me. Ollie and Gwynn were sitting on small chairs at a low table.

The instant they saw Vick they got up and yelled, 'Mummy!' and Vick was on her knees, with them in her arms, holding them, stroking their small backs desperately and covering their faces with kisses as the children gabbled and tripped over their words, hopped up and down in the safety of Vick's grip. Watching them I wondered how Ms Armstrong could still suspect Vick of any wrongdoing, so unconditional, unrestrained and joyful was their reunion.

As I turned to look at Ms Armstrong, I caught her roughly pushing a tear away from her nose with her index finger as if it was an unwelcome insect, and I realised that her job was difficult, so very difficult. The emotional toll must have been dreadful.

'Where were you, Mummy?' said Ollie, the elder child.

'I had to work,' said Vick. 'I'm so sorry.'

'Do we go home now?' he said.

'Soon,' said Vick. 'I hope soon.' She let go of her children and leaned back away from them so that she could look them in the eyes. 'Are you all right?'

'I don't like it here,' said Ollie. 'Can we go home?'

Gwynn did not say anything, watched her mother with grave eyes. Vick spoke and I could sense the effort she made to keep her voice bright, keep it from breaking.

'A bit longer here,' she said. 'Just a bit longer.'

'I want to go home,' said Ollie. His voice caught on *home* and he stood upright with his fists clenched, his eyes tight shut and his little frame shook as he cried. Vick gathered him to her but he pushed her away with rigid arms. Then Gwynn started to cry as well and I could not imagine a more helpless situation. Abruptly Ollie stopped fighting and both children collapsed into Vick's embrace and she stroked their hair, whispering, 'I'm sorry, I'm sorry,' again and again like a liturgy, although she did not have anything to say sorry for, nothing at all.

Contact was strictly monitored, supervised and time-tabled, and after an hour Ms Armstrong quietly told Vick that her time was up, that she had to go but that she could come back in two days' time if she wanted. I could not watch Vick say goodbye to her children, could not bear to see the pain that it would cause her, so waited outside, staring at the closed door of the room, trying not to picture what was going on behind it, trying not to think about how hard it must be for Vick and how brave she had to be.

I had driven Vick to the care centre in silence and I took her back to her friend's house, again driving in silence through the falling darkness. Vick did not speak for the first half of the journey and when we stopped at a red light, tired people on their way back from work passing in front of headlights, I looked across at her and saw that she was crying. My heart was beating fast, the adrenalin of the confessional.

'I'm sorry about Ryan,' I said.

Vick did not answer, turned to look out of her side window.

'I was there,' I said.

'You what?'

'I was there. Talking to him. When he... When he killed himself.'

Vick turned to me. 'You were there?'

I nodded. 'I wanted to talk to him. Get to the bottom of... this.'

'What did he say? What... Daniel? What did he say?'

The lights changed and I pulled away. 'Vick...'

'What did he *say*?'

I thought about what Ryan had told me, wondered how I could tell it, so it made sense. 'He was under some pressure. Don't know from whom. Wasn't making much sense.'

'You were there.' Disbelief in her voice.

'I'm sorry,' I said. 'I wish I could have done something. But he just... He just went.'

I took Vick back to her friend's house, came in, sat with her in the kitchen. She made coffee and we drank in silence, Vick looking out of the dark window into whatever she saw out there.

'What kind of pressure?' she eventually said. 'What kind of pressure was he under?'

I drank, considered. Came up empty. 'Don't know. Maybe he owed people money. Maybe they were getting to you, to get to him. All that's been happening. Could be it was all about him, nothing to do with you.'

'Ryan,' Vick said in frustration and anger.

'He wanted to make it stop,' I said.

'So he done himself in.' She laughed, a short, sad sound. 'Couldn't have been that bad.'

But I was not so sure. I had met Alex Blake; she hadn't. I watched her as she thought, went through recent events in her mind, shifted meanings and changed her assumptions.

'So everything's been happening,' she said, 'it weren't ghosts?'

'No,' I said. 'I don't know what it was. But it wasn't ghosts. And I think it's over.'

Vick looked angry, a brief expression of defiance before her face collapsed and she dug in her bag for a tissue, wiped her eyes.

'Why didn't you stay for the police?'

A good question. 'Whoever Ryan was involved with... Vick, it's best to leave it. It's over. Get the police involved, we'll get straight back in it.'

'But my kids. Could prove it weren't me. What happened to them.'

She was right. But she had not met Alex Blake. She did not understand.

'Vick, believe me. You don't want to get involved.'

133

She did not respond to this, gazed back out of the window.

'He was doing well,' she said eventually. 'Doing so well.'

I looked across at her, frowned. 'Doing well?'

She nodded. 'We still spoke. He told me. How good work was going.'

'Yeah, but Vick, rent-a-cop for a shopping centre? Bit of a come-down from the army, wasn't it?'

Vick frowned. 'Rent-a-what? No, Danny. Ryan weren't no security guard: he worked up at the nick. High-security.'

I did not understand. 'The nick?'

'Yeah. He was a prison guard. And doing bloody well too, if what he said was right.'

'Prison guard,' I said. I had a feeling of floating, of anchors cast off. My chest and arms felt numb and I barely trusted myself to hold my coffee.

'Loved it, he did. Reckoned he'd be running the place one day.'

I did not reply. There was a meaning here, a significance that was only barely discernible, like a dark shape submerged in murky water – a meaning that changed everything. I did not know what Vick had told me meant. But I knew that it could mean nothing good.

It did not take me long to do a search for Connor Blake, did not take me long to read four or five news stories that all carried, essentially, the same sparse information. I remembered the headlines from months ago, one more violent incident in my neighbourhood. I had not read the details, had not known the names of the people involved. Connor Blake.

On a Friday night three months ago he had been drinking in a local bar with a group of friends. The bar was open only to clientele aged twenty-five and over, in an attempt to reduce violent incidents caused by inebriated teenagers high on testosterone. That evening, though, the policy had not been enough to prevent what happened. The police described the attack as motiveless; they also described it as horrific. A young man named Karl Reece had been drinking in the bar that night. He was a medical student visiting a university friend over the Christmas holidays. He apparently exchanged words with Connor Blake and an argument broke out. Karl's friends managed to cool the situation down and both parties continued drinking. But at around two o'clock in the morning it had flared up again and Connor Blake had attacked Karl Reece, beaten him half unconscious. Then, not satisfied that the other man's disrespect had been sufficiently punished, he dragged Reece out of the bar and laid him face-down against a wall so that his forehead was resting against the bricks, his neck at an angle. He had taken a four-step run-up and launched himself at Reece, landing with both feet on the back of the other man's neck, killing him instantly.

Connor Blake was currently on remand having been refused bail due to the severity of his crime, and was waiting for his trial to begin. The prison he was being held in was Galleys Wood, about fifteen miles from my office, and was, I knew even before I called Vick to confirm, the same prison that Ryan had worked in.

I sat in my office, turned it all over in my mind. Thought about what I had done, following Ryan, talking to bookies, treating him with contempt for his gambling, his failings as a father, his weakness. But did what had happened have anything to do with that? Or was something else, something far darker, to blame?

Outside my windows the streets were quieter, commuters home from work, shops shut. Maria was at home and it was time for me to see her, even though I was in no mood for company, even hers. I was about to close up when my office phone rang. I had no urge to answer it, but after listening to it ring four times I reluctantly picked it up.

'Hello.'

'Daniel?'

'Speaking.'

It was a man's voice, but not one I recognised. He did not say anything for a moment.

'Who is this?'

He ignored my question. 'Need a lawyer. One I've got now, he's fucking useless. Won't do as he's told.'

'Okay,' I said, my hand gripping my phone tightly. 'You got a name?'

He laughed. 'You know who this is.'

I picked up a pen with my free hand, just for the reassurance of touching something familiar. 'I don't know you.'

'You will do, Daniel. You prefer Danny?'

'This conversation is over.'

'No. No, it isn't. I need a lawyer. You're it.'

'Sorry, friend. Doesn't work like that.'

'You'll do what you're told.'

'No,' I said. 'Hear me? You want legal representation, try the Yellow Pages.'

'We know all about you, Daniel. Where you live, where Maria lives. You'll do as you're—'

But I did not let him finish his sentence. Intimidation worked on power, keeping somebody on the defensive, overwhelming them. I had never been a back-foot player; was not going to let that happen. For better or worse, my instinct had always been to attack.

'You're Connor Blake. And whatever you did to Ryan, try it with me and I'll bury you.'

'You know who you're dealing with,' said Blake. 'You know what we can do.'

'This conversation is over.'

'Listen—' he said, but I had had enough.

'No, you listen,' I said and took a breath, filled my chest, let my pulse steady. 'I don't want anything to do with you. You're in prison and I hope you never see a blue sky again.'

'Oh, Daniel.'

'We're done.'

I hung up on his voice, replaced the receiver. I leaned back from my desk and my office was quiet, as if his voice had never entered. But I could still hear it in my head, could not so easily exorcise his confident swagger. What kind of a man was he? Calling me, demanding that I act as his lawyer, expecting it; his behaviour was so off the scale that for a moment I doubted what had just happened. I had opened no forbidden doors, lifted no rocks. Yet still, suddenly here he was.

But monsters do not vanish by an act as simple as finishing a phone call; this I should have known.

I was stretching my shoulders, rolling my neck and shaking off the effects of Blake's call when my phone rang again. This time I did not pick it up. I rolled my chair back to the window and watched it, listened to it ring. I had not turned the office lights on when I came back from Gabe's and it was now growing dark outside, my office gloomy, the corners in shadow. I listened to the mechanic click of my answer machine as it picked up the call, listened to my own voice as I explained that I was sorry I was not there but please leave a message. The light of my answer machine blinked red in the dimness, I heard the bleep and then I heard Connor Blake's voice again.

Perhaps it was the gathering dark or the acoustics of my office, but there seemed to be something in his voice this time, a wistful quality that made him sound as if he was calling from far away, from some unknowable, distant place.

'They want to lock me away forever, Daniel. They want to lock me away with the crazies and the kiddie killers and never let me out.'

He sighed, a mystified sadness, as if he was some kind of martyr, victim of a cruel society's ill will.

'Help me, Daniel. Ryan didn't and we had to take it all away from him. Be a friend to me. Don't make us do the same to you.'

He took a breath and I expected more, but he simply exhaled slowly, a melancholy sound, then he hung up.

I watched my answer machine as if it was a suspect device, watched its red light blinking to announce what it held. Fuck this, I thought eventually, and I got up to delete what he had left, erase his voice from my world. I would not allow the Blakes to own me. I hit delete, heard the beep that told me his message was gone, erased forever. But even as I pressed the button I knew that it would not be as simple to be rid of him, of the Blakes, that this was not the end of it. Connor Blake had driven Ryan to suicide, then tried to intimidate me. There was an intent there and I was sure that I would hear from him again, and soon.

14

'AND THAT'S IT,' I say to Gabe. 'Everything. The whole story.'

We are in his kitchen. It is only hours since we were forced off the road coming back from our fishing trip but already it seems like a distant memory: the black car in the rear-view mirror, the impact, the men in balaclavas, the guns against our heads. We have drunk the bottle of Scotch down to below the label now; it has taken that long to tell Gabe all that has happened in the past weeks. Vick, her children, Alex Blake, Ryan's suicide, Connor Blake's call from prison. The trouble I have found myself in.

'So, let me get this straight,' says Gabe. He picks his glass up, swirls what is left at the bottom around. 'All the time, it was the Blakes putting the pressure on Ryan. The furniture moving, Vick's kids. All so they could show Ryan what they could do. How they could get at his family.'

'Right.'

'Why?'

I shake my head, push my glass. 'Ryan was a prison warden. Blake must have wanted something from him.' I shrug. 'Don't know what.'

'And now?'

'And now, I'm in the firing line.'

I think again of the guns against our heads, the sound as the racks were slid back, the warning. *Last chance.*

'I told Connor Blake to go to hell.' I pick up the bottle, pour. 'Didn't take them long to send me a message.'

'So you think what just happened, that was the Blakes? Giving you a final warning.'

'I don't do what he asks, he'll kill me.'

Gabe picks up the bottle, looks at the label. 'Could be,' he says eventually.

'Got to be,' I say. 'The Blakes have got resources, you can see that. What they did to Vick, to Ryan. Running us off the road, putting guns to our heads – that's nothing for them.'

Telling the story to Gabe, I cannot help but wonder how I have found myself in this position: being manipulated by criminals, blackmailed from a prison cell by a killer. But I have to admit that telling it to Gabe is helping; as always, he takes news of my troubles with a matter-of-factness that I cannot, do not, feel. Nothing seems to surprise him. Given what he has seen and done in his life, perhaps that is not so remarkable.

'Could be,' Gabe says again. 'Question is, what do they want with you?'

I tilt my glass, look at the Scotch coat its sides, run thickly down. 'Ryan's gone,' I say. 'So I guess now Blake needs somebody else, for...' For what? 'For whatever it is he wants.' I shrug. 'Christ knows.'

'Well,' says Gabe, getting up from the table and looking a little unsteady. 'Shame you can't get your hands on him.'

'No,' I say. 'He's safe where he is.' But thinking about Connor Blake, about what he has done and what he has threatened me with, I have an urge to cause him violence so all-consuming that for a moment I forget where I am.

'These Blakes. They're that bad?'

I rouse myself from my seductive thoughts of vengeance. 'Told you what they did to the guy, Liam. Like it was nothing. Punishment, for what? For letting me follow him home? They tortured him for it.' I shake my head at my glass, confounded. 'Driving Ryan to kill himself. Yeah, they're that bad.'

The thought of them, the Blakes, some diabolical and inexhaustible force, suddenly makes all ideas of vengeance seem as pointless as weeping into a fire to put it out. What have I got myself involved with?

'Dan?'

'Yeah.' I cough, pour the rest of the Scotch in my glass down my throat, look up at my friend. 'Hell, Gabe. I don't know.'

We had pulled dented bodywork away from Gabe's rear wheel, torn off his bumper, which was dragging on the ground, and put it in his boot. The exhaust was undamaged and there did not seem to be any structural problems. The car started, and stopped, and drove in a straight line. A couple had passed us on the road and asked us if we needed any help, a man and a woman in their fifties. He had worn a flat cap and when he had asked us what had happened, Gabe had testily told him that we had hit a moose. The man had nodded in important understanding, apparently unaware that the chances of hitting a moose in Essex were infinitesimally small. Any other time we would have laughed.

We had driven back to Gabe's in silence, both occupied with thoughts of culpability, of who had attacked us and why and what we could do about it, how we could make them pay. Gabe's appearance was never approachable but, looking across at him as he drove, I had an insight into the terrible price he must have exacted from his enemies when in the army. I would not have wanted to encounter him in a fight. Would not have wanted those pale eyes to be the last thing I ever saw.

'Shame about your car,' I say.

'Yeah,' says Gabe across the kitchen from me, doing something to his espresso machine.

'Must be worth a fair bit.'

'Was. Somebody just ran it off the road.'

I am speaking to his back, which makes it easier to challenge him. 'You're up, Gabe. Time to tell me what's going on.'

'Yeah,' he says softly.

'People shooting up your house, the guy at the tennis court. All this money you've got. Your pension can't be that generous.'

Gabe turns to face me. 'As if. The British Army can't even pay for battle armour. Think they're going to pay for a car?'

'So?'

Gabe sighs. 'So, Dan, I, like any other soldier with any sense, took out private insurance. Know how much you get for a leg?'

I do not answer, cannot think of the right response.

'They all came in, the big insurance firms; cost fuck all to get covered. They must have thought the war'd be a walk-over, in and out, couple of hundred claims and they'd be quids in. Turns out the Taliban are world leaders at laying roadside bombs, burying IEDs, suddenly they're shelling out for arms, feet, legs.' Gabe allows himself a smile. 'Must have nearly finished them.'

'So that's it? You're burning through your insurance?'

'Hardly touched it. Why? Think I haven't earned it?'

This isn't fair and Gabe looks at the floor, turns back to the coffee. I do not need to say anything. I pick up the Scotch, pour another measure, pour some more.

'So,' I say. 'You've got insurance. Big deal. Doesn't explain why somebody put a bullet through your window. Doesn't explain why you think what just happened, why that was meant for you.'

Gabe smiles. 'No. No, Danny, it doesn't explain that.'

'What did you say? It was a military manoeuvre. Getting run off the road like that.'

'Still give you good odds they were after you, not me.'

'Know somebody who'd put a gun to your head?'

'I know people who'd do a lot worse. Have done a lot worse.'

'And what they said. That was a warning. *Last chance.*'

'Yeah. I think that was for me.'

I see that he is serious. It is time to find out what he is into. We have been through too much for him to keep it from me now. I've told him everything that has happened to me. Now it is his turn.

'Go on then,' I say. 'Let's have it.' I take a drink. 'The whole story. From the beginning.'

15

A LITTLE OVER three years ago, and a bare six months before Gabe had been flown out of Afghanistan in the back of a Hercules, hooked up to a drip and en route to a German hospital, he had been seconded to an infantry platoon for a rotation at a forward operating base halfway up a mountainside in the north-eastern Kunar Province. It was a place of deep valleys and high, creased mountains, green with holly trees and tall cedars and had a reputation as one of the most dangerous places in the country: hard-to-reach villages crawling with insurgents and steep trails so perfectly suited to ambushes that walking them felt like a direct challenge to Death himself.

The powers had wanted Gabe to see more combat, prior to them anointing him for greater things. They liked their majors to have seen bloodshed up close, to have a reputation for valour that, they felt, wouldn't be earned taking armoured vehicles on patrol around friendly villages. You can't order men into battle, they said, if you're not steeped in combat yourself. Captain Gabriel McBride needed to go and get his hands dirty.

Kunar Province was the ideal post: Forward Operating Base Lucifer had seen more contact with enemy forces than the next three FOBs put together. If there was going to be killing, this was where it was going to happen.

Gabe was leading the platoon and had only a few short weeks to win them over, to impose his will on them. There was an incumbent platoon at Lucifer, a battle-hardened regular infantry platoon of Rifles who were coming to the end of their rotation. It was their job during those weeks to show Gabe's new platoon the ropes, take them through the enemy positions across the valley from FOB Lucifer, lead them up the trails, introduce Gabe to the elders in the surrounding villages, and explain who could be trusted and who was, in all likelihood, concealing a cache of enemy ordnance in their home even as they looked in his eyes and shook his hand.

'This group of Rifles, 7 Platoon, who we were taking over from, they'd seen it all,' says Gabe. 'They'd been ambushed, double-crossed, pinned down. Four of their platoon had been killed and seven more evacced out with serious injuries. You could see it in their eyes and the way they spoke about the local population – pure hatred.'

Gabe has found another bottle of whisky and opens it, sets it down as he thinks back to that time, places himself back among his men. 'Doesn't usually work like that, in the army. Doesn't get personal. But these men, they'd had enough. Never expected to see the things they did, have to do what they'd done. Six months is a long time at the sharp end, isolated in a place like that.' He shakes his head. 'The place was hell on earth.'

The men of 7 Platoon had reached a point where morality took a back seat to expedience and where ordinary values of right and wrong, good and bad, had long since ceased to have any relevance. Dirty, demoralised and disgusted by the acts that they had witnessed and committed, they had crossed a line. They were now not so much professional soldiers as officially sanctioned killers.

Gabe picks up the bottle, looks at the label, but he is not reading it; he is three years and five thousand miles away on a dusty mountainside.

He looks at me, says, 'You sure you want to hear this?'

'I'm a big boy.'

Gabe shakes his head in irritation at my flippancy. 'Never told anyone before. Nobody outside the army.'

'I think I have a right,' I say. 'After what just happened.'

Gabe is still looking at me, his eyes empty. He nods. 'Fair enough. Don't say I didn't warn you.'

I nod Gabe to go on and he puts the bottle down, takes a breath as if he is about to leap from a dangerous position, and resumes his story.

It was about six days in when it happened, six days spent shadowing 7 Platoon who seemed to know the area so well it was as if they had spent a lifetime on the mountain trails, had been born in its shadow. Apparently innocuous piles of rocks and junctions of paths had particular names, after colleagues who had lost their lives there: Cooper's Crossing, Fox's Hole; Dizzy's End. Gallows humour, though any humour there had been in that platoon had died months ago.

They had been patrolling a high trail, only a few hundred metres beneath the summit, at the point where the tangle of holly trees gave way to cedars so large and ancient they seemed to pre-date the arrival of man; laid lengthways, their trunks would be taller than two men. Gabe was walking with a lance corporal named Creek who, of all the jaded 7 Platoon, was the only soldier who had retained any trace of humanity, perhaps because he was a late arrival, flown in to take the place of a fallen colleague. He was a short, slight man who still greeted the everyday horrors of life at Lucifer with an intelligent cynicism; he stood apart from his fellow soldiers and was treated by them with disdain and suspicion. Gabe believed that he feared them.

The 7 Platoon leader was up front, setting a hard pace, when a rigged grenade went off by the side of the trail, a sharp crack throwing up a shower of black dirt, which blotted out the tree-dappled sunshine for a moment. Even before the dirt fell back down to earth, they could hear the screams of the platoon leader; the grenade had shredded his legs and given him serious groin injuries, torn open an artery. But his screams were soon overlaid by the sound of incoming fire, AK rounds zipping through the air and ripping the bark off the holly trees, spitting up dirt where they fell short. Both platoons hit the ground and rolled off the trail to lower ground, looking for cover from holly trees and cedar tree logs left behind by long ago lumber companies; the weight of incoming fire was so great that they could do nothing but lie there and wait for it to lessen.

'It was like, above our heads, there was a ceiling of bullets and noise. Anyone put their heads up, they were going to die,' says Gabe, a trace of sadness in his voice. 'Nothing to do. Nothing.'

But 7 Platoon had been in this position before. Besides, the injured man was their platoon leader and a man they respected, even loved. In this foreign land of shifting rules and unfathomable morality, he was all they had to rely on.

As his colleagues put up covering fire, shooting above their heads from where they lay without taking any kind of aim, one soldier crawled up to the screaming platoon leader and stuck syringes of morphine into his neck, using first the platoon leader's and then his own, the soldier's battle-dress soon slick with bright arterial blood. He shook his head helplessly as he administered to his superior officer, knowing that there was nothing to be done, that he was bleeding so fast that he would be dead in minutes and that he was powerless to do anything except keep him comfortable. As the platoon leader's life ebbed away, the incoming fire died down until there was silence, broken only by the soldier whispering to his platoon leader, 'It'll be all right, it's nothing,' hushing him as his screams turned to whimpers and he slowly and quietly died on a shaded trail on a mountain in a faraway country he probably had not even heard of five years ago.

'You could feel it immediately,' says Gabe. 'Like a change in the weather. Nothing was said, but this, killing their platoon leader, this was it. Gloves off, blood up.'

It had been a classic insurgency ambush, fast and

unexpected and unanswerable. They had picked off the commanding officer and that had been enough of a victory for them, more than enough, a huge tactical coup. By this time helicopters were in the air and zeroing in on the platoons' position, a surveillance plane flying three thousand feet above. The insurgents wanted to put as much distance between themselves and the dead platoon leader as they could, and fast.

Still, normally the helicopters would have finished the insurgents off as they ran, firing on them from above in a display so destructive and awesome, Gabe says, it seemed as unequivocal as God's vengeance. But the brass had had enough of pointless tit-for-tat killing; they wanted warm bodies, something that could answer questions, could be paraded in front of the TV cameras and used as propaganda.

Without a word, 7 Platoon left Gabe and his newly arrived soldiers and headed off down trails they had spent six months patrolling, guided by the surveillance plane turning lazy circles above, so high in the blue sky it was out of sight. Even if they'd wanted to follow, Gabe said, half a year of life at Lucifer had honed the Rifles platoon to a level of fitness that his soldiers couldn't hope to match, their fury adding another adrenal kick to their pace. Gabe left half of his platoon to carry down the body of the dead officer; he took the rest and headed off in the direction of the departed 7 Platoon.

'We got to the village ten, twelve minutes after the other platoon,' says Gabe. 'The insurgents had headed there, didn't even realise there was a plane up above watching them. Led us to their front door.'

When Gabe and his soldiers reached the village, it was like a ghost town, every door and window shuttered, like Dodge after a gunslinger had walked into town. The 7 Platoon soldiers were dispersed, sitting or lying or crouched against walls, some smoking impassively, some drinking water, some weeping with their hands splayed over the faces in grief for their dead leader. Nobody spoke. Gabe walked to the house where the insurgents had been seen to go to, looked in the door, saw a row of untidy bodies, small streams of blood on the dirt floor, the dozy buzz of flies within the hot gloom: the aftermath of a slaughter.

'The place was so quiet, the whole village,' says Gabe, clumsily pouring a splash of whisky. 'Just us, the bodies, couple of goats bleating. I spoke to one of the soldiers, asked them what had happened. Told me they'd cornered them, got into an exchange of fire.' He lifts his glass and gazes at it but does not drink. 'Thing was, none of the dead men had any weapons.'

Strangely, Gabe does not seem particularly concerned by this detail. He imagines that they dropped their weapons off at a cache, threw them down a well, got rid of anything that could incriminate them as insurgent fighters before they reached the village. Whatever, these men were, beyond doubt, the same men who less than an hour before had killed 7 Platoon's beloved leader. They had had it coming, armed or not. This was war and Gabe was a pragmatist: he accepted what had happened without question. I do not know what this says about my friend; do not want to think about it. Perhaps, like Gabe says, it just is what it is.

But once the choppers had arrived and left, and the platoons had regrouped and the dust had settled, there was one soldier who could not accept the fact of the insurgents' slaughter with such equanimity. Creek, the recently arrived lance corporal, regarded what had happened as a war crime. If you ask me, he had a point.

'Wouldn't shut up about it,' said Gabe. 'No, he didn't say anything to his platoon; he wasn't crazy. But he kept coming to see me, asked me what I was going to do about it. Told me I could not let it drop, I had a responsibility. Mr Geneva fucking Convention.'

Gabe looks at me and there is a challenge in his eyes, as if he is daring me to agree with Creek, take Gabe to task for not having immediately condemned the Rifle platoon's actions. I do not respond. I have experienced nothing approaching what Gabe has had to go through; I am not arrogant enough to believe my opinion counts for anything. Gabe takes my silence as it is meant, nods to himself, continues.

'I told him to leave it. I was the officer in charge. It was my responsibility to look after my men, to instil discipline, to keep them safe. I told him to keep quiet, that it wasn't worth it. Told him they'd make sure his career was over if he said anything.' He sighs, deeply, a shudder in it. 'They rotated out two days later and I forgot about Creek, about that damned 7 Platoon. Three months later I come back from Lucifer and one of the first things I hear is that Creek is dead, shot through the head by a British bullet.'

Creek had been shot while out on routine patrol. But despite being killed by a British bullet, his death had been ascribed to enemy action. So many British weapons had been taken by the insurgents it was assumed that this was the explanation; no shadow of suspicion ever fell on the other members of his platoon. Nobody ever suspected he had been killed by his own.

'I told him to keep it quiet,' says Gabe, his eyes on the table and his voice, which since a child I have rarely heard so much as waver from its precise and cold delivery, is barely a whisper. 'I didn't help. Refused to. And he was right, of course he was right.' Gabe shakes his head slowly at the table, still unable to reconcile himself with what he had done, what he had not done. 'I was his commanding officer.' He looks up suddenly, his eyes tortured with grief. 'My fault. Hundred per cent. On me.'

Massacring a dozen insurgents in cold blood, Gabe could live with. But not the premeditated murder of a soldier who he had liked, respected, and let down when in a position of power, a position to make a difference. He had started to investigate, asked questions, lobbied officers higher up the chain of command to conduct a proper inquest into the shooting of Lance Corporal Creek. He'd had, Gabe says, some success. Then he had walked past an IED disguised as a lump of camel shit and the next thing he knew he was in Germany and he was missing a leg and he would never see active service again.

'Ever wondered what creates monsters?' says Gabe, holding his glass up to his face. 'Six months at Forward

Operating Base Lucifer. That's what.' He downs his drink and blinks slowly, shuttering those blue-ice eyes, and I have never seen anybody look so desolate.

16

THAT OUR SOCIETY no longer executes its citizens for misdemeanours is something that I believe is to our collective credit; as a lawyer I do not accept that justice is served at the end of a rope. But as I sit in the waiting area of Galley Wood high security prison, the idea of incarceration does not seem much more humane.

Galley Wood was constructed in the late nineteenth century when criminology was in its infancy and earnest reformers were looking for alternatives to execution, finding rational solutions for monstrous acts. It is a Victorian building that has been added to and added to but which retains its solid and baleful façade. Back then, prison was intended to be as abhorrent as possible, a deterrent every bit as effective as hanging – a hell on earth. I wonder how much more tolerable it is today.

I entered through a visitors' entrance, rather than the main white metal gates that prisoners pass through on their way to years of captivity. I had my photograph and fingerprints taken, was patted down, my briefcase opened and examined, and a spaniel dog was brought over to check that my shoes contained no drugs or other contra-band. The other visitors had been through this procedure before, probably on many occasions, and submitted to it in sullen silence; just one more petty humiliation in their joyless lives.

Now I am sitting on a hard green plastic chair that is fixed to the wall of the waiting area, watching a woman in a tracksuit tell a child to shut the fuck up, this is the last time. It was the last time the time before, and the time before that. She has four children with her, their ages ranging from about three to fifteen, and she has a stunned expres-sion on her face as if her present situation has occurred overnight, rather than being the gradual accumulation of hundreds of poor decisions. There are old and young people waiting to visit prisoners, men, women and children, their skin yellow and sickly under the tube lighting. But they all share a quiet anger – at the prisoners they are about to visit, at themselves, at the world in general. A prison is a terrible, dehumanising place, for prisoner, visitor and guard alike.

It is three days since Gabe and I were forced off the road and had guns placed against our heads. It has taken this long to arrange a visit to see Connor Blake, to get the paperwork organised. He is on remand, which made things easier. Had he been serving a custodial sentence, getting access to him would have been near impossible. Now I am waiting to see him. I have no idea what to expect.

As I wait I think back to that night with Gabe, the memory compromised by the amount of Scotch we had drunk and, I now suspect, the shock I was suffering at what had happened to us. Still, I remember enough to know that Gabe is in trouble every bit as deep as mine.

Gabe might have recovered from the wounds he suffered out in Afghanistan, but the guilt at what had happened to Lance Corporal Creek still troubled him months after his release from Selly Oak hospital. He had made phone calls, contacted members of his old platoon and any soldiers he could find connected with the Rifles; he had lobbied superior officers to reopen Creek's inquest, cajoled, finessed, threatened.

'Course,' Gabe had said, 'nobody wanted to know. Why would they? I had no proof, no grounds at all to get it reopened. They just thought I'd lost it, another PTSD loony.'

It turned out that nearly all of the soldiers of the Rifles platoon had left the service. They had followed the path of many ex-soldiers in search of the adrenalin rush the army could provide, coupled with the kind of salary it could not, and gone freelance for private security companies.

'Mercenaries,' I said.

'It's where the money is nowadays,' said Gabe. 'Britain, the US, they go into countries to liberate them, then lose the stomach for the fight. All the western companies committed to infrastructure work, building motorways, oil exploration, suddenly they need protection from the pissed-off locals. You know how much an ex-sergeant can get a day out in Iraq?'

'Don't they need, I don't know, some kind of licence?'

Gabe laughed. 'Giving them away like pizza menus. Another thing ex-soldiers like. Fuck-all oversight. They can run around shooting whoever they want, nobody says a word.'

I imagined the veterans of the Rifles, unleashing their brand of savagery across the world with nobody to apply the brakes.

'Turns out this wasn't enough for them,' said Gabe. 'Bunch of them got together to create a company – Global Armour. Already won some lucrative contracts. Been out in South Sudan for six months.'

'Doing what?'

Gabe shrugged. 'Christ knows. Whatever they want, I expect. Anyway, doesn't matter. They're back now.'

'The guy at the tennis court?'

Gabe nodded. 'He's one of them. Horrible shit called Banyan. Proper little killer.'

'And the other night? The shooting?'

Gabe smiled, swirled his Scotch as he thought back to their misjudged attempt at intimidation. 'Yeah, that was them. Thought they could scare off a cripple. Should have seen their faces when I went after them.' He laughed at the memory.

It was now full dark and the events of that afternoon seemed something that had happened in the distant past, separated from the here and now by drink and exhaustion. I frowned, my mind working slowly through the fog of alcohol as I tried to piece it all together, cause and effect. 'It's not a bit... drastic? What they're doing?'

Gabe shrugged. 'Private security companies run on reputations. All they've got to trade on. If you've got a reputation for shooting your own kind, you're dead in the water.'

'So you really think that was them?' I said. 'Earlier?'

Gabe nodded slowly. 'The way they got us out of the car – fast, aggressive – it was good work.'

'Could be,' I said. 'Still think it was Blake.'

'One way to find out,' he said.

'Yeah.' Go and see him. Not something I wanted to do. 'So, what's next?' I said to Gabe.

'That guy you met the other day. Shaved head. Major Strauss. He was my superior officer and he's on the case. We're going to nail them. It's going to happen.' He drank the remains of his glass, pushed it away from him. 'It's going to happen.'

The room where I am waiting for Blake has walls of drably painted brick. There is a window high up and I am sitting at a table, an empty chair on the other side. The rules have been explained to me and my almost empty briefcase examined again; I know that I must not give anything to the prisoner or offer to bring anything in for the prisoner or pass on messages from proscribed persons to the prisoner or knowingly provide information to the prisoner that could result in harm to any other prisoner.

The room has two doors on opposite walls and there is a rattle in the lock of the door facing me, the door I did not come in through. The door opens and a man is walked in, a guard holding him by the arm, high up under his armpit.

'Connor Blake,' says the guard, and he says it with a curl of disgust as if the name has tasted bad inside his mouth. He lets go of Blake and looks at the hand he was holding him by and I half expect him to wipe it on his shirt.

'We'll be outside. If you need us. Hammer on the door.' The guard gives Blake the stare as if to warn him to be on his best behaviour but Blake does not respond, does not meet his eye. He appears to be in his own world, unaware. The guard turns and walks to the door, pauses in the doorway, takes a last look at Blake and then shakes his head and closes the door behind him. Now it is only me and Blake, him standing and me sitting, and for a moment there is silence as I look at the man who I believe has been at the root of the recent evil I have experienced.

Connor Blake is so good-looking that I do not recall ever encountering anybody who comes close. He has black hair in gentle waves and the bluest eyes I have ever seen, bluer even than his father's, and his features are so regular, his nose so straight and jaw so strong, that he would not look out of place in a Hollywood movie or on the cover of *Vanity Fair*. He is wearing prison denims yet on him they look almost stylish, as if this season's fashion is jailhouse chic. He has his sleeves rolled up and he is wearing handcuffs, his hands in front of him. He is standing casually, relaxed, as if wearing handcuffs is nothing, as if it is something he has chosen to do.

He pulls out the chair across the table from me and sits down, leans back and makes himself comfortable, as relaxed as if he is in his own home. He clasps his hands and puts them on the table in front of him, the handcuffs making a metallic sound on the table's surface. I watch him, wait for him to speak.

'Never hang up on me again,' he says.

'What makes you think you can give me orders?'

Blake ignores me. He carries the contemptuous air of a man who acknowledges only that which he considers worthy. When I worked in the City, one of my clients had been the son of a sheikh connected to the House of Saud, a young construction billionaire who drove a Lamborghini and was surrounded at all times by a retinue of deferential advisors he treated worse than unwanted pets. For some reason, Blake makes me think of him.

'The people in here,' he says. He shakes his head. 'Wouldn't believe it. Dogs. Animals. The stink of them.' He makes his eyes go big in mock panic. 'Man, you've got to get me out of here.'

'How will I do that?' I say.

'Course,' he says, and I wonder whether he hears anything I say, 'they don't touch me. They know who I am. But still. You know what I think the problem is?'

'What's that?'

He leans forward, whispers conspiratorially. 'Place is full of criminals.' He leans back again, smiles, delighted at his joke. I watch him without expression.

'Come on, man. Lighten up.'

'Don't think so.'

'We're going to be working together. Give me a smile.'

'Not going to happen.'

Blake closes his eyes, puts the cuffed heels of his hands up to them, sighs in frustration. 'Okay. Okay, Daniel. Let's have it. What's the fucking problem?'

He takes his hands away, frowning, and his bemusement

seems genuine. I wonder whether he even understands that intimidation and blackmail are hostile acts, that they cause resentment in those it is visited upon.

'You threatened me. My girlfriend.'

'Maria? Nothing'll happen to her. Not unless I say.'

I can feel my pulse hurrying, heat rising from my chest. 'Mention her again and I'll break your jaw.'

'Probably could too. You're a big, ugly bastard, anybody ever tell you that?' He smiles, presumably to rob his words of any offence. 'Listen, you're on the team now. Nothing to worry about.'

'I wasn't worried.'

Blake gazes at me for some seconds, watches me as a bird of prey would tall grass, looking for movement. There is something hypnotic about his stare, an assuredness that seems unassailable.

'You fucking well want to have been.'

His words are delivered with such measured threat and contain such a promise of malice that for a moment I am unbalanced; they are so at odds with his affability of moments ago that I do not know how to respond. By the time I am ready for a comeback the moment has gone and he is smiling again.

'Daniel, hey. Start again, okay? Okay?'

'Running me off the road,' I say. 'Holding a gun to my head. No. No, it's not okay.'

Blake frowns, looks behind him as if asking his counsel for advice. He looks back at me, confusion in his eyes, his composure threatened for the first time.

'What?' he says.

'Please,' I say.

'No,' says Blake. 'What the fuck are you talking about?'

I look at him and he is looking at me in incomprehension and I realise that he has no idea what I am referring to. He had nothing to do with it. What happened on that road, the guns to our heads, the warning – it was all about Gabe. A military manoeuvre, that's what Gabe had said. They'd been after him, not me.

Too late I realise that Blake has done nothing except make some empty threats and rattle my cage. All I want to do now is get away from his odious presence. But I need some answers; I owe Vick that much.

'Tell me,' I say. 'Ryan Lowrie. What did you want from him?'

Blake looks surprised. 'Want? Wanted him to get me out of here.'

'How was he supposed to do that?'

Still that look of surprise, as if I am asking questions that he cannot be expected to answer. 'Fuck would I know? He's the screw, not me. Was,' he corrects himself, smirking. 'I told him to find a way. Get me transferred, give me a day release, whatever. His problem, not mine.'

'But...' I say, and for a moment I cannot think of the words for this man. 'Did you really think he could do that?'

'I'll be honest,' he says. 'Towards the end, I think he was stalling. Bullshitting me, saying he could do this, do that.'

I thought of Ryan, of him hearing of furniture moving, of Vick waking outside; being shown shots of his children tied up, unconscious. Of the relentless pressure put on him and his desperate response; empty promises, assurances that he would find a way to get Blake out, if he'd just give him time. Saying anything to keep Blake and his men at bay, away from his family.

'What did you expect?' I say. 'You were blackmailing him, harming his kids.'

Blake shrugs, looks bored. 'Anyway, gave him a week. Told him he didn't get me out, we'd kill his wife. Ex-wife. Do it properly this time.'

'So he took his own life.'

'Yeah.' Contempt in Blake's voice. Contempt like I had shown Ryan, to my shame. 'Little prick.'

This is enough for me. 'We're done,' I say, pushing my chair back.

'Sit down,' says Blake, amused.

'I have nothing more to say to you,' I say, standing up. 'I've seen all I need.'

'You're going nowhere. You need to get me out of here.'

'How?'

'Ryan couldn't. So now,' he points the first two fingers of one cuffed hand at me, takes a shot, 'I've got you.'

'We're done,' I say again. 'Goodbye.'

'You can't leave.' He shakes his head as if he cannot believe that I am acting so foolishly. 'You don't walk away from the Blakes.' He pauses, closes his eyes as if invoking some all-powerful entity. 'My father.' He looks at me. 'Don't tell me you want to meet him again.'

I do not, never want to, ever. But this is not a moment

165

to show weakness. I think of Ryan, of what he had been reduced to. 'Send anyone after me,' I say, looking at him, giving away nothing, 'and I'll put them in a grave.'

'You've got no idea what we can do.'

'I've seen what you can do.'

'Nothing compared to what we'll do to Maria.'

I step around the table and take a handful of Blake's denim shirt, lift him and push him backwards over his chair, rush him up against the brick wall behind him. He hits it hard and I feel the breath leave his body, feel his ribcage give under my hand. My face is inches away from his and I am looking directly into his eyes. Amusement in their blueness, delighted by my loss of control. There is no fear. Most men, if I did this to them, would be begging. He only smiles.

'Daniel. What are you doing?'

'Never threaten me.'

'Give me a beating? There are guards outside the door. You're in prison, Daniel.'

I take a firmer grip of his shirt, lift him so that he is on tiptoes. His eyes widen slightly as he senses my strength and there is an excitement there. He is enjoying this.

'You'd like to hurt me. I know. But you can't, Daniel. You really can't.'

I let go and back up, turn away from him as I pick up my briefcase.

'There's nothing you can do. Me, it's different. I can make one call and destroy your life.'

I hit the door with my fist and the sheet metal makes a dull booming sound. I can hear Blake laughing quietly.

'Daniel, if you walk out of that door then it will all change.'

I turn and Blake is leaning back in his chair, smiling at me.

'We will take it all from you,' he says.

'Listen—' I begin, but the door opens and the guard who had walked Blake in enters, looks at Blake, at me, says, 'All right?'

'Fine,' I say, and walk past him. As I do I hear Blake's voice say, 'Everything, Daniel. Everything.' Another guard is outside and he asks me to follow him, leading me through a maze of corridors and locked doors and out of this place and back into the light.

17

MY VISIT TO Connor Blake has disturbed me more than I care to admit. I spend the rest of that day considering him, trying to work him out and understand what kind of upbringing or psychological flaw would cause somebody to act as he had. I once had a teacher who maintained that nobody was beyond redemption; that everybody had some good in them. Her name was Ms Dawson, who I came to know as Rachael, a woman who had discerned some intelligence beneath my rough exterior and had encouraged me to apply for a scholarship to public school, which paved my way to university and a career, if you could call it that, in law. She has been dead over a year now, a victim of breast cancer, and her memory is one that I cherish and mourn. But still, I cannot agree with her. Some people are simply bad. They harbour no goodness, possess no virtue.

I pick up my phone, make a call. 'Dean? It's Danny.'

'Danny, son. How you doing? How's your old man? I ain't seen him in here for a while.'

'Same as normal.'

'Fucking horrible.'

'Right.' Dean grew up alongside me and saw first-hand how I had been treated. Even though he's happy to serve him in his pub, he has no respect for my father.

'Know Connor Blake?'

There is a silence on the other end and I take my phone away from my ear, check it is still connected.

'Why d'you want to know about him for?'

'Case I'm working on. Need some background.'

'You want to steer clear of that lot.'

'Just background. Don't worry.'

'Anyway, Danny son, I don't know him, don't want to fucking know him.'

'But you know somebody who does.'

'Might.' Silence again, then, 'You know he killed someone?'

'I know. So go on.'

'Hang on, thinking.' I listen to Dean's breathing and think about how first my father and now Dean have tried to warn me off the Blakes.

'Danny?'

'Yeah.'

'Can only think of one person. Might want to talk to him. But Danny?'

'Yes, Dean.'

He hesitates. 'Nothing.'

Dean gives me the name of a man who he tells me is a chef at a hotel called Thorndon Manor and had been tight with Connor Blake for years, called Ade, said like Maddy. He asked me to come round the pub one day, have a drink, but behind this I could feel his discomfort at what I had asked of him and he seemed anxious to get off the phone, end the conversation. I thanked him and told him I'd see him around and he hung up before I did, leaving me with a dead phone to my ear.

That night Maria and I drive to a seafood restaurant on the coast that has a reputation across Essex and further, a dark candlelit place with heavy wood tables overlooking a small harbour of fishing boats and modest yachts. Maria knows the owner and he embraces her, shakes my hand and gives us a table in the window where we watch a full moon float above the sea, scraps of cloud blowing across its pocked face. We eat green-lip mussels and oysters, share a lobster, drink white wine recommended to us by the owner. In the warm flickering light Maria looks beautiful, her dark hair and skin merging with the shadows so that she seems a part of them and I can barely delineate her form, watch only her shining eyes and lips as we talk together.

The place is so peaceful and removed from reality that for a brief time I can push the events of the day to the back of my mind, exist in the here and now. But towards the end of the evening the inevitability of returning home intrudes and my thoughts turn back to Connor Blake. Maria catches my change of mood and reaches across the table, puts a hand on my wrist.

'It's work, isn't it?'

I have not told Maria what has been going on. I do not want her to know, as if by telling her any details she will be involved, put within touching distance of the Blakes. I nod, settle for a half-truth.

'Vick. The way she was with her kids. Hard not to think about.'

Maria leans across the table and takes my chin in her hand, gives it an affectionate tug. 'You're a good man, Daniel Connell. Don't let anybody tell you different.'

I do not know what to say to that, so say nothing.

Maria sighs. 'Listen, Daniel, you're a lawyer, not a social worker. There's nothing you can do.'

I nod dutifully but cannot shake the worry that I am already in too deep, past a point of no return. We pay and drive home with the radio playing songs from a generation ago; I do not speak more than ten words along the way. Maria keeps looking at me and I want to speak to her but I cannot think of anything to say. She cannot know what is happening, can never know. Some secrets are worth keeping.

I drive out to the hotel the next morning. The sky is blue and it is very cold, a ground mist on the flat fields, the sun golden and dazzling on the horizon, casting long shadows. Thorndon Manor is an upscale country house hotel at the end of a long gravel drive, which crackles sharply in the chill air as I drive up it. I introduce myself at reception, tell them that I am a lawyer and that I need to speak to Ade regarding a case, and that I am sorry to come to his place of work but that it is urgent.

The woman behind the reception desk looks at me suspiciously and asks me if he is in any trouble. I tell her that it does not concern him but that he might be needed as a character witness; she seems satisfied by this nonsense and asks me to sit in the lounge and that she will fetch him.

Ade is black and a huge man, his chef's whites only making him seem more immense. When I offer my hand to shake it seems small in comparison to his, his fingers the size of sausages. But despite his size he finds it hard to meet my eyes, and in his hunched and reluctant posture I can read a life spent outside society, the natural reticence of the congenitally disenfranchised.

I ask him to sit down. I am sitting on a leather sofa and he sits opposite me on an identical sofa, a coffee table between us.

'I'm sorry to trouble you,' I say.

'What do you want, man?' he says quietly.

'Just a little help.'

'You know my boss out there? He's counting the seconds I'm away from the grill. Going to make sure I pay them back, every one.' Ade's voice is soft and gentle, and it sounds strange coming from such a colossal frame. He talks down into his hands as if he is in a confessional, owning up to something shameful.

'It concerns a case I'm working on,' I say. 'Involving Connor Blake.'

'Oh fuck no, man,' says Ade. 'I don't want none of this.' He looks away across the room as if I have given him bad news and clasps his hands together, squeezes them against each other.

'Ade? I'm sorry if this is something you'd prefer not to speak about.'

'You know I've just come out? Three years. Not allowed to fraternise with the man. So how can I be talking about him with you? Fuck that noise.'

'Okay,' I say. 'Listen, I just want to get a sense of him. What he's like. It would help.'

'Should be cooking.'

'I won't keep you long.'

'Counting the seconds. Lose my job, 'cos of you.'

'That won't happen.'

Ade looks at me for the first time. 'Why d'you want to know?'

'You know he killed somebody,' I say.

Ade laughs softly, blows air from his nose. 'Big surprise.'

'You used to be friends with him.'

'I used to run with him,' Ade says. 'Before.'

'I'm getting the impression he's bad news.'

'He know you've come to see me?' A rush of panic, a rising edge to his soft voice.

'No. I'll never mention it. He'll never know.'

This seems to reassure Ade. He relaxes, his huge shoulders slumping in relief. 'Bad news. Could say that.'

'Why?' I say. 'What did he do?'

'You know who his dad is?' say Ade.

'I know.'

'Connor Blake,' says Ade, as if summoning up a name from a scarce-remembered legend, some cautionary tale. 'Worst person I ever met.' He sighs, looks at me reluctantly

173

and briefly closes his eyes, opens them again. 'Had a taste for ladies. You meet him?'

I nod.

'Yeah, the girls – never a problem for him. But, you know, maybe 'cos it was so easy for him, I dunno… But they weren't enough. Normal things weren't enough for him. He wanted to…' Ade frowns. He shifts on the sofa and the whole frame moves under his weight. He must have been close to thirty stone. 'Dunno how to say it. Play with them. Own them.'

'Okay,' I say. 'He liked the ladies.'

'No. Fuck no, man, listen. It was like… like they were *his*.'

I am trying to follow him but I do not know what he is trying to get at.

He blows out air in annoyance, sits up, elbows on knees, tries again. 'Sex weren't enough. He'd pay girls to let him hurt them. But that shit, that went wrong. He'd lose control, think he could do what he wanted.'

'Hurt them?'

'Cut them. Anything under the skin. Getting inside them, couldn't leave it alone. He don't think people are people. He thinks they're… *things*.'

Ade looks as if his memories are causing him physical pain, as if looking back at what he has witnessed is a form of torment.

'One girl, I don't know what he wanted but she said no, no way she was doing that. He lost the plot, cut up her face with a blade.'

'What happened?'

'Her and her dad, didn't have no mum, they both just moved away. Don't know where. Just went.' He pauses. 'This beautiful girl, man.'

I think back to Connor Blake, his astounding eyes and chiselled features. If I saw him in a photograph, I would imagine nothing but goodness, a man of virtue.

'He once said to me he wondered how it would be to put his hands inside someone here.' He frames his belly with both hands. 'Deep inside. He was serious.'

My mind skirts briefly over this image, of Blake elbow-deep in another person's innards, the heat, the blood. I am not surprised that Ade flinches from the thoughts of what he has seen and heard. I accept that there is a spectrum of human desire and that the idea of a norm is notional at best. But some people inhabit the outer limits and their most mundane desires would horrify any ordinary person.

Ade tells me that he had run with Connor Blake partly through fear of what he would do to him if he did not. He tells me that Blake liked to be surrounded by people who had some physical quirk, unusually tall or large or misshapen in some way; freakish. Ade tells me that he weighed twenty stone by the time he was fourteen and that Blake had been fascinated by his size. He sighs, the uncomprehending sound of the duped and brainwashed, trying to understand how he had fallen under such a man's influence.

'And nobody said anything?'

'Got away with it all. Didn't matter what,' Ade says. 'Always had done. His dad'd buy witnesses, make sure they didn't say nothing. Paid Connor's victims off, made it all go away.'

'All of it?'

'Untouchable, always had been, Connor. Couldn't do no wrong. You seen him. Fucking film star.' For the first time I sense aggression from Ade, an anger deep inside him. I look at him, his size, and choose my words.

'And now? You don't see him?'

'Don't have nothing to do with him. Ain't allowed anyway. Parole, and all that. Besides, them Blakes scare the shit out of me, always did. Soon's I can, I'm leaving. Moving away. Another country. Can't get far enough away.'

I thank Ade, apologise again for taking up his time and for asking him difficult questions. Ade shakes his head, says it's okay, whatever, long as he still has a job to go back to.

I stand up but Ade stays seated. When I leave the hotel I look back through the window of the lounge and Ade is still sitting on the sofa, massive in his chef's whites, looking down at his hands. His lips are moving and I think that he might be praying, to who and for what I do not know.

18

I FIND GABE working on his car in his garage, the door pushed open. Working next to him is the shaven-headed man I met days ago, who Gabe had called Gavin. It turns out his official title is Major Strauss and they served together in Afghanistan, where Major Strauss had been the battalion commander to Gabe's platoon leader. He is popping out the bodywork of Gabe's car and while he does it he tells me that he has worked on Land Rovers in Northern Ireland, that he cannot recall the number of dents he has repaired. He tells me that British soldiers are worse drivers than Italians. Watching them work I see that they have an easy camaraderie, a product of years serving together; a part of Gabe's life I know little about.

As they work they explain the situation to me as it stands, 7 Platoon and Lance Corporal Creek, recount it in crisp sentences as if they are briefing a junior officer who is still green and needs everything spelling out. But they are right: I have no idea of the world they are dealing in.

'So the platoon all went into private security?' I say.

'Most of them,' says Gabe. 'At least twenty.'

'Unusual,' says Major Strauss. 'For all of them to go at once. But after what they'd seen in Kunar they'd had enough, wanted the easy life.' He tested the electric window on the back rear door and it did not work. 'Fuse,' he says.

'So what they're doing, that's easy?'

Gabe laughs, counts off on his fingers. 'Better pay. Better weapons. More respect.'

'And they get to do whatever they want, make up their rules of engagement,' says Major Strauss. 'In the British Army, before you pull the trigger you need to be damn sure you understand the politics of what you're about to do. Shoot the wrong person, at the wrong time, in the wrong place, you're going to jail.'

Gabe shakes his head. 'Joke.'

'Getting that way,' says Major Strauss, who is now the other side of the car, poking around underneath Gabe's steering wheel. 'But in private security, there's no rule book.'

'All depends on where you're willing to go,' says Gabe. 'A group of mates can win a massive contract in the first year or two of trading, just because they're the only ones'll go there.'

'South Sudan,' says Major Strauss. 'There are regulars with two, three years' army experience cleaning up over there.' He stands up. 'It's not the fuse. My guess is that window's buggered.'

'Mostly about reputation, though,' says Gabe. 'Think about it, you're some white-collar boy from a multinational – petroleum, minerals, something like that. Living in a gated compound in Lagos or Khartoum, hostile locals, you're going out in the field three, four times a week. You want people you can trust looking after you.'

'The Americans like ex-Rangers, the Brits go for Special Forces or, if not, then regular infantry with combat experience,' says Major Strauss. 'All about reputation.'

'So the boys from the Rifles have got it all going on,' says Gabe. 'Masses of combat experience, decorations, ready-made command structure. Good to go.'

'Global Armour?' I say.

'That's what they're calling themselves,' says Gabe. 'And the word is they're up for some huge contract in Iraq. Word gets out about what happened in Afghanistan, there's no way they'll win it.'

I nod. For the first time I have a sense of what Gabe is involved in: taking on a group of battle-hardened soldiers, threatening their chances of getting rich, of hitting the big time.

Major Strauss pulls off the trim around Gabe's rear door and looks at the assembly underneath. 'This,' he says, 'looks fuck all like a Land Rover.'

We give up on Gabe's car and move to his kitchen, make coffee, sit at his table. Gabe sits opposite Major Strauss and as I sit next to Gabe I once again have a feeling of intrusion, of encroaching on private territory and history. They drink and reminisce about Afghanistan and Gabe reminds Major Strauss of an Afghan army recruit who had arrived at their base fresh from having been given rudimentary training at the army centre outside Kabul. The first thing he had done when on routine manoeuvres was shoot a cow with an RPG;

he had missed the first time but had got it on the second attempt, scoring a hit in the cow's centre mass so that it rained steak and there was little left of the cow but hooves and a head. Apparently the recruit had been disappointed as he had wanted the cow for food and the RPG had done too much damage.

'Why didn't he just shoot it?' says Major Strauss. 'He had a sidearm, right? Could have walked right up to it, shot it in the head.'

'Don't know,' says Gabe. 'Maybe he just liked the feel of the RPG.'

'He last long?'

'Gone the next day. Like he'd joined the army just to blow up a cow, soon's he'd done that, *adios*.'

Major Strauss and Gabe laugh and I smile with them; I have never heard Gabe discuss his time in the army like this, treat it with such wry amusement. My initial impression of Major Strauss had been unfair; I had been hostile, jealous that Gabe had put him before me, assumed he was something he was not. But he seems a good man, urbane and jovial but with the strata of hardness running through him that has got him to the rank of major, has made him able to command men on the battlefield.

Gabe stops laughing, turns his empty coffee cup with his fingers. 'So, Gavin. What's the situation?'

Major Strauss looks at me, back at Gabe. Gabe shakes his head. 'Daniel's on our side. You can talk in front of him.'

Major Strauss nods and I feel strangely privileged to be included, but also out of my depth in the company of these two men who have seen combat up close, who have taken lives without compunction or guilt.

'So,' says Major Strauss, 'Corporal Creek's inquest. I'll be honest, Gabriel, it's not looking great. Not great at all.'

'You spoke to the generals?'

'Got as far as their secretaries.' He sighs. 'They've pulled the drawbridge up, Gabriel. Closed ranks. You know what it's like.'

'No reply?'

'Left messages, written letters. Nothing. Right now it's a dead end and I'll be honest with you, I'm not sure what's left to do.' Major Strauss takes a deep breath, lets it out. 'It's the situation out there, much as anything. Helmand's going under and there are more casualties every day. The government in Kabul is a joke, an embarrassment. We tried to rebuild a nation and it's worse than under the Taliban.'

Gabe nods. 'We're pulling out?'

'Probably. Soon as we can convince everybody that we're not running away from it.' He smiles without humour. 'Which we will be. But the point is, last thing the army needs is any more bad publicity. Reopening an inquest? They don't want to know.'

'Anything left to do?'

'Unless you can dig up a witness. We need to apply pressure, give them no choice. Right now, they couldn't give a shit about us.'

Major Strauss picks up his jacket and we walk with him out to Gabe's hall. He shakes our hands, puts his arm across Gabe's shoulders.

'I'm sorry,' he says to Gabe. 'I understand why you want this to happen. But you may need to make your peace.'

Gabe nods. 'Thank you, sir,' he says. 'I'll be in touch.'

Major Strauss leaves and Gabe turns without speaking, heads back to the kitchen. I think perhaps he wishes to be alone, put my head around the door but he beckons me in.

'Coffee?'

'Okay.'

Gabe takes down coffee, filters, talks to me as he is doing it. 'You go to see this Blake guy?'

'I saw him.'

'And?'

I shake my head. 'Man thinks he owns people. Never met anyone like it.'

'What's he want from you?'

'Wants me to represent him.'

'Why?'

'Search me. Didn't get that far.'

'You hit him?'

'A bit.'

Gabe laughs, fills the coffee machine. 'Enough to scare him off?'

'Don't know. Hope so.'

I sit in silence at Gabe's table, thinking about Connor Blake. 'I asked him about Ryan. What he'd wanted from him. He told me he wanted Ryan to get him out of prison. No idea how, no plan. Put it all on Ryan. Asked the impossible.'

'Can understand why he killed himself.'

'Yeah.'

Gabe sits opposite me. 'This is all happening because you agreed to help, what was her name?'

'Vick.'

'Yeah, Vick. Listen, Dan, you're a decent man. Things'll work out.'

I do not reply. Instead, unbidden, a string of images pass through my mind: of Vick, her kids, Maria, all the ways in which things could not work out, could end in catastrophe.

'She all right? Vick?' Gabe says.

I bring myself back to the here and now, blink the thoughts away. 'She's seeing her kids. Thinks she'll get them back soon.'

I had spoken to Vick earlier and she had seemed better. Nothing more had happened in her house, she was getting regular access to her children and, she told me, the events of the last few months were beginning to seem like a bad dream. A bad dream that had caused her ex-husband to take his own life.

'See?' says Gabe. 'Things'll work out.'

He pours coffee and we sit and drink and plan our next matches, discuss opponents' strengths and weaknesses, formulate strategies. As always with Gabe, I feel stronger, more of a formidable force alongside my old partner. His kitchen is warm and as familiar as my own and eventually I convince myself that I might have seen the last of the Blakes, that they might leave me alone. I am stronger than Ryan, bigger and uglier; I could be more trouble than it's worth. But at the same time, I cannot help but think of Alex Blake. A man who would do anything for his son: cover up crimes, make it all disappear. Where will he stop?

19

THE NEXT MORNING a slight warmth has at last overcome the cold and the sun is shining, giving a sense that spring is finally marshalling its vast green reserves. Maria and I drive into the countryside with the windows open, the breeze snatching at our hair and the flat land opening out in front of us like an invitation to participate in a worthwhile future.

A friend of Maria's from school is getting married and Maria is maid of honour; we have booked a room where the wedding is being held, are staying overnight. Two days away from the events of the last weeks – the relief I feel is like taking deep breaths of air after having been smothered. Maria catches the lift in my mood, sings along happily to whatever songs come on the radio, makes up words that make little sense but which make me laugh.

The wedding is at a brick country house built in the sixteenth century by Sir Somebody and had been visited by Queen Elizabeth I, a man in a white suit tells us as he shows Maria and me through to the reception, carries our bags to our rooms and points out the view, the four-poster, the bathroom, the mini-bar, until I give him a tenner to go away. Maria is hanging up her dress and it strikes me that this must be what all couples do: go to weddings and stay in hotels. That we are a couple, just like any other; the feeling is something I cannot describe.

The hotel provides bathrobes of thick white towelling, and seeing myself in the full-length mirror, part of me cannot help feeling that I look as if I've broken into somebody's palatial home and am trying the bathrobe on for size before taking off with the jewellery.

Maria apparently agrees with me, says, 'You know, you're not really the fluffy bathrobe type.'

She is lying back on the bed, stretching, twisting around like a cat on the white sheets and she has a crafty look on her face.

'No?'

'No.' She sits up, sniffs the air. 'Are those bubbles you're putting in?'

'I thought I'd try it.'

'Daniel Connell in a bubble bath. Well I never.' She cocks her head, regards me with suspicion. 'Are you going soft?'

'I don't think so,' I say, and I cannot help but smile at Maria, at her pointless provocations.

'I don't do soft,' she says, stretching out on her back again. 'I like my men hard. And stupid,' she adds, kicking her legs at the high ceiling.

'You can have it if you want,' I say. 'The bath.'

'Or,' she says, rolling onto her front and resting her chin on her hands, raising an eyebrow. 'Why don't we hop in together?'

Maria can say things I would never dare, say them as

if they are the most natural things in the world, and I am momentarily speechless, not trusting myself to answer. Maria rocks her head from side to side and sighs as if regarding a lost cause.

'Tell you what, you dope. You get in, and I'll sneak in when you're not looking.'

I smile at Maria's rough kindness, the depths of her understanding and affection. I turn and go into the bathroom and my whole being feels limned by a charge of delicious possibility, all the better for it being so alien, so unexpected, and so good.

The weddings I have been to often bring two different worlds together, divided by class or religion or culture, playing out as miniature social experiments, though lubricated by drink and good wishes. Maria's friend Jade is pure Essex. Her guests are builders, taxi drivers and men with money and vague occupations, accompanied by dolled-up beauties in skimpy designer labels and outrageous heels. The groom, Rufus, on the other hand, is a City banker and old money: Harrow and Oxford and a seat kept warm around the boardroom table. His guests are groomed and dressed in understated suits and frocks that whisper of class and wealth. The reception is held in the Great Hall and half of the room are talking loudly, laughing heads thrown back, expansive hands gesturing and slopping Champagne over the parquet; the other half are looking on with faint puzzled smiles on their smooth faces, as if they are watching a difficult performance they do not quite understand.

'Okay,' says Maria, snatching a glass of Champagne as it passes by. 'Could be interesting.' She holds her glass up in front of her face. 'Cheers.'

I knock my glass against hers, take a drink.

'You seem better,' she says. 'Less detached.'

I nod. 'Getting there.'

'Maybe you're just better when the sun comes out,' she says. 'Like a lizard.'

'A lizard?'

'Cold-blooded,' she says. 'Needs warming up.'

I shake my head. 'Never been my problem,' I say.

Maria looks at me in amusement. 'No. No, Daniel, I'll give you that.'

'Just happy,' I say. 'To be here. With you.' The words come out haltingly, but they come out nevertheless. Maria's face lifts, her eyes open wider, and I think of a time-lapse film of a flower blossoming.

'Well,' she says, and doesn't say anything more. It is not often that Maria is lost for something to say. She drinks and looks about the room and smiles at what she sees: people talking, drinking, laughing, and a young man at a grand piano gently playing a tune that I cannot place but which I have heard before, have heard many times.

'There she is,' says Maria, just before a tall, pretty woman in a sleek white wedding dress prances up in heels like a skittish pony, followed by a handsome, nervous-looking man who is glancing about him as if he expects to find a sniper in the crowd.

'*Maria!*' Jade screams and hugs her, turns to me, hugs

me as well. She has big white perfect teeth. I can see most of them. 'You must be Daniel! You're so *big*!'

I do not know how to respond to her observation, smile and nod. Rufus puts out a hand and gives it a firm shake.

'Enjoying yourself?' he asks.

'Thanks, yes,' I say, and it is true. I don't ask him the same question; he looks as if he would rather be anywhere else.

Young women marrying money has a long tradition and in my neighbourhood has never appeared to go out of fashion, feminism never having gained a convincing toehold in Essex. To strike gold there were, broadly, two options: find a local up-and-coming self-made man, or get a PA diploma and head for the City, as Jade had done. Villains or bankers – in the final analysis, the money was equally grubby. It would still buy a mansion, furs, pay for summers in St Tropez, so really, who cared?

But perhaps I am being uncharitable. Jade seems happy and I am sure that Rufus will be as well, just as soon as the immediate threat of Jade's friends and relatives is removed, driven back to wherever they came from and out of his life.

I have been placed at a table at which sit relatives of the bride, along with a young man whose place name says Bellamy, although I cannot tell if that is his first or second name. Maria is at the top table. I can see her talking to Jade, laughing. A big man with cropped silver hair is talking to Bellamy and the rest of the table is listening; the big man is called Stan and has told me he is in the building trade. I saw him earlier helping his wife climb out of a year-old specced-up jet-black Range Rover. He must have been building a lot of houses.

'So go on, what you driving, Bellamy?'

'Oh, well,' says Bellamy modestly. Bellamy has told me that he trades in derivatives, that it is actually quite tedious, mostly just spreadsheets. He called me 'chap' when he addressed me and has a lazy upper-class drawl and unruly hair and I disliked him immediately.

'No, go on,' says Stan with a smile that tries at angelic but fails. His head is huge and his florid face is so dark it is almost purple, as if he has been holding his breath for too long or is being invisibly throttled.

'A Ferrari,' says Bellamy, as if he is ashamed of it, which I am sure he isn't.

Stan smacks his hands together, looks around the table. 'Fuck me, he don't look like he's started shaving.' He turns his attention back to Bellamy, who is looking uncomfortable. 'Three five five?'

'Three sixty Spider,' says Bellamy. 'Black.' He cannot help but let the smugness creep into his tone. I dislike him more than ever.

'Now then, you know what they say about young men in sports cars, dontcha?' says Stan. 'Know what it means, driving a motor like that?' The whole table is almost reverentially following the exchange, a circular table with a rapt audience of sixteen people around it hanging on Stan's every word.

'Yes, yes,' says Bellamy, a little testily. 'I know what it is supposed to mean.'

'Means,' says Stan, leaning closer in to the table. The rest of the table leans in too, all part of the conspiracy. Stan holds up a little finger, waggles it. 'It means... You're an arsehole.'

Stan laughs with an abandon that is almost demented, smacks his hands together again, looks around in delight. Everybody apart from Bellamy and me obviously know Stan well and join in the laughter. I cannot help but smile too.

Bellamy, however, is a son of privilege, privately educated, working a six-figure job in the City: he is not used to this kind of rough ridicule, cannot help but take offence, is intrinsically unable to see it for what it is, normal wedding sport. I know he will react badly, misjudge the situation woefully.

'Now steady on,' Bellamy says. 'There's no need for that.' He sounds as prim as a Victorian vicar.

'No, no,' says Stan, holding his hands up in apology. 'No, you're right, Bellamy, son, that weren't on.' He nods seriously and the table waits for what comes next, a collective holding of breath. Stan points at Bellamy. 'You're a rich arsehole.'

This time the laughter around the table is unrestrained and I watch Bellamy's face blush with impotent rage; I am willing to bet he has never been spoken to like this before in his entire charmed life.

He stands up abruptly, says, 'Cigarette,' turns and leaves, walks stiffly to the exit of the function room. He will stew over this for a week.

Stan's wife, a tanned middle-aged lady with big hair, enormous diamond earrings and garish make-up, slaps

Stan on the arm affectionately. 'You are a cunt, Stan,' she says.

'I am, ain't I?' Stan says, grinning proudly, taking his sweet time to make eye contact with everyone at the table. I cannot imagine him being more pleased if he had backed the winner of the National. 'I really am.'

Stan runs a book on the length of the speeches, which is won by a lady two places down from me called Lisa who had guessed twenty-eight minutes, Stan handing over the £150 with comic unwillingness. He has also been disappointed by the lack of controversy and dirty jokes, has attempted to heckle the best man, but his wife put her foot down at that.

Now the formalities are over and Maria comes to save me from Stan, takes me by the arm. As I leave the table, I hear Stan call after me, 'You drive a Ferrari 'n'all?'

'Having a good time?' says Maria.

'Yes,' I say.

Her face is glowing with happiness and drink. She kisses me and then whispers, 'Let's explore.'

She takes my hand and leads me out of the dining room, down a vaulted corridor, into what might once have been a library. I have the feeling I had as a boy, sneaking off with a girl for an illicit make-out session. Maria must feel the same because there is nobody in the library and she immediately kisses me again, this time long and hard, and after some moments I feel her body melt against my hand around her back.

'Can't beat a good wedding,' she says afterwards. 'Let's not stay too late. Get back to our room.'

I smile once again at her unashamed frankness, can only nod dumbly. She steps back, looks at me, looks around her. The room we are in is large and panelled, lined with mounted heads of different animals: deer, elk, boar, a wolf, a tiger.

'Poor beasts,' says Maria. 'Reminds me, there was a crow in my bedroom yesterday. Dead. How weird's that?'

'What?' I say. The noise of the wedding is gone. I am aware only of the humming contours and limits of my body, of the heaviness of my hand; of Maria's face, white and blurred and indistinct.

'Nearly stepped on it. Think it got down the chimney?'

'In your room?' I say.

'Beak open, wings spread. Freaky deaky. Let's get something to drink.'

Maria moves away, heads back towards the wedding party. I do not move. At the doorway she stops, turns. She seems ethereal, barely there. 'Daniel? Daniel? Hey. Daniel?'

There is dancing and drinking, laughter, a woman in tears followed out of the room by a gesticulating boyfriend or husband in a kilt, more laughter, the evening underpinned by the unconditional goodwill people bring to weddings along with their best suits and dresses. But throughout the evening my anger grows and grows until a deep well of rage fills my body. I am so tense that people watching me standing rigidly at the margins may believe that I am undergoing some kind of seizure.

Somebody put a dead bird in Maria's bedroom. While she slept. What else did they do to her? I want to find the people who did it, make them pay, cause them to suffer. I can think of nothing else.

'Dance?' Maria asks me. She has picked up on my mood and there is a forced enthusiasm in her voice like a mother cajoling a recalcitrant child.

'No thanks.'

'Come on, Daniel. Show me what you've got.'

'No.'

Something in the way I refuse, an irritable jerk of my head, stops Maria, freezes the teasing smile she has tried on.

'What's up?'

'Nothing.'

'So dance.'

'Yeah, listen. I don't fancy it.'

'Okay. Understood.' Maria searches my face, comes up with nothing. She is a little drunk and infuriated by me, and is not going to let me hijack her fun. 'Just have to find somebody who does.'

At some point I head upstairs to our room. It is still in the state of disorder that Maria left it in: scattered make-up bottles, discarded tights, towels and an abandoned pair of heels in a corner where they were disdainfully flung. This was the room that so recently had seemed to serve as a validation of our status as couple; we were like everybody else, as entitled to happiness as they were. Now it just seems to mock me. What had I been thinking?

Maria comes in much later. I can hear her say goodnight to somebody outside the door. The other person laughs and stumbles away down the corridor. She closes the door and turns on the lights, sits down on the bed, ignores my pretence at sleep. She shakes my shoulder gently, folds herself over me so that our cheeks are together, hers on top of mine. She smells of Champagne.

'Is it me?' she says softly. 'Have I done something?'

I do not reply. She lifts her head and looks at me with eyes that are fearful and confused. I cannot meet her eye. I shake my head, do not trust myself to speak.

'Maybe the wedding freaked you out. It's okay, it's not like I expect—'

'It wasn't that.' God, I have not even thought of it. Maria, marriage. Never considered it.

She is silent, makes patterns on the bedspread with a fingernail. 'You can tell me,' she says at last. 'Whatever it is, you can tell me. Daniel?'

But I cannot. Of course I cannot tell Maria that there are men out there who are putting dead birds in her room while she sleeps, the same men who injure children in their beds and burn down homes; that I attract the threat of violence like a magnet attracts iron and I may be putting her in danger.

For all the love I want to think Maria feels for me, I have never managed to shake the suspicion that she also retains a vestige of caution, a wariness that I might be too hard, have too much history, hold inside too much capacity for wayward aggression. A big dog that you cannot entirely trust around people. I do not want to risk it, do not want to give her reason to fear me, fear being around me. I cannot bear to lose her.

'It's nothing,' I say. 'I'm sorry. It's just... with what's going on. Vick. I can't get it out of my head.' It is not a lie, not entirely; but nor is it the truth.

Maria leans down, puts one hand on each side of my face, turns it so that I am looking at her. She gazes at me and again I struggle to meet the honest goodness there, the depth of feeling.

'I love you, Daniel Connell,' she says. 'Whatever happens.'

I wish so much that I could believe it. But later, lying next to Maria sleeping, feeling my heart beat against the weight of her arm across my chest, I know that whatever it is that we have is too fragile; that very soon something terrible will happen to make it disappear forever.

20

MARIA IS ASLEEP and she looks peaceful, her lips slightly parted, one hand half open, palm up, next to her ear. Her hair spills across the pillow in luscious waves. How many times, I wonder, have I looked at her in such a pose, amazed that she is with me, that I have the privilege of watching her sleep? But there is another hand in the picture, and it is holding a screwdriver that dimples the skin of Maria's throat, the suggestion of pressure. It is this that I have been gazing at for the last I do not know how many minutes, wondering how things have reached this stage, what I could have done differently. And wondering, ultimately, if I am capable of protecting her from the men who have taken the photograph and put it through the door of my office, where I picked it up from the floor on entering this morning.

Intimidation relies on the safety net of anonymity, the certainty that no links exist back to whoever is applying the pressure. The assumption is that they know what it is about, you know what it is about, and there should be an end to it. I know who sent the photograph, know what they want. But even if I had been in any doubt about who was behind it, I would not have had long to wonder.

I am pouring coffee in the corridor outside my office when my phone rings. I pick up though I do not recognise the number.

'Yes?'

'Daniel. Where do you think this will end?'

'What do you want?'

He ignores my question. 'There is nothing we cannot do to you,' he says.

'What do you want?' I say again. I can think of nothing else to say.

'Only what I always wanted,' he said. He sounds frustrated. 'Daniel, there was no need for any of this.'

'You were in Maria's room.'

'Not me, Daniel. I'm in prison.'

'If you weren't, I'd break your legs.'

Connor Blake laughs. 'Magnus wanted to cut her ear off,' he says. 'You should be thanking me.'

The statement is so abhorrent that I do not trust myself to respond and there is a silence during which I can hear him breathing.

'So come on, Daniel. You going to be my lawyer?'

'Why me?'

'That other lot, big City lawyers. Hard to persuade. You show up out of the blue, might as well have come tied up with a ribbon.'

'What makes you think you can intimidate me?' But even as I say it, I realise how empty my words sound. Blake does not even answer but I can hear him laughing softly.

'What do you want?'

'We'll talk about that. When you come to see me.'

I have an impression of doors closing all around me, leaving me in a dark place, alone. 'Come to see you,' I say.

'We have a lot to talk about. You're going to get me out of here.'

I close my eyes and I cannot think. My mind seems frozen, starved of possibilities and choices. They got into Maria's home. Took photographs. What could I do?

'There are procedures,' I say eventually. 'You need to sack your current defence team. We'll need to go to court, a judge will need to sign it off.'

'See,' says Blake, condescension in his voice as if he is geeing up an uncertain child. 'That's what I pay you the big bucks for.'

'Give me your lawyer's name,' I say, and it is as if I am casting off the last rope mooring me to my old life, drifting away into a vast unknown place of malevolence and menace. He gives me a name and I say, 'I'll see you in court.'

I cut Blake off, push my mobile across the desk far away from me. I look about my office, at my familiar surroundings, and I have no idea what to do, none at all.

While I was contemplating a dark and violent future, Gabe was taking the fight to 7 Platoon, showing a tenacity and appetite for the fray, which only recently I believed he had lost for good. While 7 Platoon may have fired bullets into his home and held a gun to his head, these acts, if anything, only seemed to spur him on. I had always known that Gabe was a contrary man; I had not appreciated quite what little value he put on his own life when there was a mission to be completed.

With the help of Major Strauss, Gabe had tracked down as many members of 7 Platoon as he could; those who had been attached to the platoon at the time of Lance Corporal Creek's death and those immediately before. He had called them, visited them, appealed to their sense of duty, to their better natures. But few had wanted to talk, and those who did had nothing to reveal, other than a deep and abiding hatred and fear of 7 Platoon, of what they had become and what they had done out there in Afghanistan.

But he had spoken to one man who had asked Gabe to stop by and visit. He had not been with 7 Platoon when Gabe was shadowing them in Kunar Province but he had served with them shortly afterwards, up until just before Lance Corporal Creek's death. He gave Gabe an address, told him he was there all day every day, that anytime was fine.

Ex-Private Shane Foster was a small man with a restless energy he could not quite contain; he ducked and weaved as he spoke as if he was sparring with Gabe, rather than simply talking. He was wearing a t-shirt with the arms cut-off and had crude tattoos on his wiry arms, but around his eyes were lines left by an easy laugh and he emanated an aggressive goodwill. Foster worked at a boxing gym, a small building with a flat roof and two full-size rings inside, punch bags and speed balls and weights at the far end, smell of sweat and leather and vapour rub. Two boys in headgear were throwing jabs at one another in one of the rings, and while Foster spoke to Gabe he kept an eye on them, throwing instructions and profanities their way as they slipped or shipped punches.

'Creek, right, I heard he was killed. Fucking shame. He was a good man, I liked him. Phil, fuck's sake cover up. You like getting hit?'

'Yes,' said Gabe. 'He was a good man. Knew him well?'

'Well enough. Enough to know he was different.' Foster started to walk around the ring and Gabe had to follow, speak to his profile as Foster watched the boys box.

'Different?'

'Yeah, not like the rest of them, of us. Always thinking, always asking questions. Phil, don't slap, you ain't a girl. Are you? Phil? You a girl?'

One of the boys who Gabe presumed was Phil looked down at Foster and shook his head. The other boy took the opportunity to hit him, a crisp right to the temple. Phil staggered sideways and Foster laughed.

'Gal, you're a little shit, know that?' He turned to Gabe. 'So. You reckon, what? He weren't killed kosher?'

Gabe nodded. 'But nobody's talking. Can't get anywhere. You hear anything, see anything?'

Foster shook his head. 'I'd left by then, and not a day too soon, I'll be honest with you. Banyan, Burgess, Shine, all of them, gone over the other side, hadn't they. Gone.'

'Think they could have killed Creek?'

'That lot?' Foster stopped walking, was momentarily stilled. 'Reckon they'd kill anything.'

Foster climbed into the ring and spoke to the boys, made sure they met his eye as he told them what they had done well and what they needed to improve on. He dismissed them, cuffing both across the back of the head as they escaped, wriggling through the ropes. He did not come down, spoke to Gabe from up where he was.

'I wanted to see you, check you out before I spoke to you,' he said. 'Never know.'

'Worried about 7 Platoon?'

'Never want to see them again.'

'So you've got something to tell me,' said Gabe.

Foster nodded down at Gabe's leg. 'You exercising?'

'Tennis.'

Foster nodded again. 'You want to box, that leg won't stop you.'

'I'll bear it in mind.'

'There was a guy, a soldier, don't know how he spelled it but think he was called Petroski. Came in on attachment, don't know where from either. Him and Creek, you know what Creek was like, didn't have many friends, did people's heads in, if I'm honest. But this one, Petroski, they were tight.'

Foster threw a body shot at the ring's top rope, making it quiver, then put out a hand to still it as he thought.

'He knew something. Said something, talked about how wasn't any way it was legit, Creek getting shot. Said he knew something about it, said it needed to be known.'

'Petroski?' It was not a name Gabe had heard before. 'Know where I can find him?'

'Got flown out. Caught up in some incident, roadside bomb, never got the details. Last I heard of him.'

'Know where I can find him?'

'Wouldn't have a clue. How many Petroskis can there be?'

Foster took a mop from the corner of the ring and started to clean the canvas floor. Gabe stood there for some moments but it seemed as if the meeting was over.

He turned and headed for the door but as he reached it, Foster called, 'Sir? Serious. You want to box, you come back here.'

Gabe called in favours and spoke to army personnel staff, who turned up only one Petroski – James, a private who had recently been discharged from service, invalided out. They pointed him to a hospital, told him that was the last record they had of him. But when Gabe called the hospital, they told him that Petroski was no longer with them and that no, they could not tell him his whereabouts, that that information was limited to family and he was not family, was he?

Gabe pulled rank, turned on the charm. No joy: dead end. Petroski might as well have dropped off the planet.

He tells me this sitting across from me in my office the following day, asks me if there are any legal channels he can pursue, issue a subpoena.

'Doubt it,' I say. 'On what grounds? That he may or may not know something about the death of somebody who may or may not have been wrongfully killed? You'll need a lot more than you've got.'

'He could be important.'

'"Could be" isn't something the law takes very seriously.'

Gabe puts his hands behind his neck, eases out some tightness. 'Understood.'

'Strauss can't help?'

'Civilian matter now is what they say. Family only.'

'Phone book? Voting registers?'

'Nothing. Guy's just disappeared.'

'Sorry.'

'Yeah.' Gabe looks about my office. 'And you? What's happening?'

I have not told Gabe about the photograph of Maria. What could he do? I shrug, affect nonchalance. 'Not much.'

Though, if I am honest, not much is the only answer I can give. I have contacted Blake's solicitors and have made a date to stand before the judge to take on his case. Maria and I have seen each other, and although I have tried to appear normal, I know that she has sensed a difference in me. I am unwilling to touch her, want to keep her at arm's length as if getting close to me will put her at more risk. Over dinner she seemed on the verge of saying something, readying herself to confront my behaviour, how it is affecting us. But she said nothing and we are maintaining an uneasy peace.

'Not much,' I say again. I think of Maria, the photograph, the screwdriver. Of how I have capitulated to Connor Blake, agreed to represent him. Of how cowardice and love seem inseparable, one a companion to the other. 'Nothing at all.'

21

EVERYTHING SEEMS TO be happening very quickly. I feel as if I should say something, ask everybody to slow it down. Take five. Give me time to think, to try to come to terms with what is going on, accept this new reality. But the judge clearly has better things to do. Perhaps he is wanted on the golf course, or this procedure is eating into an expensive lunch. Blake's previous solicitors cannot get out of this courtroom fast enough. They have not looked at me once. Only Blake seems to be enjoying himself, standing and smiling broadly as if it is his birthday and we are all here for his benefit. We are nearly done and I am not prepared for this, nowhere near ready.

'One last time, Mr Blake,' says the judge, an old man with red-veined cheeks and clear grey eyes. 'You are absolutely sure that you would like to change your solicitor?'

'Sure.' He winks at me. I watch him with no expression.

'Mr Connell. You are happy to take Mr Blake on as a client?'

Happy? Nothing like it. Not even close. But I nod, say, 'Yes, Your Honour.'

'All right. We're done. But Mr Blake' – the judge lifts a hand, points at Blake – 'I do not want this to happen again. You cannot simply change solicitors as if you are changing cars. Understood?'

Blake nods happily and the judge gets up, sighs and shakes his head at us: myself, Blake's previous solicitors and Blake, who is flanked by two prison guards. The judge turns and leaves by a door behind his high desk. As soon as the door closes behind him, the guards take Blake away. He looks back, gives me one last wink before he is led through another door. I turn to Blake's previous defence team but they are already halfway out of a third exit and have still not looked at me or acknowledged my presence. They have washed their hands of Blake, citing 'irrevocable differences', dropped him like a hot coal.

All that is left in this courtroom is me and a box containing all of Blake's notes, evidence, disclosure – everything needed to defend a case. It is on the table where his previous defence team were guiltily sitting. It is not a big box; I can easily carry it. But I do not want to touch it, want nothing to do with it. I look at it, cardboard, unremarkable, and cannot help but think of Pandora's box, waiting to spill out all the evils of the world. How is it that I have become its custodian?

I finally pick it up, put it under one arm and head out of the court. I have just picked up a high-profile client, am working on a case that will attract national headlines. I walk down the steps outside the courts and a man I know walks towards me. There. It has started.

'Heard you were going to be here,' he says.

'Jack.' Once Jack had been a star reporter on Fleet Street, an Essex boy done good, mixing it in the serious world of journalism. But his need for a stiff drink soon eclipsed his eye for a good lead. He had come back to Essex to dry out and now wrote for the local paper, a hard-luck tale writing second-division stories. But I knew him of old and liked him; he never complained about his downward trajectory, faced the world with a cynic's wry smile.

'You're representing Connor Blake?'

'Yeah.'

'Not your usual area.'

'Pays to diversify.'

I continue walking. I do not want to talk about it. But Jack keeps pace, knows me well enough to know that there's got to be more to the story.

'Know about the Blakes?' he says.

'Some.'

'Course you do.' He is familiar with my background. 'How's the old man?'

'He's all right.'

'Danny.' He puts a hand on my arm and I stop, look at him. He is studying me, his eyes concerned, and I am reminded of how much I like this damaged but ultimately honest and good man. 'They're bad news, the Blakes. And Connor Blake, he's the worst of the lot. Well,' he says. 'Apart from his father.'

'Heard that before.'

'You know what you're doing?'

'I'm a big boy,' I say.

'Yeah. Yeah, Danny, you are.' Jack does not smile. 'But no matter how big you are, there's always somebody bigger.'

Later that day, Gabe called me from his car as he drove back from the hospital where the movements of Petroski, James, Private Infantryman, had last been recorded by the bureaucracy of the British Army.

St Luke's Military Hospital was not officially a hospital for convalescents, which had not existed for decades, becoming relics from the First World War. But the number of soldiers surviving wounds that until recently would have been fatal meant that many hospitals were practically indistinguishable. St Luke's looked after soldiers who, thanks to body armour and battlefield surgeons, had suffered terrible wounds but had made it back home alive. There were men walking on prosthetics or pushing themselves in wheelchairs, burn victims and men in plastic masks and wrapped in soft bandages. Some of them would never leave.

Gabe had come in person to try to achieve what he had failed over the phone: to find out where James Petroski was now living. But he had met another dead end here. The man in charge of records had refused Gabe access to Petroski's details with the smug satisfaction of the irrevocably institutionalised – he wasn't family, nothing to be done, out of the question, end of, move along, next.

Back in the car park, he was about to get into his car and head home when he had heard a voice call out, 'Sir?'

Gabe turned around and saw a man he recognised. He thought for a second, placed him, said, 'Robbie?'

Robbie Jackson was in a wheelchair but he had seen Gabe arrive as he looked out of the windows of the hospital's sunroom – something, he told Gabe, he spent a lot of time doing now that he could no longer walk. He had been injured in an explosion while driving a Land Rover without armour, although the last time that Gabe had seen him, he had been an active sergeant.

'Beat you,' said Jackson. 'You only lost one.'

Gabe looked down at Jackson, at his cut-off tracksuit bottoms which revealed the stumps of his legs. 'Christ, I'm sorry, Robbie.'

Jackson smiled up at Gabe. 'Makes two of us. You looking for someone?'

'Petroski. James Petroski.' Gabe's pulse spiked with hope. 'You know him?'

'Before my time,' said Jackson. 'Sorry, sir. Listen, you want to join us up there? Got a card game starting.'

Gabe hesitated. He had seen enough of hospitals in recent years, did not wish to revisit their sharp smell and quiet, subdued atmosphere only broken sporadically by pain-filled or simply enraged patients. But he saw a flicker of desperation and anticipated disappointment in Jackson's eyes; realised that a visitor from outside was an infrequent and longed-for event.

'What are you playing?'

'Texas Hold 'Em.'

'Play for money?'

'Sometimes.'

'Hope you've got deep pockets.'

Looking at the men sitting about the table out in the hospital's long sunroom, they seemed works in progress, unfinished projects of some modern-day, cowboy Frankenstein. There were men missing hands, legs, eyes, arms, and men with burns who lacked hair – a workshop's worth of prosthetics awkwardly wielded. Yet there was also an air of mordant humour, jokes about players losing hands, laughter. After two decades in the army, Gabe felt as if he had returned home.

Two decades in the army had also taught him how to play poker, but it was not long before he had lost all of his money and was offering his adapted Nike trainers to a man who shared the same prosthetic.

'So you left, sir,' said Jackson.

'Didn't fancy a desk job.'

'You miss it?'

The suddenness of the question, and the atmosphere of camaraderie around the table that Gabe cherished like long-lost family, caught him unprepared. The thought of just how much he missed army life, and the grief he endured away from it, brought a sharp lump to his throat. He tried to cough it away but Jackson noticed.

'It's hard, sir.'

'Don't need to call me sir,' said Gabe. 'I'm a civilian.'

'Yes, sir.'

Gabe could not help but smile at this. He threw in his hand. 'I'm done.'

A man with a prosthetic arm and a pile of other men's

money in front of him laughed. 'Officers. Never could play poker.'

'Hey, Diggs,' said Jackson casually. 'You knew James Petroski, didn't you?'

'Yep,' he said. 'Poor fucker.'

'Know where he is now?' Gabe said.

Diggs was raking in money but at this he stopped, looked at Gabe with suspicion. 'Why?'

'Want to find him.'

'Why?'

The other players were still, aware of the change in Diggs's attitude, his sudden hostility.

'A man under my command, something happened. I'm looking to put it right.'

'That right.'

'Yes.'

Diggs began raking the money in again, stacking coins. 'Got a number?'

Gabe took out a piece of paper, pen, wrote down his mobile number, his home number, slid it across to Diggs. Diggs took it. 'Captain...?'

'McBride. Captain Gabriel McBride. Ex-captain.'

'I'll try and get in touch with him.'

'Thank you.'

'Not promising anything.'

'Thanks anyway.'

'Yes, sir.'

*

Driving back, Gabe told me what had happened, what he had discovered. There was an edge to his voice, a purpose and energy; the mission was back on and he could see an end to this, a possibility of justice for Lance Corporal Creek. I could tell that, for the first time in many months, Gabe realised the future may hold something for him; that his existence was not unequivocally damned by the loss of his leg. Driving back to Essex, the sun dipping behind him and the wounded soldiers still at their game of poker, perhaps he came to realise that of all the soldiers left on the battlefield or flown home from war zones hooked up to morphine and life-supporting machines, he was one of the luckier ones.

22

I KNOW A man who smuggled a bar of gold into Thailand by inserting it into his anus. When he got to Thailand he must have aroused suspicion and the Thai border police made him strip off his clothes, then told him to stand on a table and jump off it. The impact on landing caused the bar of gold to drop from his rectum and fall onto the floor with a guilty clank. He told me this story after serving fifteen years in a Thai prison, which he described as inhuman – filthy and diseased and worse than footage he'd seen of battery farming.

I am thinking of that man, trying to remember his name, as I pass through the security of Galley Wood prison on my way to see Connor Blake. I am trying not to think about exactly what I am doing. I do not want to arouse suspicions as that man had done. I hope that the breath mint that I have just sucked on will mask any smell for the spaniel that is sniffing about visitors' ankles. I am concentrating on swallowing carefully, and praying that nobody tries to engage me in conversation. Because in my mouth, between my upper back molars and my cheek, I have four grams of cocaine, and if I am caught with them I am going down: game over.

The morning after taking over Connor Blake's case, I left home early and drove to my office. I told myself that it was because I had a backlog of work to catch up on, which I had been neglecting recently. But the truth is that I also did not want to speak to Maria, did not want to feel her reproachful, hurt gaze.

I turned on the office lights. It was dark outside, streetlights still on. As the tubes flickered on, the first thing I saw on my desk was the box containing Blake's case documents that I had not opened yet. Within it was the story of Blake's crime and it was not one that I wished to know about, even though I knew that I must. I had no choice.

I worked for an hour until the post arrived, walked out to pick it up and make coffee. While I was pouring my coffee the office phone rang. I considered ignoring it. If it was Blake, I did not want to speak to him. But I walked through to my office and picked up.

'Hello?'

'Daniel?'

It was Aatif, the Pakistani national whose visa I was supposed to be sorting out. I had done nothing to make that happen, nothing at all.

'Yes, Aatif.'

'Danny, those bastards... What have you heard? They have said yes, no? They bloody better have.'

'Nothing yet,' I said. 'I'll be honest, Aatif – it's not looking good.'

'Bloody shits,' he said. He worked at his cousin's builder's merchants and had picked up the vocabulary like a natural. If the visa requirements were as simple as the ability to swear like a scaffolder, Aatif would have little to worry about.

'It's this Somali stamp, Aatif. They don't like it. And your explanation, why you were there... They're not having it.'

His claim that he had been visiting relatives in Somalia would not wash; he could not supply names and addresses or, crucially, an exit date. Now I knew that the Home Office suspected he had been there for political reasons, connecting with jihadists. If I was honest with myself, theirs was the more likely explanation, although I found it hard to accept that Aatif, a short plump man with a big moustache and deep brown doleful eyes, was capable of waging serious holy war.

Aatif did not reply, and I had nothing more to say to help him. 'Listen, Aatif, I'll call you back soon as I hear anything.'

I hung up to him swearing. Aatif's problems felt very small and distant right now. But I was his lawyer and I took his file out, began drafting a letter to the Home Office to ask for due consideration to be given to his personal circumstances, his good character and excellent employment record. My heart was not in it and the words looked empty and ineffectual on the screen.

I sat gazing at Blake's box for I do not know how long and eventually my phone rang again. I picked it up slowly and brought it to my ear as if any sudden movement and it might blow.

'Hello?'

'Connell?' The voice was high-pitched and one I recognised.

'Speaking.'

'Got a message from Connor.' The voice had a quaver to it, a just-suppressed excitement.

'Yes?'

'He wants to see you.'

'Okay.'

'And he wants you to bring him something.'

I picked up a pen. 'Go on.'

Magnus told me what Blake wanted me to bring him, said it with relish. He was enjoying this, enjoying intimidating a man over twice the size of him. It could not be a feeling he had had often in his life.

'Are you insane?' I said.

'He wants you to do it.'

'And if I get caught?'

'Aren't you a lawyer? You won't get caught.' He laughed, a soprano giggle. 'Probably.'

'You're asking me to bring drugs into a prison.'

'Not asking. Connor isn't asking. Connor's telling.'

'He must know I can't do it.'

Magnus was silent for a moment. 'See the photograph of your girlfriend?' he said.

'No, you—' I begin.

'Should see who was holding the screwdriver. Supposed to have deported him.' Again, that excitement in his voice.

'Listen—' I said, but he interrupted again.

'Even I'm scared of him. You don't want him anywhere near.'

I looked out of my office window. Just beyond the glass people were getting on with their lives, going into shops, buying groceries, placing bets, talking, laughing. Beyond the glass felt like another world.

'Connell? You need to do this.'

'Tell Blake I'll see him,' I said, and I put the phone down before I had to hear Magnus's voice again. There was something in his childlike depravity that made me want to wash myself clean, as if it outraged my very skin.

Billy Morrison was sitting on the one swing that wasn't broken in the children's play area of The Angel, a pub on the outskirts of town opposite a sprawling and neglected housing estate. I had helped Billy in the past, saved him from a local gangster he had found himself on the wrong side of. I had hoped that perhaps that experience would have forced him to grow up, get his life together; but Billy was one of those people to whom the future was as far off as another planet, and could only see as far as the next deal, the next score, the next hit.

But I knew about Billy's upbringing and the misery he had been surrounded with since birth: the 'uncles' and strangers who had haunted his childhood with their mysterious appearances and vanishings, who had caused it to be full of uncertainty, fear and the daily expectation of abuse. Could I be surprised if the future held no special allure for him? I looked down at him where he swung gently on the swings and could still see the lost child in him, though he was now nearly thirty.

'How many?' he said.

I wished I did not have to ask him this, for both of our sakes.

'Four.'

'Four?' he said. 'No worries.'

'Got them on you?'

'Yep.' Billy was wearing a puffa jacket and he unzipped a pocket halfway up, pulled out a plastic bag full of wraps.

'How much?'

'For you, Danny, hundred and sixty. Can't say fairer. Fucking pure as you like.'

A cold wind blew across the playground and Billy shivered.

'You doing okay?' I said softly.

'Me?' He smiled up at me. 'Blinding, Danny. On the up.'

I doubted that, doubted it very much. I handed him notes, took the drugs from him. 'Thanks, Billy.'

'No bother.' I turned to go and Billy said, 'Danny?'

'Yes?'

'Ain't like you. All this. Drugs.'

'No.'

'You want to be careful. Don't want to get into all that.'

He looked at me with frank concern, as if it had not been him who had, only seconds ago, willingly supplied me with drugs, as if it was not him £160 better off for something which he had likely cut so heavily he was clearing a 70 per cent margin. Morality was something missing from Billy's life like other people lacked sight. I raised a hand and left him rocking on his run-down swing, surrounded by broken glass and weed-cracked tarmac and suburban deprivation, convinced that he was doing well despite all appearances to the contrary.

It is my turn in the line of visitors. I put my briefcase on a metal table and open it. A prison guard in latex gloves goes through it, opens files, picks them up by the spine and shakes them. He is being more thorough than the guard last time I was here. I have more in my briefcase this time but still I am worried. The cocaine in my mouth feels big and I am sure that I will not be able to talk. Across the room from me, a young woman in a short denim skirt is being patted down by a female guard. The guard takes a torch from her pocket, asks the young woman to open her mouth and shines her torch into it. I have not seen this happen before either.

I look back at the guard going through my briefcase. He has seen me looking at the young woman and is now looking at me curiously. I raise my eyebrows – *Will that be all?* – and he pushes my still open briefcase across the table towards me. I close it and he holds an arm out, showing me to another guard at a further table. This other guard is a middle-aged man, short and overweight with a scrubby beard. He too has latex gloves on. He puts his hands up under my armpits and I lift my arms to accommodate him. He squats down, runs his hands up and down my legs. He steps back and asks me to empty my pockets. He is irritated. I should have done it before. I nod, look apologetic.

He looks at me suspiciously and I say, 'No problem,' and I think it sounds normal. I wonder, if I do everything slowly, if he will be in more of a hurry to search me and get onto the next person. But slowing down might make him suspicious. He holds a grey plastic tray out and I put coins on it. He puts it on the table beside him and squats back down, goes over my pockets and trouser legs more thoroughly.

'Shoes off,' he says.

I frown. 'This necessary?' I regret saying it as soon as it has come out of my mouth. It sounds thick and wet, not like me. I untie my laces, take my shoes off and he picks each shoe up in turn, examines it. He looks at me.

'You're a lawyer?'

I nod.

'There a problem?'

I shake my head. He frowns. 'No. None at all.' The drugs in my cheeks make me sound as if I have a lisp, as if I have never mastered speech.

He nods over to the guard with the spaniel and the spaniel comes over, tail wagging, and puts its nose into my shoes. I try to look nonchalant but my pulse is hammering and I can feel my heart against my chest.

The dog does not seem interested and the overweight guard looks at me, up and down, gives me back my shoes. I bend to tie them and when I stand up he is looking at somebody behind me. Some colleague, back-up. This is it. I'm going to be pulled.

He looks back at me, frowns. I don't move, do not dare.

'You're done. Move along.'

I look down, do not look at him. I walk towards the end of the security hall and am nearly at the door, which a woman prison guard is opening like a beautiful invitation to a magical kingdom, when I hear his voice say, 'Wait.'

I turn around and he is holding the grey tray with my coins in it. 'Always said you lawyers are paid too much,' he says.

If I am honest, Connor Blake is so handsome that it seems like a miracle. I have never seen anybody who has such perfect features. But underneath that external beauty, I cannot help but imagine a different visage, something rotten and ugly and deformed writhing just beneath the flesh. Perhaps that is why he surrounds himself with freaks; perhaps, despite his good looks, he identifies only with the blighted and grotesque.

But amateur psychology will get me nowhere. I can only deal with the man across the table from me, and right now he is looking at me with amusement lighting up his start-lingly blue eyes, a smile on his lips.

'*You got the stuff?*' he hisses, a parody of a juvenile drug deal.

The guards have left us alone in the same room as before. I dig with my forefinger, tease the tiny packages out from behind my back teeth.

'What the fuck was all that about?' Now that I have run the gauntlet of the prison security I am no longer nervous, only angry.

'Ah,' says Blake, nudging the wet packets with his index finger where I have put them on the table. 'A little initiation.'

'If I'd been caught,' I say, 'you'd be looking for another lawyer.'

'They don't search lawyers, Daniel,' says Blake. 'Calm down.'

'They had my shoes off,' I say. 'Went through my briefcase.'

Blake looks surprised, then laughs. 'Joking.'

'Do I look like it?'

Blake scoops up the packages with one of his cuffed hands, pushes his chair back and bends down in his seat, tucks them into his sock.

'It's what we do,' he says. 'Test people out, to see how... obedient they'll be.'

'That fucked-up little goblin of yours threatened Maria.'

'Ace up our sleeve,' says Blake, unmoved by my quiet fury. 'She's safe for now. After all' – he straightens up, smiles at me – 'we've got four grams of cocaine covered in your DNA.'

It is like chess, dealing with Blake, only he has all the pieces and he is casually blocking off escape routes one by one, zeroing in on mate. I do not have the ammunition to do anything about it.

'So,' I say. 'What is it you want?'

'I want out of here,' says Blake. He takes a deep breath, looks about him, the small painted brick cell that we are in. 'They feed on each other in here. You know that?'

'Oh?'

'Eat each other's spirit. Yesterday a kid hanged himself, some pretty little slim-hipped boy, had victim written all over him. Couldn't take it any more. They'd been taking turns with him.'

'And that bothers you?'

'No,' says Blake. 'No, Daniel, I like it. I like to eat people's spirits. I ate Ryan's. I ate his brain.'

'He killed himself.'

'He did. My fault.' He nods in reluctant acknowledgement. 'Definitely my fault.' He grins suddenly. 'Should have seen his face, when I showed him the photographs of his kids.' He lets his face fall loose, mouth working like a fish. *My children. My babies.*

I look at my briefcase because it belongs to me and I know it and it is familiar, some touchstone of normality, sanity. I will not allow this man to get inside my head, to sink his teeth into my brain.

'Still want out,' says Blake. 'They can't keep me here. Not me.'

'How'd you do it?' I say. 'Moving the furniture? Hurting those kids?'

Blake smiles, the smile of a parent whose child has won a sporting event – complacent and satisfied. 'My boys. Might as well have moved in to her house. Set of keys and a cylinder of dentist's gas. In and out like it was their local.' He laughs, a sound that is as mechanical and devoid of humour as an unwilling car starting.

'The birds?'

223

'The what?' He frowns, then smiles. 'Magnus. He thinks it'll freak people out. You've met him. He's a sick little puppy.'

I take care not to show any reaction but I cannot help but think of Magnus and other men, cruel and damaged and barely human, walking through Maria's home, placing a mask over her mouth as she sleeps, holding in their hands instruments of pain and disfigurement.

'All right,' says Blake, and he takes a deep breath: back to business, enough small talk. He clasps his cuffed hands together, places them on the table. 'As you know, they have accused me of murder.'

I do not say anything, just watch him.

'Isn't this when you ask me if I did it?' he says.

'I'm sure you did,' I say. 'You malicious little fuck.'

Blake smiles. 'Course I did. He had it coming.'

'What did he do?'

'Laughed at my shirt.'

'That's all?'

'It was the way he did it,' says Blake. 'As if he didn't know who I was.'

'He probably didn't.'

'Could be right.' Blake shrugs. 'Whatever. Still couldn't let him get away with it.' He closes his eyes again. 'His neck went like it was nothing. Like a rotten stick.'

He seems to be enjoying the memory, lingering over it like some would a hat trick scored on a Sunday morning. 'The problem is, Daniel, there's a witness.'

'Must have been a lot of witnesses,' I say.

'Most of them knew not to say anything. Only one person's talking.' He stops. 'You haven't read the files?'

'I was getting to it,' I say. 'Wanted to speak to you first. Get your side.'

'My side,' says Connor Blake, and he gazes at me with those bluer than blue eyes. They lack focus and I do not feel that he is looking at me, but rather at some distant, unknowable place. 'My side is anyone laughs at a Blake, on his manor, they're going to get killed. It's the way it is.' He says this last almost wistfully, as if it is not he who is responsible for this immutable law.

I nod. 'I'm happy to take that to the judge.'

Blake ignores me. 'The reason I want you as a lawyer is you're going to tell me who that witness is.'

'Okay,' I say. 'But you don't need me. Any lawyer would tell you that.'

'That last one I had said he couldn't.'

'He say why not?'

'No. Said it was impossible.'

I stop, think. Normally a witness's name is disclosed to the defence team. It gives them a chance to check the witness's background, whether they've got any reason to lie, any axe to grind against the accused. No reason why Blake shouldn't know the name of the witness against him: it's his right under law. Unless his or her identity was protected.

'Don't know,' I say. 'I'll look into it.'

'You'll do more than that,' says Blake. 'You'll find that name, then tell me what cunt thinks he can testify against me.'

'Let's be clear,' I say to Blake. I take a deep breath. 'If I suspect that you will use this information to harm the witness, I cannot give it to you.'

Blake looks at me for a long time and a smile spreads across his handsome face and into his eyes. He just looks at me, does not need to say anything, and I understand. Protesting is pointless. This man, this depraved poster boy, can ask of me anything he wants.

23

I AM GOING through Blake's files the next morning when my mobile rings. I look at the number and see that it is Gabe. I pick up. I have just read the coroner's report of Karl Reece's death and already I have no wish to read any more, to delve any deeper into this awful story.

'Gabe.'

'Morning, Danny. You all right?'

I lie. 'Yeah.'

'I need a lawyer.'

'What've you done?'

Gabe laughs. 'No, not like that. I've found him. Petroski. Says he's willing to talk.' He sounds energised, excited. A new Gabe. Or back to the old Gabe I once knew.

'That's good.'

'It's excellent. Need to get something official.'

'Right.'

'Do you do affidavits?'

'For you, I'll even cut you a deal.'

*

We drive out in Major Strauss's car through a cold, spiteful rain, under low, ragged dirty-white clouds hurrying across the sullen slate sky. In the front, Gabe and Major Strauss swap stories and I sit in the back, try not to think about Blake and what he has asked me to do. As a lawyer, much of the work I do is good and useful; I am about to swear an affidavit from this man Gabe has found, use his testimony to force the army to reopen Lance Corporal Creek's inquest. But what Blake has asked me to do – supply him with the name of a hostile witness so that he can intimidate him or her, or worse – is unethical at best, probably illegal and certainly morally abhorrent. If I do what he asks, I do not believe that I will be able to look in the mirror again. If I refuse, then I expose Maria to the sick acts of Connor Blake's entourage. I do not know how many men he has to do his bidding, no idea of the depth of his resources.

Maria. Her name alone is ineffably precious. Maria. I cannot let anything happen to you. I will not let anything happen to you.

I sit back and watch as we hiss past articulated lorries on the two-laner, their huge wheels churning dirty spray, black water cascading in filthy ribbons off their bellies. There is a killed deer at the side of the road, lying forlornly on its side in the rain. My internal debate is pointless. The reality is that I have no choice. I cannot defy the Blakes. If I do, they will crush me and everybody I love like roadkill beneath a sixteen wheeler.

*

228

James Petroski lives in an isolated farmhouse on the north Essex coast, a flat region of long grass, marshland and very little else. The only sound is the reluctant suck and sigh of the ocean coming from beyond where the land drops off. The only sign of civilisation, apart from Petroski's farmhouse, are massive wind turbines out at sea like some forgotten alien artefact, their blades pearlescent and indistinct in the afternoon's shabby light.

Gabe leads the way, but before he can knock the door to the farmhouse opens and James Petroski is in the doorway, backlit by his home's interior lighting. The gloom outside means that he is almost in silhouette, but even in the indistinct light I can see that there is something terribly wrong with him. He steps out and I see that his face is badly burned, so much so that one ear is completely gone, melted away; one eye is sightless and the skin on the damaged side of his face is ridged and shiny, like a red plastic bag that has been screwed up and hastily smoothed. He is bald apart from some ragged clumps of hair and his lips are shrunken, exposing his teeth and gums.

'Hey,' he says. 'You found me.' From something so damaged, I hardly expect human sounds to emerge, but James Petroski sounds as genial as if he is welcoming friends round to watch the game. The contrast is so unexpected that I half expect him to pull off his mask, reveal a normal-looking man with a winning smile underneath. 'No problems?'

'No problems,' says Gabe, putting out a hand to shake. 'It's good to meet you.'

Petroski puts his out, but his wrist is just a stump so shiny with scar tissue that it looks as if it is wrapped in cling film. He looks at it ruefully then smiles at Gabe, and although the smile looks ghastly in that wrecked face, there is also a warmth in his eyes that softens the horror of it. He holds out his left hand instead and Gabe swaps hands, shakes.

'Some pair,' Gabe says. 'I lost a leg over there.'

Petroski laughs and I can see his molars. 'Not grown back?'

'Not yet,' says Gabe. 'Give it time.'

Petroski looks at the stump of his wrist again. 'Grow,' he tells it. Then he looks at me, looks at Major Strauss. 'I'm James Petroski,' he says.

We introduce ourselves and Petroski salutes Major Strauss with his stump before he catches himself, remembers that he is now a civilian, that he no longer has a hand to salute with. He smiles, shakes his head.

'Old habits.'

'Once a soldier,' says Major Strauss.

'Tell me about it,' says Petroski. He steps aside. 'Go in. I'll make tea. Then we'll talk.'

James Petroski tells us that the military is in his blood: his great-grandfather had escaped Poland and flown Spitfires in the Second World War, claimed to have shot down nine German fighters although Petroski suspects that was an exaggeration, probably an outrageous one. Petroski had decided to go into the army rather than the air force and

230

had been a sergeant posted in Afghanistan when his career had ended.

He tells us that he had been in the back of a Warthog armoured vehicle, crossing a bridge over a river in Helmand Province when the bridge had been blown up by an IED and the vehicle had tipped into the river. It landed upside down and falling equipment and unconscious soldiers had blocked the doors, leaving them trapped and disorientated in the dark as it sank beneath the water.

'Burning fuel was leaking, I don't know where from, and it was all over me. I couldn't move, couldn't even lift a hand to beat out the flames.'

Soldiers in following vehicles had climbed down the banks of the river to get to the soldiers, to pull them out of the wreckage. But the Taliban had hidden a sniper up in the hills above the river and every time a soldier got close, the sniper shot him.

'They were doing their best but they couldn't get to us. Inside soldiers were screaming, some were already under water, nobody could move. The smell of burning people...' He shakes his head. 'The vehicle kept filling up with water, soon it was up to my nose and I couldn't move my head, could only lie there until it covered me.'

Petroski is sitting on an armchair in his living room, Major Strauss and Gabe across from him on a tired yellow sofa that looks as if it was rescued from the side of a road. I am standing, as there are no more chairs. His living room is lit by a bare bulb and there is little else in the room: a low table, a TV on a pile of magazines. Petroski drinks tea and smiles at us.

'Yep. First I caught fire, then I drowned. Could say I was having a bad day.'

He tells us that it is good for him to talk about what happened; that the more he talks about it, the less it eats away at him. It is something the psychiatrists had suggested: a way to demythologise the events of that day, take away their power.

'Eventually they located the sniper and put down machine gun fire, dragged us out. Some of the soldiers needed resuscitating but nobody died inside that vehicle. Two were killed trying to get us out.' For the first time the vitality and warmth leaves Petroski. His head lowers in unconscious respect as he remembers their sacrifice. 'Got to remember that I was one of the lucky ones.'

Looking at him, at what is left of his face, it is hard to believe that luck has shone on him. But I suspect that James Petroski is one of those men to whom every day is a blessing, who deals exclusively in silver linings. I can feel only admiration for him.

'So,' says Gabe.

'Right,' says Petroski. '7 Platoon.'

'I've brought Daniel so that he can witness what you say. Make it official. Are you okay with that?'

Petroski nods.

'That way, they've got less room to manoeuvre. Can't really refuse to reopen the inquest.'

'7 Platoon,' says Petroski. 'I never served with soldiers I didn't like before. But that mob, I hated being under fire with them.'

'Didn't trust them?' says Major Strauss.

'I'll be honest,' says Petroski. 'Most of them, they fucking terrified me. Sir.'

'You don't need to sir me,' says Major Strauss.

'Sorry,' Petroski says, nearly adds 'sir' again, swallows it in time. 'I don't know what it was. What they'd seen, what they'd done. But they'd lost that humanity that any decent soldier needs.'

He tells us some of the stories he'd heard from them; an Afghani interpreter who had travelled with them and they'd befriended, who was later kidnapped, beheaded and left at their base's perimeter. Members of their platoon who had been killed or injured by IEDs, always the IEDs, placed on roads and made with low metal content so that they were almost impossible to detect. The daily gamble they all took as they patrolled booby-trapped streets, death always just a step away, meted out by an enemy that rarely showed its face.

'But we all faced the same dangers,' said Gabe. 'All of us. They didn't have it any different.'

Petroski nods. 'I know. Sometimes I think you just get a bad bunch. All the wrong people together. They feed off each other. Spent too much time on their own and...' He runs out of words.

'Went bad,' says Gabe. 'I know. Felt the same thing.'

'Just hardness. Killing was all they cared about.'

'So you heard them talk about Creek?' says Major Strauss.

'Right,' says Petroski. 'Yeah. Overheard them talking about killing him. Creek shouldn't have been mixed up with

233

that lot. He was a good man, an intelligent soldier, stubborn like you wouldn't believe.'

'Yes,' says Gabe. 'Wouldn't be told.'

'Like a dog with a bone, that boy,' says Petroski. 'They hated him.'

'Tell us what happened,' I say. 'Keep it simple. Just the relevant details.'

Petroski nods, silent as he goes back over what he heard, organises it in his head. 'I wasn't with them long,' he says. 'But I was with them when Lance Corporal Creek was killed. We'd been out on a patrol and got into contact just outside a village. Half of us were behind a wall, the other half were taking cover a few hundred metres away in the trees. Returning fire, nothing unusual. It was all over in minutes; the enemy just took off. Probably only been four or five of them, saw us, thought they'd have a pop.'

Petroski pauses, drinks tea. 'They didn't seem concerned, 7 Platoon. About Creek. He'd been with the group in the trees and he was dead, shot through the head. Nobody said much. A couple of them carried him back to base, but there was no atmosphere. Usually with that lot, one of them got hurt and they'd want revenge. There wasn't any of that.'

'Okay,' I say. 'But was there anything specific you saw or heard?'

'When we got back to base, I heard Banyan talking to a couple of others.'

'Who?'

'Shine and Burgess. They were laughing. Banyan said, "Yeah, I gave Creek the good news." Shine said to him, "Got to the front of the queue?" and Banyan said, "Man had it coming," and Shine and Burgess both agreed.'

'That's it?' says Major Strauss.

'That's enough,' says Gabe. 'If he's prepared to swear to it.'

Petroski nods. 'Course, sir.'

'One thing,' I say. 'A credibility issue. How come you've never said anything before?'

'I had an appointment with the colonel in charge of the company,' says Petroski. 'It's not like I wasn't going to say anything. Then, next day...' He shrugs, puts his spread fingers up to his ruined face. 'Never got to see him.'

We are ready to leave, standing in Petroski's hall. The wallpaper is peeling off the ceiling and there is mould in the corners; it looks like a ninety-year-old man recently died here. The place needs work, a lot of it.

'You bought this place?' says Gabe.

'Yeah,' says Petroski. He looks about him. 'Estate agents call it potential, right?'

'You're a long way from people,' says Major Strauss. 'Is that healthy?'

Petroski shrugs and I see a sadness in his good eye. 'I guess not. But you know? I can live with looking like this. It hardly hurts any more and sure I've got a missing hand, but...' He stops, and this is the first awkwardness I have felt in his company.

'I shouldn't have asked,' says Major Strauss. 'Not my business.'

'It's just,' says Petroski and again he falters. His face does not betray his emotion but as I look at him a single tear escapes his eye, runs down his creased and melted skin. I wonder if he has parents, what his mother feels when she looks at the legacy of the awful pain he has been made to suffer. It must be heartbreaking. He blinks, clears his eye. 'Other people. The way they stare. It's not fair on them. On me.' He breathes in, a shudder of grief in his throat. 'Other people,' he says.

Gabe puts a hand on Petroski's shoulder, grips him hard. 'I think you are remarkable,' he says. 'It's a privilege to have met you.'

Petroski smiles, bares his gums, shakes his head, but Gabe has got him in his gaze and will not let him get away, will not allow Petroski his self-deprecation. 'You are an example to me. Thank you.'

At this Petroski smiles for real; coming from a man with Gabe's reputation and rank, I guess that it must mean something. He does not answer but I hope that Gabe's words register, and that they help sustain him. I cannot imagine how hard it must be for him just to wake up every day, face a world that flinches rather than look at him.

He watches us go, raises a hand as we pull away, once again backlit by his hall's bare bulb.

None of us speak in the car, driving through the darkness in silence, each occupied with his own thoughts. I cannot help but dwell on James Petroski's injuries, examine them and what they must mean for him. He is dreadful to look at but he is a good man – honest and warm and aware only of his luck, not his misfortune. I compare him to Connor Blake – spoilt, indulged and impossibly good-looking – and it only makes me hate him more. How is it that of the two of them, it is Blake who has become such a monster?

24

HOW MANY EYEWITNESSES can you fit in a toilet? It is a question I am asking myself as I look through the witness statements collected by the police following the murder of Karl Reece, allegedly at the hands of Connor Blake. They are piled on my desk, thirty-two accounts of what the customers at Jamie's Bar saw that night, what they had to say about the brutal act that had played out right in front of them; an act which, I was sure, none of them would ever be able to forget.

I am in my office and it is early, not yet light outside; I again left Maria asleep, drove though empty streets full of the previous evening's debris, broken glass and spilled blood. But now, with Blake's file in front of me, my mind is on that night, the dark early hours when a promising young man was beaten to death for an imagined slight so trivial it would have gone unremarked by the majority of people. There is no light in this story.

Jamie's Bar has been around for years, decades even – a smart storefront bar visited by locals who, generally, know one another and have grown up together. Anyone they don't know, chances are they'll know a brother, father, cousin. Clearly, everybody there knew the Blakes; knew what happens if you crossed them, if you dared implicate one of them in murder.

Of the witness statements I have read so far, twenty-eight of them claim to have been in the toilets while it happened and could not recall having seen anything, neither the build-up to the attack on Karl Reece nor the aftermath, as if it had all happened in another place entirely. Three simply did not say anything, refused to speak. All the accounts are written in the elaborately formal style of police statements: witnesses 'have no knowledge of the assailant's identity' or 'confirm their presence in the premises' facilities during said assault'. But behind these statements is another, less precise sentiment: a fear of speaking out, a fervent wish to have been anywhere but there, to have witnessed anything but that.

That, the coroner's report confirms, is the savage beating of Karl Reece followed by a stamp to the back of his neck, which snapped two vertebrae and killed him instantly. The coroner was sure that it was a stamp that had been the cause of death. The tread of the killer's shoes was clearly visible on Karl Reece's skin. Prada, she concluded. This season's. I would expect nothing less of Connor Blake.

Throughout all of this detail I can sense Blake's presence in the gloom of my office, as close as if he is smirking at my shoulder. This wall of silence, the abject excuses of the witnesses, the prosaic details of the coroner's report that somehow only make the reality of what happened more unpalatable; the box that Blake's former solicitors gave me seems a documentation of all the indifference, cruelty and self-interest that society so often stands accused of. And at the centre of it is Blake – arrogant, entitled and as close to evil as I can imagine.

I push the papers aside and pick up my cup of coffee long gone cold, wondering what exactly I am going to say to Blake when I see him. Whether there is any way I can get out of this mess that I am in.

Connor Blake has one black eye, although it is not closed and I can see a glint of mischief in it as he is pushed through the door of our interview room by the same guard who had manhandled him in last time. This time the guard pushes Blake with more force and Blake nearly loses his footing, cuffed as he is.

Blake looks at me, frowns. 'You going to say anything?'

'Is there a reason for this rough treatment?' I ask the guard mildly.

'Yeah,' the guard says. He is in his fifties with short white hair, has the nose of an ex-boxer, big hands and a neck as wide as his head. 'Your client's been causing trouble.'

'I notice he has a black eye,' I say. 'Care to talk me through that one?'

'Can do,' says the guard. 'If you insist.'

In truth, I do not care either way; I have only been playing the role of concerned advocate. But I nod all the same. Since I have started, I might as well play the role convincingly.

'Fight in the kitchen couple of days ago,' the guard says. 'Where Blake's been working. I say working.'

Blake sniggers and I wonder how the guard can resist hitting him. I am struggling myself.

'Seems your client's taken against an inmate called Chambers. Big black fella, in for armed robbery. So Chambers has hit him. Fucking fair play, I say.'

'Okay,' I say. 'If you could get to the point.'

'The point,' says the guard. 'Right. Point is, Chambers give him this black eye. So next day, Blake's heated up a wire on the gas stove and put it through Chambers' eye. Right through the middle.'

'I did no such thing, by the way,' says Blake. He is leaning up against the wall opposite me and grinning as if he is in possession of a marvellous joke he can barely contain.

'Well, Chambers ain't talking,' says the guard. 'Won't see out of that eye again either.' He shakes his head and looks at the floor, and I half expect him to spit. 'Fucking Blakes.'

'What was that?' Blake has his arms folded but he is no longer smiling and his chin is tilted up in challenge. 'What you *fucking* say?'

Perhaps it is because the guard has had enough for one day and lacks the will to challenge Blake. I hope so, do not want to consider the other possibility – that the Blakes' reputation is such that this guard hesitates to speak ill of them even within the sacrosanct walls of this prison. Whichever, he turns away from Blake, says, 'Nothing.'

'What I thought you said,' says Blake.

The guard is pushing open the door but at this he stops, perhaps recalls who he is and what he stands for. He raises his shoulders, turns deliberately and says to me with a glance of frank disgust, 'How you can stand to work for scum like that.'

He walks through the door, pulls it to quickly behind him, and as it closes I feel as if it is me rather than Blake who is the prisoner in this place.

'So,' Blake says, taking a seat. 'Name. Address. Go.'

'What was it your previous lawyer said to you?'

'Said he couldn't give it to me.'

'He was right. He couldn't.' Blake is watching me closely. This is his shot at getting out of here, his chance to get at the only witness against him. He is perfectly still and I sense that he is holding his breath. 'I can't give it to you either,' I say.

Blake closes his eyes, does not say anything for a moment. 'Daniel. You don't want to do this.'

'Not me,' I say. 'They've got him or her in special measures. Protected identity. I don't know who it is.'

'No.' Blake shakes his head. 'No, no, fucking no, no, no.' He raises a finger, points it at me. 'No.'

'Listen,' I say. 'This is what happens when the police have reason to believe a witness might be intimidated.' Blake has his eyes closed but he is still pointing his finger at me like a drunk trying to make a point. 'They protect their name; give them an initial. No address, no name, nothing.'

'You know I can do anything. Kill her, hurt her. Make it so you won't recognise her. Anything I say will happen.'

242

'Are you listening? What you're asking me to do – I can't do it.' I cannot get through to this man but I need to, need him to understand. He must understand.

'They always do what I say.' Now he has his eyes open and his clear blue gaze is an invasion; I can feel it under my skin, probing places he has no right to be.

'Connor, I am going to go now. I cannot help you.'

'I'll make the call today.'

'No.'

'Yes, Daniel.'

'You won't touch her.'

Blake laughs. 'Daniel. Look at me. Look at me and wake the fuck up. I'm in prison. You think there's anything we won't do?'

'She has nothing to do with this.'

'You'll find out who that witness is. You know what we can do.'

After reading the statement of Witness A, I have a better idea than ever. His was the last I read and was unique in that it was more than a single page long and it contained more than a simple denial of all knowledge. His interview had been transcribed, set out in impersonal black and white across five pages; but his outrage and disgust at what he had witnessed that night came through as if he was speaking out loud.

Witness A had been drinking with friends. Their names were blacked out in the transcript, all ties to his identity meticulously erased. What was clear was that Witness A had been close to the events, that he had seen everything, that he was a good and brave man, one of the rare few who refuse to allow atrocities to go unchallenged on principal, regardless of personal risk.

So how did it start?

Blake, his gang and these other lads were just talking, laughing. Taking the piss, I don't know. Wasn't paying attention, just knew they were there. Weird-looking bunch. There was some short guy with strange eyes.

Good-natured?

Seemed to be. You know, with that edge. Group of men, pissed, giving each other shit. Way these things can go.

Do you know what triggered it?

Can't say. I heard a change in the voices, anger. Blake's holding his shirt, pulling at it, saying something to him. Christ, that poor kid.

Do you know what was said?'

No. Yeah. Don't know. Him, Blake, just rage really. Shouting. Up in the kid's face.

You mean Karl Reece?

Yeah.

What did Reece do?

Nothing. Looked confused. Like he didn't understand. His friends tried to calm things down, were talking to Blake and his people.

So things settled down?

Yeah.

You okay?

No.

There are people you can speak to.

How can these things happen?

Sir, I wish I could tell you.

Where do people like that come from? It was over nothing and he killed him and he liked it.

If we could—

No. Understand this. He wanted to do it and he liked it. It gave him pleasure.

Sir, you're upset.

It gave him pleasure.

Although the transcript does not indicate it, I imagine that this last word was delivered with a bewildered, questioning force. At this stage I think it likely that Witness A was in tears, his mind replaying the moment of Karl Reece's death and the transcendent look on Connor Blake's face, wondering how it could be, how men like Blake could exist among us.

The interview was suspended at this point and the time code shows that it took Witness A over thirty minutes to resume.

Okay to continue?

Yes.

So. They have an argument, then things calmed down. Tell me what happened next?

Nothing. Not for a while. Some of Karl's friends left, think there were only one or two still with him. He went to the bar – that's where I was – and Blake said something to him and, I don't know, maybe the kid had had one too many, gone to his head, said something back to Blake and that was it. Bang. All kicked off.

Blake attacked him?

Hit him, glassed him. I saw him stabbing at him with the glass but the kid, Karl, he didn't have time to fight back. He was out of it from the beginning. Just taking it. The blood looked black it was that dark.

Would you like to stop?

Everybody moved back, gave them room. Blake's crew holding back the kid's friends. It felt like minutes, just Blake kind of working on the kid. Yeah. Working on him. No hurry.

Nobody did anything?

We did. Our group. Told him to leave it, that was enough. A girl, other side of the bar, she was screaming for him to stop. Don't think she knew the kid. His friends just kind of moaning, 'Leave him, please, leave him'. But mostly, just… quiet. Like we were spectators.

Okay to go on?

Just... We could have done something.

You are doing something.

No. Weren't right. What happened. These things
shouldn't happen.

Sometimes they do.

Why?

They just do.

Blake eventually tired of what he was doing to Karl
Reece and helped him up, half-carried him outside like he
was supporting a fallen comrade, carrying him to safety.
Nobody knew what was happening but some followed them
outside as if sucked into Blake's current of violence. There
Blake carefully arranged Karl Reece so that he was on his
front and his head was against the wall. He took four, five
careful paces back like a footballer lining up a penalty. Karl
Reece's friends were now struggling but were held by Liam
and other members of Blake's entourage.

Witness A tells the interviewing officer that Blake had
looked, he couldn't describe it, euphoric maybe, in the
second he was still before he launched himself at the back of
semi-conscious Karl Reece's neck. He grunted as he landed
but that did not mask a sound that the witness could not
describe but assumed it was Karl Reece's neck snapping.
Karl Reece dying.

And then?

And then Blake went to his people and they formed up and backed up like they were a pack of wolves. Nobody dared approach them and Blake was looking, making eye contact, looking into the eyes of everybody standing on the street. Absolute silence. Blake looked into my eyes and he was pleased with what he had done. You could see that. Pleased.

Anything else?

He looked at us to tell us, give us a message. Not to say anything. That was the message.

Yet here you are.

Couldn't let it stand.

You're very courageous.

Don't say that.

Really.

Don't.

We need people like you.

I did nothing and now he's dead.

'I could show you photographs that would make you weep,' says Blake. Still that gaze, as if he knows what I am thinking, can read my darkest fears. What was it that he had said? That he had eaten Ryan's brain.

I return his gaze; do not say anything.

'I'll give you six days,' says Blake. 'After that, we'll come for her.'

He has my pen in his hand and he is writing on a piece of paper. He finishes, caps the pen, pushes paper and pen across to me.

'Six days,' I say.

'You'll call this number. With the name.'

'I cannot get you the name.'

'I'm trying to be patient.'

'Even if I had a year,' I say.

'My father has men on his payroll, can make women wish they were dead. Or the kids she teaches.' He taps his finger on the paper, the number written there.

'If you touch her, I will make you pay.'

'I'm in prison, Daniel. What can you do?'

'There's always a way.'

Blake sighs. 'Still not getting it. There's nothing you can do. We have you' – he holds out his cuffed palms, closes his hands into fists – 'like this.'

'Connor—' I say, and I am ashamed to hear my voice betray me, sound a note of entreaty.

'I know, I know, you're frightened, don't know what to do, where to turn. It's a nightmare, right? I understand.'

'Six days. I can't—'

'But, Daniel, this is nothing. Nothing to what it will be. I promise you that. I absolutely fucking guarantee it. Daniel? Look at me.'

I stand up, close my briefcase. I will not stay here and listen to this; do not trust myself, how I will react.

'We take the gloves off, let the dogs off the leash, then there's no going back.'

I cross to the door and knock on it. I do not look at Blake who is leaning back in his chair, cuffed hands behind his head. The guard opens the door and I pass him by as quickly as I can, but not before I hear Blake say, in a voice that sounds as relaxed as if he is confirming a long-standing arrangement: 'Six days, Daniel. Call that number. Six days.'

I drive back to my house with the sun sinking through clouds full of the threat of rain, so purple they look putrid, backlit by the sun's weak yellow, the ripe colours of a neglected wound. I park outside and there are lights on inside my home, which means Maria is there and I think back to just weeks ago when this would have been a wonderful sight. I sit in my car for some minutes, wondering how it is I am going to face her. Since Blake invaded her flat, took her photograph, I find it hard to look her in the eyes; my sense of culpability has created a tension between us that she cannot understand and which I cannot bridge.

She has dressed up for me and she kisses me in the hall, greets me with a smile that is wider than her usual smile though less certain for all that. She is so beautiful and blameless that I feel a moment of panic. What have I done to her?

'Hi, handsome.'

'Hey.'

'Bad day?'

I shake my head, less in answer than to discourage questions. But Maria will not let me avoid her so easily.

'I thought we might go out.'

'Oh.'

'Do something.'

'Maybe another time.'

'Might do you good. Us good.'

'Another time.' I see her smile falter and again feel that panic. I cannot treat her this way, cannot cause her pain.

'Maria...' I begin.

'Have I done something?' she says, a forced brightness to her voice.

'No,' I say. 'Course not.'

'I wonder...' she starts but stops. 'You just need to tell me. Hey? I'm here.'

I look into her eyes and I want so much to reach across and touch her, tell her everything, confide in the goodness and wisdom I see there. Vick, Ryan, Blake, his dreadful family – how all that has happened has been a consequence of my good intentions. How all I had ever wanted was to help an old acquaintance who had once meant something to me. Perhaps she would understand. Then I picture her running upstairs, packing a suitcase, frantically flinging in clothes, the things she leaves in the bathroom, fleeing from my life as she realises that I am a man who is surrounded by malevolence, who has caused men to hold a screwdriver to her throat as she slept. I cannot tell her anything. She would be gone in minutes.

'It's nothing,' I say. 'Give me a break.'

'A break,' she says. She is on the verge of a comeback, things she wants to say about to spill out. But she catches herself and she only narrows her eyes as if she has come to some internal decision, nods slightly. 'Whatever you say, Tarzan.'

She goes upstairs and I sit at my kitchen table, wondering why she is here, why she does not just go home to her flat. There is nothing for her here, not right now. Then I think that perhaps she loves me and is not willing to give up on me just yet, and this thought causes me to close my eyes for some moments as I realise the enormity of what I am risking.

I have to subdue an urge to upend my kitchen table, tear cupboards from the walls, cause damage that can never be undone. Six days, Blake said. What could I do in six days?

25

IT IS TOO early for Jamie's Bar to be open but I knock on the closed smoked glass door which reads *Over 25s Only* anyway. There is no answer so I hammer on it with my closed fist, making it shudder in its frame and passers-by stare at me; they look away as soon as they meet my eye. I stand back and look up and see movement in one of the windows overlooking the street. I walk back to the door and hammer on it some more. At some point somebody is going to answer. I have nowhere else to go, nothing else to do but raise whoever is inside. It is day one of my six-day deadline and here, the scene of the crime, is the only place I can think of to go. I have to start somewhere.

This morning I had woken up and Maria had not been next to me and I thought that she had left me, given up on us. I had come to bed late the night before and she had been asleep, or pretended to be. We seemed to exist in separate worlds, superimposed onto one another, unable to connect. In the morning I had lain in bed and could still smell her hair conditioner on her pillow. I had got up and gone down-stairs and there she had been, quietly drinking coffee at the kitchen table with her back to me. Seeing her long hair, her stillness, then her shoulders hunching as she brought her mug to her lips, made me feel grief as if she was already gone and I was only watching her ghost.

I approached her from behind and touched her shoulder. She slowly put her mug down and reached up to put her hand on mine. But she did not turn around as she would normally, did not give me her smile, bathe me in her gaze. Instead she patted my hand as if she was comforting me for some mutual regret, got up and left the kitchen. Some minutes afterwards she left my house and during those minutes all I did was stand there, in my kitchen, trying not to think of anything at all.

I see indistinct hands behind the dark glass of the door of Jamie's Bar, hear the sound of bolts opening, the jangle of keys. The door is pulled open and a man in a faded black Jack Daniel's t-shirt leans towards me, both hands on the frame of the door, a cigarette in his mouth. He is big, has a scar next to his right eye and his eyes are hangover pink.

'Fuck do you want?'

'I want to speak to whoever runs this place.'

'Well, he ain't here.'

'No?'

'No. Fucking nearly broke the door.'

'You work here?'

The man takes a pull of his cigarette, flicks it past me into the street. 'Fuck's it to you?'

'Mind if I come in?' I walk past him and he watches me into the dark bar, says, 'Yeah, yeah as it happens I fucking do.'

There is a woman sitting on a bar stool wearing running

bottoms and a tight t-shirt which shows her cleavage and a roll of her stomach. Her hair is tied back and she looks tired. She looks at me without curiosity and drinks from a bottle of beer. Jamie's Bar has banquettes along the wall opposite the bar and it opens out at the back where there are tables and chairs.

The man is still at the door and he calls out to my back, 'What do you want, man?'

I stop and turn and wait for him to come to me. 'Wanted to see the size of your toilets.'

'You what?'

'Were you working the night Karl Reece was killed?'

'Louie?' says the woman.

Louie turns to the woman. 'Call Del.' The sleeves of his t-shirt are cut off, showing arms that are not muscular but are big, heavy with flesh, and his shoulders are large.

'Because the night he was killed, the whole bar was in them. Your toilets.'

The woman at the bar has picked up her mobile and called a number. She whispers into it.

'You a copper?' Louie says.

'No. I work for the Blakes.'

'Yeah?'

'That's what I said.'

He leans across the woman and takes a cigarette from a packet in front of her, lights it. 'So, again – what do you want?'

'Somebody's talking,' I say. The words sound strange. These are not words I should be saying. 'A witness. Wondered if you knew anything.'

The woman turns to me now and takes a good look. I smile at her but she does not smile back. She slides off her stool and wanders behind the bar. Her running bottoms are low on her backside and I can see a tattoo fanned above her buttocks.

'You serious?' Louie says.

'I don't look it?'

Next to the bar a door opens and another man comes in, who I assume is Del. He must have been upstairs. He is overweight, his belly stretching his white t-shirt. His face is shapeless and full of puppy fat and he looks subnormal in some way. He is probably seven foot tall. I have never seen a more massive person. Between Louie and Del, they probably make two and a half of me, and I am big.

'You're not one of the Blakes,' says Louie. It is not a question.

'No.'

'So who the fuck are you?'

Del is behind me and Louie in front, blocking the way to the door. The woman is behind the bar, watching the action unfold with lazy interest, chin in hand, cigarette to mouth.

'I work for the Blakes.'

Louie laughs. 'We are the fucking Blakes,' he says. 'Least, near enough. Affiliates.'

'Who taught you that word?' I say.

'He's lying,' says Del behind me. His voice sounds wet and clumsy.

'It speaks,' I say.

'You're a copper,' Louie says.

'I told you. I'm working for Connor Blake.'

I hear Del move behind me and I palm the ashtray from the bar, turn and hit him with it. It breaks on his forehead but this does not seem to bother him. I back up because I know that if he gets hold of me there will be nothing I can do. Louie is standing watching, which he shouldn't. Del might be enormous but it will need them both to take me down. Now he has lost the advantage.

I assume that Louie will expect me to retreat from the massive threat of Del, which is why he is standing waiting. Instead I walk up to Del and duck under his haymaker and hit up beneath his chin. He is so tall that some of my shot has lost its power by the time it hits his bottom jaw but I still hear a sharp enamelled crack as his teeth meet. I put my crossed forearms into his soft chest, which is the height of my head. I push him and he is so tall it is as if I am pushing up. I have momentum and he stumbles back, faster and faster until he reaches the tables and chairs at the back of the bar. He falls over them and twists and his head hits the end wall with the sound of a hammer on steak.

The woman is reaching for something under the bar, a weapon of some kind, I expect. But the bar is too small to swing anything and besides, I am on Louie before she can give it to him, landed three headshots before he can defend himself. He puts his arms up like a child in the playground, but I hit him under the ribs, once, twice, and his legs go. I stand back, take a breath, prepare to go back in.

'That's enough,' says the woman behind the bar. 'Fucking leave it.'

I stop. I am breathing heavily. I look at her.

'If we knew who was talking,' she said, 'he'd be a dead man.' She shakes her head, confounded by my stupidity. 'Now go on, whoever you are. Do one. Before you get yourself in real trouble.'

I look at Louie, who now has blood down the front of his Jack Daniels t-shirt. He is looking up at me, his expression fatalistic, and already one of his eyes is beginning to swell and close. At the end of the bar Del is still and quiet, lying on his front among fallen chairs, his legs bent carelessly like a huge sleeping child.

I have found nothing; this has been a mistake. I nod to the woman behind the bar, who smiles sarcastically back at me. I turn to leave and can feel the throb in my knuckles. So much for that. I am going to need a new plan.

I had spent the day going through Blake's file, looking for something, anything that could help me find the identity of the sole witness against him. But I had found nothing; all I discovered was that Connor Blake was responsible for the death of a young man who emphatically had not deserved it. Karl Reece, the file told me, had been a twenty-two-year-old medical student at Oxford who was visiting college friends over Christmas. He came from the north of England where his father owned a farm. He was scholarly and gifted and originated so far from the aggressive brash world of suburban Essex that he might as well have been born on the moon. He had never encountered a man like Connor Blake, never imagined that good-natured banter could go so wrong, so quickly. He did not know the rules. And because of that he was dead. Karl Reece undeniably deserves justice, and I am doing my best to see that he does not get it.

If I am honest with myself, what has just happened was partly a result of this, my feelings of culpability and helplessness. Louie and Del had not deserved what I had unleashed on them; Connor Blake was my real target. But he is untouchable. And along with the shame I feel for what I did to them, the truth is that I also feel calmer. Violence has its uses, disgraceful as it is to admit.

I do not want to go home, cannot face Maria. At times like this there is only one place for me to go; only one person who can help. Someone who is as hard as anybody I am dealing with, probably harder, who sees the world with an eye even more cynical than my own. I get in my car and head for Gabe's.

Major Strauss is in Gabe's kitchen when I arrive. They are drinking and talking, and I do not want to intrude, but Gabe looks pleased to see me, waves me in. The last thing I should be doing is drinking. I have too much to do, too many things to sort out. But one drink clears the way for another and before long I am halfway in the bag, yet with the reptilian part of my brain still sober and alert, keyed up way too tight.

Much of what Gabe and Major Strauss are talking about is beyond me so I just sit and listen as they discuss their time in Iraq, Afghanistan, the difficulty of raising a domestic army in a foreign land, issues of ethics and logistics, politics and tactics. I can see by the way he talks about it how much Gabe misses the army; how its rules and challenges ignited his imagination, still do.

At some stage Gabe is silent for a little too long and he sets his glass down abruptly, says, 'Bed,' gets up and leaves.

I imagine that Major Strauss will now leave but instead he refills his glass with Scotch, pours more into mine, looks over at the door Gabe has just left through and sighs.

'That, Daniel, is one of the tragedies of my career.'

'Gabe?'

'An excellent soldier. Excellent. Would have ended up my boss. No doubt.'

I nod, do not reply. I know so little about his time in the army that I have no contribution to make.

'Fighting?' says Major Strauss, looking at my knuckles.

'Something like that.'

But he has already lost interest, mind back on Gabe. 'Always first. Always. In the lead vehicle. Didn't have to be. Led by example.'

'His men liked him?'

'Loved him. You can't imagine. Be next to his men, on his front, looking for IEDs, prodding at the ground with a bayonet. Tell me how many other commanding officers'd do that.' But he is not asking a question, does not want a response. There is a genuine sadness in his voice. 'If a bomb went off under a vehicle, he'd be the one hosing it out, fishing out body parts, pieces of soldiers. Him. Not his men. Every time.'

'He misses it.'

'Course he does.' Major Strauss laughs without humour. 'Doesn't understand what it's like now. They blow his leg off, we're not even allowed to shoot back.'

'That bad?'

Major Strauss shakes his head, downs his drink. 'He's a good man. Involved in all this, that dead corporal.' He sighs again, something wistful and regretful in his face. 'Such a shame.'

'How's that going?'

'Getting there,' he says. 'Reaching a resolution.' He stands up, looks down at me. 'I'll see you.'

'Yeah.'

He walks unsteadily out of the kitchen and I hear the front door close and shortly after his car leave, headlights through the window painting the wall of Gabe's dark kitchen. He should not be driving. Neither should I. But I know where Gabe's sofa is and I head for it, take out my phone and keys, notice that I have missed two calls from Maria, and fall asleep.

26

THE FIRM OF lawyers I worked for in the City before my public disgracing and banishment back to Essex owned an office building near London Bridge, had been there for nearly a century. The firm was run by men of privilege, privately educated sons of the social elite; looking back I find it hard to understand why they hired me. Perhaps they enjoyed the idea of having such a brute in their midst, a caged beast to wheel into meetings and put the frighteners on recalcitrant clients. But maybe I am being hard on myself. I was a competent lawyer and made them a great deal of money. Though it is also true that I never felt at home in their hushed book-lined corridors, always saw myself as an imposter.

About five years ago I worked on a case there with a junior solicitor named Charles, a fundamentally decent man but weak and easily turned. I soon discovered that he was fiddling his time, claiming hours that he had not worked. I confronted him about it and he told me in a cracked voice that he had been instructed to do so by one of the senior partners, Gideon, a florid-faced man with long white curled hair who affected brightly coloured bow ties and braces. Gideon was a loud and unpleasant bully who had carved himself out his own fiefdom, which he ruled with spite and greed. Charles told me that Gideon had threatened him, told him that he would be out of the firm if he did not do as he was told. Charles had a demanding wife and children in private schools, and he could not afford to lose his job. As he told me this he had taken off his glasses and elaborately cleaned them without looking at me, but I had seen that they had begun to fog from his tears.

At a firm golf day several weeks later, I had been paired with Gideon, consigned to spending three hours hacking at a golf ball in his unpleasant, hectoring company. He had spent the first nine holes filling me in about his younger girlfriends and how much his house was now worth, how it had doubled in value in little over three years even though it was in a neighbourhood that had a lot of blacks.

On the tenth hole he had knocked his ball off the fairway into the rough and close to a small lake. I followed him as he went to find it, and next to a small stand of trees told him that if he did not promise to stop bullying Charles and the other solicitors under his jurisdiction, then I would drag him over to the water, hold his head under until he nearly drowned, then do it again and again until the point at which he saw things my way. His initial outraged reaction had been to question my sanity, then threaten me, then mock my heritage. But I had held him by the balls and looked into his eyes until he nodded in sullen, cowed agreement. We had played the rest of the holes in silence.

Whether it was the pain in his groin or his chagrin at what I had said to him, I could not tell; but on that back nine his golf swing went to hell.

Now I am sitting in a café over a cup of expensive cappuccino, looking at Charles. He has not changed much; he has new glasses but his shoulders still slope and his chin is still weak. He does not look happy. I cannot blame him, after what I have just asked him.

'It's impossible.'

'It's difficult, I accept that,' I say. 'But please. Don't tell me it's impossible.'

Charles no longer works in private practice; the pressure eventually became too much. He now works as a prosecutor for the CPS, and while he is not working on Connor Blake's case, I have no doubt that he knows somebody who is. Somebody who knows the real identity of Witness A.

'You owe me,' I tell him, not for the first time. But it is at least true. I had said nothing to anybody about his dishonesty back then, about what Gideon had told him to do. And after our golf day, Gideon had left him alone.

'But Daniel.' He looks at a passing waitress as if he is considering asking her for help, to save him from the nasty man. 'It's beyond illegal. We'd both go to prison.'

'I won't tell.'

'Daniel.'

'Listen, Charles. I wouldn't ask if it wasn't necessary.'

'But why? You know you're not allowed to know.'

'I just need it.'

'I can't do it.'

'You need to,' I say. I have never felt as low and contemptible and I despise myself for what I say next. 'Or you want me to go to the Law Society with what you were up to back then? It'd finish your career.'

'Daniel.' The way he says it, as if he had held me up as some kind of paragon and is devastated to see that I am human after all; the disappointment of a child discovering his favourite football star is a drug user. 'Why are you doing this?'

He's not getting it. He still cannot believe what I am asking of him. He needs to understand I am serious.

'Your wife, what's her name?'

'Ophelia.'

I should have remembered. 'What's she going to do when you lose your job, can't get a new one because of what you did?'

'Christ, Daniel...'

'Kids still in private school? Want to keep them there?'

'This isn't fair.'

'No. No, it isn't. But Charles, it's happening. So. Can you do it?'

'No. Don't know. Maybe. Daniel, this... this is insane.'

'Look at me, Charles.'

Charles tries to meet my eyes but he cannot, ducks back down over his pot of Earl Grey.

'Charles, I just need a name. Then I'll leave you alone.'

He shakes his head at his tea. 'A name.'

'Two words. All I need.'

He is still shaking his head. 'Can't believe this. Not you, Daniel.'

'Just nod if you can do it.'

Charles stops shaking his head, is still for some seconds. Then he nods slowly, but still does not lift his head, still does not look at me. I put one of my cards on the table and wait until he picks it up.

'Need it soon, Charles. Need it yesterday.' Charles just nods again. I stand up and look down at him, a small man huddled over a small teapot, and I feel sick at myself, as much of a bully as his old boss Gideon. No, worse. I turn to leave and Charles does not even look up to watch me go.

Back at my office I put a call in to Jack, my acquaintance on the local paper. Gabe had asked me if I could find out anything about Global Armour, told me that he had tried but that their accounts were held offshore and he did not know where to look, who to ask. Jack had done his share of investigative journalism on Fleet Street until the bottle had beaten him. He probably still had contacts he could lean on.

'Danny. How you doing?'

'Good, Jack. You?'

'Decent, pretty decent. You still acting for Connor Blake?'

'Yeah.'

'You all right?'

'Yeah. Think so.'

'Tread carefully, Danny. Those Blakes, you know? Not a lot they won't do. Not a lot they haven't already done.'

'Got you.'

'So what can I do you for?'

I tell him about Global Armour, tell him that they might be involved in something and that if they are, he'll be first to know. Tell him it could be juicy. Jack listens in silence.

'So,' he says.

'So.'

'What do you want from me?'

'Anything you can find out. Who they are, who's backing them. Be good to know what we're up against.'

'Say they're registered offshore?'

'Apparently.'

'I know some people. I'll get back to you. Juicy, that what you said?'

'Fat and.'

'My language. Leave it with me.'

I hang up and my mobile tells me that I have missed four calls and that they are all from Maria. I cannot hide from her any more. But I do not know how I can face her. I call her number and close my eyes as it rings and I am relieved when it goes through to her voicemail. I hang up without leaving a message, before I hear her greeting. I would not have known what to say anyway.

By the time I get home it is late, nearly the end of the second day. Only four left to go. Maria is not there, although she has cooked. It is possible to reconstruct her evening from what is in the kitchen: the unwashed pans, the two place settings at the table and the opened but untouched bottle of wine. I do not need to look into my waste bin to know what is in there. She has not left a note and there is no message on my phone. I am trying to protect her from

Blake, but I cannot help but wonder what I am destroying in the process.

Four days to go. Charles had better come through with that name.

27

IT IS ASTONISHING to me how little there is in Connor
Blake's file, how thin the evidence against him is, considering
he committed a brutal murder in public before over thirty
people. No forensic evidence, nothing physical to incriminate
him, no CCTV footage. Just the word of one person. I spend
the morning once again scrutinising all of his paperwork,
looking for something, anything that can point me to the
identity of Witness A. I reread the coroner's report, go back
through all of the witness statements. Then I read Witness
A's statement again, his disbelief at what he had witnessed,
his unwillingness to accept that evil like Connor Blake's
could exist in our purportedly modern and civilised society.
I read Connor Blake's interview, his relentless denials. I can
almost hear his pleased tone, his smug assertions that he
had nothing to do with what had happened, that they had
the wrong person. Within these pages is nothing to give me
any idea of who Witness A is: no clues, no indications, no
indiscretions that might betray his identity.

The last pages are a list of the names of the witnesses
in total: everybody who had been there that night. I have

looked at it before but not examined it. Witness A is not on it and every other witness has denied everything. Still, I place them on my desk and look at them. A list of names, no more. No addresses, no photographs, just names in black and white.

I get up and refill my coffee cup in the entranceway, sit back down, take a drink. There are thirty-two names on the sheet and they are listed in alphabetical order. I read through them and I do not recognise any of them. I stare at the paper and unfocus my eyes. One of the witnesses is called Leighton, which is not an unusual name but not a common one either. Leighton Finch. I do not recognise the surname but the first name stirs something. I cannot place it. I lean back in my chair and think. But the more I think, the more elusive it becomes, like reaching for something in a tight space and accidentally pushing it out of range, and eventually it is gone and I wonder if I was mistaken. Perhaps it is the name of somebody on TV or in a film.

It is no good. There is nothing here. My future now rests on the actions of Charles, a spineless, weak man who I hope is desperate enough to do what I have asked him. But, if I am honest, I doubt his nerve.

Maria has not called and I have not been in contact and when my mobile goes I think that maybe it is her. But I do not recognise the number and when I pick up it is Jack.

'Global Armour, Danny. Those boys like to keep themselves to themselves.'

'Guess that's the way with mercenaries.'

'Way with everyone, my son. Who wants to pay tax?'

'Did you find anything?'

'Registered overseas, like you said. Tricky to find anything but I have a mate. You know how it is.'

'I know you're connected, Jack.'

He laughs. 'I wish. But yeah, I've got a mate. He did some digging, turned up a few names. The directors. Not a lot else.'

'Okay. Whatever you've got.'

'You'd think, wouldn't you. British nationals running round the world, got every kind of weaponry you can imagine, you'd think there'd be somebody keeping an eye on them. Instead, they're registered offshore, hardly exist. Making a ton of money.'

'Blood money.'

'All smells the same, Danny boy.'

'So what've you got?' I ask again.

'Okay, so. Names and addresses. Four directors. Got an S. Connor?'

'Writing them down.' Gabe might know them. 'Who else?'

'P. Mitchell, two Ls. Hang on.' I hear him speak to somebody, say thank you, he'd take care of it, leave it on his desk. He came back. 'Sorry, Danny. Right, next. Got an F. R. Pieters, spelled P, I, E, T. South African, I'd say.'

'Got it.'

'Last one, G. Strauss. Like the composer.'

Gabe had called him Gavin. Major Gavin Strauss. 'He's a director?'

'Says here. Mean something to you?'

'Jack?'

'Yep?'

'Thanks for this. Got to go.'

Gabe is not answering his phone and when I get to his house his car is not there, and there is no reply when I knock on his door. I know that Gabe is capable and highly trained, but Major Strauss has the backing of most of 7 Platoon, and besides, Gabe does not know what I know. Strauss has the advantage of surprise over Gabe and I cannot help but worry for him.

I call Jack back at his office and his line rings and rings, and I am about to give up when he answers.

'Yes?'

'Jack, it's Daniel again. You said you had addresses with the names.'

'You want Strauss's.' A statement, not a question. Jack has been a newsman too long not to pick up on a story.

'You got it?'

He reads it to me and I thank him again and get back into my car. Strauss lives in a village twenty miles away and I can be there in a few minutes, although I do not know why I feel the need to hurry. Gabe not answering his phone is the norm rather than the exception; he is a man who is always hard to pin down. It would be better to wait, to face Strauss together. But I have a feeling of disquiet, of things not right. It may be linked to what is happening with Blake and Maria but I cannot sit and wait for Gabe to resurface. I need to do something.

*

Major Strauss lives in a red-brick and clapboard cottage with a thatched roof, which sits behind a low hedge on a narrow lane in the village of Gamble's Green. When I get there it is still light, although it is fading. Strauss's car is on his gravel drive. I pass his house and park on the road further up next to a gate giving into a field. I can see his house in my rear-view mirror and for some time I just sit and wonder what I should do. Knowing Gabe, he would want to sort this out himself, would not want somebody to act for him. But he is still not answering his mobile and I cannot be sure that Strauss hasn't already done something to him, dramatic as that sounds to me.

No cars pass and the village feels deserted as night falls. I spent the previous evening watching the Blakes' home, playing out revenge fantasies in my head that I lacked the strength to carry out. I will not do the same tonight. I am about to get out of my car, walk to Strauss's house and see how things play out, when his car's headlights come on and he pulls out of his drive, onto the road and past me.

I start my car and pull out to follow him. He drives fast. He knows these roads, has driven them many times, and I have trouble keeping up as he takes narrow bends at fifty, sixty miles an hour. We are heading back the way I had come and I wonder whether he is headed for Gabe's, but he takes a small lane that climbs up under a canopy of leaf-less trees. At the end is a restaurant, a sign lit up saying The Black Horse. It has big glass windows and has been modernised and inside it is bright and I can see tables inside, can see people eating.

Strauss turns a corner and enters the car park. I park on the road outside, sit and wait. Soon Strauss comes back into view on foot and walks to the entrance of the restaurant, goes inside. He speaks to a waitress who nods and leads him to a table. He passes out of view. Sitting in my car I feel anger, a rage building, for how he has misled my friend, for what he may have done to him, for his lies. I get out of my car and I feel as loose and purposeful as I would before a tennis final, almost elated by my anger; after so much helplessness I have a target and it feels good.

I push open the glass door and the waitress smiles at me. Her smile drops when she sees the set of my face. I walk past her and over to Strauss's table. He has his back to me and I walk around the table, which is set for two, and sit down opposite him. He is surprised to see me and for a second his face gives him away – he looks as guilty as a cheating husband.

But he quickly recovers, smiles, says, 'Daniel. What are you doing here?'

I reach across the table and get my fingers inside his collar and tie, my knuckles brushing his Adam's apple. I grip and stand up, haul him over the table. Cutlery and crockery spill onto the floor, a wine glass smashes. He is bracing himself with both hands on the table, trying to stop me from pulling him all the way over. His face is up against mine, his chin over the back of my wrist. I could bite his nose off. His eyes are not as frightened as I would like.

'Where's Gabe?'

'You imbecile.'

'Where is he?'

Strauss looks amused. 'I think he needed to visit the men's room.'

'Danny?' The voice comes from behind me and I know it well. I turn and Gabe is standing looking at me, a confused smile on his face. 'Problem?'

Everybody in the restaurant is watching us, although when I meet their eye they look away. I let go of Strauss and he sits back down, smoothes the front of his shirt, adjusts his tie.

'What's going on?' says Gabe.

'Your friend wants to join us for dinner,' says Strauss, but Gabe cuts him off.

'Asking Danny,' he says. 'Danny?'

'Ask the major about the directors of Global Armour,' I say.

'Ah,' says Strauss.

A man who I presume is the manager of the restaurant comes over. He is short and French.

'Gentlemen? Please, not in here.'

'We're leaving,' I say.

'Right,' says Strauss. 'Things you need to hear. Follow me.' He has lost none of his composure, has assumed control despite what I have done to him, as if he is the one calling the shots. He gets up and walks to the exit.

Gabe frowns at me. I nod slowly and he nods once back, and although no words have been exchanged I know that Gabe is behind me, that he is in my corner.

We follow Major Strauss outside. He walks around the

side of the restaurant, through a gate into the car park, which has three rows of cars parked on the gravel. I can see Gabe's near the entrance.

'Where are you going?' I say.

'Follow me,' Strauss says.

'Why?'

'It's in my car.'

'What is?'

'You'll see.'

I slow up. I do not like this. Gabe stops at my shoulder.

'We'll wait here,' I say.

There is a dark van next to us. Suddenly its side door slides open. I can see figures inside. As I turn to look, two men approach us from the other side of the van, one from the front, one from the back.

'Shit,' says Gabe.

'In,' says one of the men. It is the man from the tennis court. Banyan, Gabe called him. Called him a killer.

I back up slightly, tense my arms. Gabe shakes his head at me.

'In,' says a voice from inside the van.

For a second Gabe does nothing. I hear the sound of the rack of a gun being slid back. I don't know whose gun it is.

'Your friend,' says Banyan to Gabe. 'He's nothing. We'll shoot him now.'

Gabe nods and steps up into the van. I cannot believe he is giving up. Then I look at the two men, their guns. Gabe is right. What choice is there? I step up as well.

Banyan and the other man climb in after us. Major

Strauss watches us from below as the door slides closed. Somebody steps onto the back of my calf and suddenly I am on my knees. The floor of the van is hard. It is very dark.

'Go,' says Banyan. I recognise his voice. The van starts and pulls forward, and I almost lose my balance on my knees. I put out a hand to steady myself and it touches somebody. Whoever it is takes my hand and bends my fingers and thumb. The pain is incredible.

'Sit,' a voice says, and I sit. My back butts up against the side of the van. I can make out Gabe next to me. Then somebody turns on a light and I can see that Gabe and I are sitting against one side of the van and three men are in with us. They are wearing jeans and boots and jackets. Banyan is standing, smiling, one hand on the ceiling of the van to steady himself. The other two, sitting, have the capable air of hard men. They watch us without interest. Gabe does not seem curious either. He is breathing evenly, relaxed. The van turns corners, slows and speeds up and we rock with it. It is quiet.

'Couldn't leave it.' Banyan breaks the silence.

Gabe shrugs, does not reply.

'Fucking boy scout,' he says. 'Why'd you give a shit anyway?' He sits down next to his comrades, legs stretched out.

'He was under my command.'

'He was a little prick.'

Gabe just looks at Banyan. Banyan looks back at him but I have never known anybody who could meet Gabe's gaze for any length of time. Banyan looks away.

'Where are we going?' I ask.

'Shut up,' Banyan says. He watches me in silence but he is a man who enjoys wielding his power and cannot stay quiet. 'Taking you somewhere you won't be found.'

Nothing more is said and Gabe seems to have lost interest. He has his eyes closed. All four of them seem to be used to silence, to managing situations without speaking. I suspect that this is something the army teaches you. We continue driving and for a long time we are on a straight road. I can hear other vehicles coming from both directions – a two lane. Then we slow, turn to leave it and for some minutes, perhaps five, we slow, speed up, turn tight corners.

Gabe yawns. 'Much longer?'

One of the men opposite laughs. 'Come too soon for you, don't worry about that.'

Gabe just nods, closes his eyes again. His composure is incredible. Banyan watches him with irritation.

We drive on a little further and stop. The engine dies and the light goes off. We wait in the dark and silence, then the door slides open and Major Strauss is there.

'All right. Out.'

We climb out and stand in what looks like a picnic area. There are wooden tables, an earth track. I can hear the sound of the sea. It is very cold. The moon is out and the sky is clear. Strauss's shaved head is big and pale in the light.

'I'm sorry, Gabe,' he says. 'Have to admire your tenacity. But this, it's got to end.'

'Didn't have you figured for a traitor,' says Gabe.

'Here.' Strauss holds up a bottle of Scotch, unscrews the top. 'Need you to drink this.'

'Oh?'

'Just drink it,' says Banyan.

'We having a party?' says Gabe.

'Something like that.'

Strauss hands the bottle to Gabe, who takes it. 'So it's true? You're part of Global Armour?'

'Drink,' says Banyan.

Gabe shrugs, takes a drink, makes a face. 'Why?'

'You don't need to know,' says Strauss.

'No,' says Gabe. 'But I want to.'

Strauss sighs, walks away from us.

'Drink,' says Banyan again.

'More?'

'All of it.'

Gabe holds the bottle up, looks at it. 'Blended. Cheap wankers.'

I hear the sound of a car approaching. Headlight beams light us up and make our shadows swing. The car passes us and I think it is Gabe's car. Its headlights show that beyond the picnic tables is nothing, just black sky. We are on the edge of land. I can still hear the sea. Strauss comes back.

'You know what to do?' he says to Banyan.

'Yes, sir.'

'Leave it for half an hour. We want that alcohol in his bloodstream.'

'Got it.'

'Come on,' says Gabe. 'You owe me an explanation.' The

way he says it, as if he knows that this is it – that we are dead men.

Strauss sighs, looks at Gabe. 'Nothing to do with you,' he says. 'I'm sorry. I really am.' He rubs a hand over his shaved head. 'You know how the army is nowadays. Rules of engagement, politics. If it's not the US telling us what to do, who to shoot, it's the UN. We don't do soldiering any more.' He stops.

'And?' says Gabe. There is an edge to his voice.

'Drink,' says Banyan.

'Fuck sake.' He drinks. He has drunk maybe a third of the bottle already.

'I'd had enough. Wanted more. The private military, it's like it used to be. You get things done. Clear missions. No politics.'

'More money.' There is contempt in Gabe's voice.

'Wasn't about the money,' says Strauss.

'You don't drink faster,' says Banyan, 'I'll shoot your friend.'

'Spare me,' says Gabe to Strauss. He drinks.

'For what it's worth, this will live with me for the rest of my life,' says Strauss.

Gabe laughs, a short sound that conveys nothing but disdain. 'Cheers,' he says, waves his bottle at Strauss, drinks.

Strauss shakes his head and walks away. As he passes us he stops, thinks of something. Then he changes his mind and walks on, gets to his car, starts it up. He drives off and we listen to the sound of his car fading away into the distance.

'Sorry about this, Danny,' says Gabe. His speech is imprecise and he has drunk well over half the bottle.

'Don't worry about it,' I say.

'Probably won't be all right. You know that?'

I feel dread in my stomach. I always imagined Gabe was invincible. 'Fuck it.'

'Yeah,' says Gabe. He laughs without humour. 'Yeah.'

'Keep drinking, soldier,' says Banyan. One of the other soldiers laughs, says, 'Fucking soldier.'

'Hey, Burgess,' says Gabe. I had not realised he knew the other men; he had treated them with such indifference. 'I remember you, remember how you were in contact. Learned to shoot yet?'

'Fuck you.'

'Had you for a coward back then,' Gabe says. 'Looks like I was right.'

Burgess takes a step toward Gabe but Banyan gets between them. 'Leave it,' he says to Burgess, then turns to Gabe. 'Just get it down you.'

'Why?' says Gabe.

'D'you think?' says Banyan. 'So everybody'll figure you're just another pissed arsehole drove off a cliff.'

Nobody says anything for some time. I watch Gabe in the moonlight silently working on the Scotch and feel a deep sadness that this is happening to him. A hero, reduced to this. Being forced to drunkenness by honourless men. By men inferior to him in every way. Rendered powerless and humiliated. I love Gabe and being witness to this is breaking my heart.

Burgess gets into Gabe's car and drives it to the edge of what I guess is a cliff overlooking the sea. He gets out and walks to the van. He drives the van so that it is just behind Gabe's car, nosing the rear bumper.

'All good?' says Banyan.

'Should be. He drunk enough?'

'Got to be. He's done the whole bottle.'

Gabe turns and his head moves slowly and stupidly. He has trouble focusing on me. 'I'm sorry, Danny.'

I nod and an arm is put around my neck from behind, another around my head. I reach around but cannot get to whoever is holding me, so I rush him backwards. He is not big enough to stop me but he has seen this trick before and he does not fight the momentum, uses it to drop and turn. Suddenly I am falling and he still has hold of my head and neck, then he has me on the grass. His grip is strong and he squeezes and squeezes. I try to use my legs and arms to get up but already my vision is darkening and I cannot breathe. I feel panic and struggle but there is nothing I can do.

I can see Gabe. I am looking up at him. Things get darker and darker and the last thing I see is Banyan taking the bottle of Scotch from Gabe almost gently while another man hits him on the back of the head with the butt of a gun and he collapses slowly to the ground.

28

'RACK THE SEAT back, Dan. Dan, Dan, listen. Rack the fucking seat back. Now.'

Gabe's voice seems to come from a long way away but I open my eyes and I am sitting in the passenger seat of his car and he is next to me. How did I get here? I look across at Gabe. His face is shining, his hair on fire.

'Dan. Rack your seat back.'

His hair is not on fire. It is lit up by something. I look behind and am blinded by headlights. There is a lot of noise. A car's engine screaming. This car I am in. I look at Gabe and it feels like slow motion.

'Rack your seat back.'

I reach under my seat. There is a handle. I pull it, push with my legs and my seat slides backwards. Gabe leans over, puts his hand under the seat. The whole car is moving, juddering. The van is trying to push us over the cliff. The noise is amazing.

Gabe sits back up and he has a gun in his hand. He points it behind us. It is next to my head and so close. He pulls the trigger and the rear window explodes. The sound of the gun is huge in my ear. He shoots once, twice, three four five times and hauls on the wheel of the car. We shoot forward and turn. I look out of my window and all I can see are waves far below me, their white tops. I cannot even see the cliff we are on. We are hanging in space. There are rocks in the sea below and they are hundreds of feet down, dizzyingly far. The chassis drops. One of the wheels must have gone over. We are going over. My weight is against the door and I am looking down at the sea below. Gabe floors the accelerator but nothing happens. The van that was pushing us over is coming towards us again. We aren't moving. It is going to hit us side on, tip us over. I hear the enraged snarl of the engine, its furious impotence. The lights of the van are inside the car. Everything is lit up, shocking white, black shadow. Then like a goat finding its feet on a steep rock face, the tyres bite and we leap forward. Gabe struggles with the steering wheel like it is alive. The back wheels slide out and now we are heading away from the cliff. Gabe leans across me and shoots through my window, the gun going off in front of my face. I can feel the explosion, escaping gases slapping my skin. Then we are off and bouncing over the grassy area and then onto gravel, Gabe turning and the car skidding onto a road. He floors it and we barrel down a lane lined by high hedges, twisting through the bends until we reach a junction onto a bigger road, two lanes. Gabe does not speak. The needle is nudging eighty, ninety, a hundred, and we listen to the road unreeling under the tyres until there is a small lane on our left. Gabe swings into it, kills the engine and lights.

He turns to me. His eyes have difficulty focusing. 'Danny. I'm going to need you to drive.'

We stop at an all-night services and Gabe walks unsteadily to the toilets where, he tells me, he intends to vomit. When he comes back he drinks four cups of coffee, one after the other, from a machine. I cannot help but notice that his hand is shaking.

'You hit any of them?' I say.

'Don't know,' says Gabe. His speech is still imprecise. 'My aim was off. What a bottle of Scotch will do.'

'You always keep a gun under your seat?'

'That's a new thing.'

I nod, watch Gabe drink under the harsh light of the service area. He finishes his last coffee, crushes the plastic cup in his fist. 'We need to move.'

'Where are we going?'

'Petroski. Where they'll go next. They'll call Strauss, he'll point them there. He's their next problem.'

'Now?'

'Right now.'

We get back into Gabe's car. It has no passenger window and the back window is smashed; Gabe has, I suspect, an unregistered handgun under his seat. I hope that we do not get pulled over by the police. I drive. At least the person behind the wheel is sober. Must count for something.

It is incredibly cold even though we have the heater turned up full. Outside the moon is still bright and we drive without speaking, the flat land of Essex spooling past. It is two in the morning and it feels as if we have the land to ourselves.

Petroski's home is some miles to the north and we arrive at his isolated farmhouse just after three. We knock on the door and Petroski opens up so soon it is as if he was waiting for us, although we did not have his number and had not called. In the moonlight his face is even more ghastly, the ridges silvered and the hairless skin like polished marble. But he smiles when he sees us and once again I am struck by the goodness he seems to radiate despite his appearance, and despite his desolate surroundings. He does not seem surprised to see us.

'Gabe, Daniel. Fancied a drive?'

'James, I'm sorry,' says Gabe. 'I need you to collect clothes, anything you need. We need to get you out of here.'

Petroski looks at us for a moment then nods, says, 'Right away,' and disappears back into his house. He is not gone for more than two minutes and when he's back he is dressed and carrying a green military tote bag.

'Going anywhere nice?' he asks.

On the way back to his house Gabe explains what is going on to Petroski, how Major Strauss was involved from the start, how he believes that Strauss was taking an interest in Gabe's investigation so that he could monitor the risk he posed to Global Armour.

'He say why?' says Petroski. 'Why he'd sell out the army, his comrades?'

'Claimed he was sick of the politics,' says Gabe. 'But it's always about the money, right?'

'Reason they're called mercenaries,' says Petroski.

'They tried to kill us,' I say.

'Doesn't surprise me,' says Petroski. 'We're talking about 7 Platoon.'

'I'm sorry,' says Gabe to Petroski. 'I've got you into this.'

'No drama,' says Petroski. 'Could do with the excitement.'

'What makes you think you'll be safe at yours?' I say. 'Strauss knows where you live.'

'In the middle of town,' says Gabe. 'No way they'll try something there. Too urban, too public. And they know I'm armed, already shot at them once. They won't risk it.'

I do not reply, hope that he is right.

'And Danny,' says Gabe. 'I'm sorry.' He sounds subdued, exhausted.

'Told me that already,' I say. 'Enough now.'

We drive in silence for some miles and Gabe nods off next to me, a troubled doze in which he fidgets and groans. I look at Petroski in the rear-view mirror and he looks as unflustered as if we are off on a fishing trip. Gabe is still asleep when I pull into his drive and I shake him awake gently. He opens his eyes fearfully.

'We're home.'

'Thanks, Danny.'

'Nice place,' says Petroski.

'You're going to need to stay here,' Gabe says. 'For a few days. Till we get this sorted.'

'Happy to,' says Petroski.

'You know they're not going to give up?' says Gabe. 'You realise that? I've got you neck-deep in shit.'

'Thought had occurred to me,' says Petroski. 'But you know what? I never liked that mob. We'll think of something.'

'Yeah,' says Gabe. But he does not sound sure.

He turns and walks to his door, opens it and disappears inside. He looks tired and his limp is so pronounced that his walk is more of a dragging lurch. This night has taken it out of him. I cannot help but wonder, after all that has happened, all that he has suffered, how much he has left to give.

29

I MANAGE AN hour's sleep at Gabe's and then he drives me to The Black Horse to pick up my car. In the cold morning light, the events of the night before seem unreal, the restaurant car park empty and innocent. Neither of us has much to say and we nod goodbye to each other, wrung out, exhausted.

I get home, shower and wash away the confusion and stink of the night's events. When I am dressed again I feel better, tired but functional. But I do not have time to relax or take time out. This is day four and I am no closer to finding who Witness A is, no closer to keeping Maria safe from the threat of the Blakes. There are two days left. Somehow I need to make them count.

By the time I open up my office it is gone eleven and there are two messages on my answering machine. I put on coffee and pick up my post, then pour a cup and walk back into my office, hit the button.

The first message is from Charles, left at eight that morning. He is struggling to hold back tears and his voice is weak and uneven. I wonder how a man like him has managed to perform in the legal profession for so long; he lacks any kind of backbone.

'Daniel, I can't. I just... I can't do it. Please. For God's sake, Daniel, I can't do it. What you're asking me... Please call me.' A pause. 'Just call me.'

There is a bleep and the voice of my answering machine tells me that the second message was left at nine-thirty. It is Maria and as her voice fills the room, I feel a hollow free-fall feeling of grief in my chest. How I have missed her voice.

'Daniel, eight-thirty at Fratelli's. You will be there.' Her voice carries little warmth and it is clear that she is giving me no choice. If I am not there then that will be it: we will be finished. Even Maria's patience and goodness has a limit. I erase the messages, drink my coffee and look out of my office window at the bleak street outside. I am looking forward to nothing that this day will bring.

Charles picks up on the second ring with a strained whisper and I imagine that he is at work, among other people. 'Daniel?'

'Charles.'

'Daniel, wait.' He does not speak and I hear ambient sounds, perhaps of an office, then a door swinging closed on hinges that want oiling. When Charles speaks next, there is an echo and I guess he is in the gents.

'Daniel, please.' His voice is a whine, a schoolboy protesting at an unjust punishment.

'Give me good news,' I say.

'I can't do it. I can't. I tried but... It's impossible.'

'You have to,' I say.

'There's no way.'

'You know what I can do,' I say. On the other end I hear a sound from Charles, which I think is a sob. I am coercing a helpless man, using intimidation. I am no better than Connor Blake.

'Charles?'

'Yes?' He sniffs, a wet, pitiful sound.

This is a man I could bend to my will with no difficulty; he is as malleable as clay, weak as straw. But then I think of Ryan, a man driven to the edge of despair, and what had happened on the roof of that car park. Of the contempt I had shown him. Of my culpability. I close my eyes, exhale a long breath, speak without opening my eyes.

'Okay, Charles. Drop it. Forget it. Get on with your life.'

'Really?'

'Yes. Really. Go on. You're in the clear.'

I hang up on his obsequious thanks, lean back in my chair and close my eyes. I am so tired, I cannot think straight. I lean forward, rest my head on the desk and try to block out all thoughts. Perhaps if I can just sleep for a few minutes. I have let Charles off the hook, let my only lead slip away. There are men out there who will hurt Maria. There is nothing I can do. There must be something I can do.

A passing lorry shudders my office windows and I wake from my sleep that was not really a sleep. But though I had my eyes closed for only minutes, I feel slightly better and the cycle of dark thoughts that I had not been able to escape from has finished. There is always hope; there must be.

I once again take out Connor Blake's files and spread them out on my desk. They are now so familiar that I do not need to read them to know the contents. I pull out the final pages, the list of witnesses, the thirty-two names. I line them up in front of me. Again I stop at the name Leighton. There are not many people called Leighton and I have encountered somebody of that name, I am sure. I have an image of the outdoors. Green. A fresh smell. I almost have it.

My phone rings and I pick up.

'Hey, Dan, it's Jack. Just catching up. You have any joy with that address I gave you?'

'Joy? Yeah. No, not exactly. Getting there.'

'Not holding out on me?' Jack the newsman, determined to get his story.

'No, nothing like that. Soon's I know anything, you'll be the first in line.'

'Good. See I am.'

'Yeah, Jack. I'll be in touch.'

I hang up, rub my eyes, my forehead. I look back at the list, back at Leighton Finch. Whatever I had in my mind before Jack called is gone. I get up, refill my coffee cup, try not to think, try not to force whatever connection I am attempting to zero in on. I sit back down and empty my mind, take a deep breath. I look up the list and, there, my heart beats a little faster as I see another name. Darren

Wilmott. The surname means nothing to me and Darren is not an unusual name at all, but still, there may be something. I feel a nagging excitement, the feeling a lottery player might have if he sees three numbers come up, scarcely daring to believe what may be about to play out. Leighton Finch. Darren Wilmot. Neither of their surnames holds any significance and I acknowledge to myself that I am reaching at straws, that these first names on their own mean practically nothing. But at the same time, in the goldfish bowl of my home town, it would not be unusual for me to have come across at least one of the people on this list.

I pick up my phone and call my father. I grip the handset tight in anticipation, will him to answer. He picks up on the third ring.

'Yeah?' No niceties with my father.

'It's Daniel.'

'Pick a time to call, dintcha?'

It is four in the afternoon. I cannot understand why this time should be especially inconvenient. 'You busy?'

'Don't matter. D'you want?'

'The men who do your garden. Tree surgeons.'

'You mean landscapers?'

I probably do. 'Yeah.'

'What about them?'

My father is proud of his garden, keeps it in perfect condition. In summer it is a marvel. It is something I have never been able to reconcile, this love of gardening with his essentially inhuman nature. 'One of the landscapers is called Leighton,' I say.

'You telling me or asking me?'

I close my eyes, take a breath. Dealing with my father is as thankless as putting down people's pets. 'Just tell me their names. Could you do that?'

'Leighton, yeah. There's Roy, some short prick called Darren, Phil's their guvnor.'

'What I thought.'

'So what you asking me for then?'

'I'll see you.'

I put the phone down, look back at the list. I scan the columns and at the very top is Roy Atkins. They came around every summer to my father's garden. Leighton, Darren, Roy, Phil – the four of them crammed into the cab of their flatbed lorry. I scan the list, mark each name so that I am sure, but there is no Phil there, no Philip or Phillip. This could mean one of three things. The first and most likely is that I have seen three first names and made a wild, desperate connection that does not exist. The second is that Phil was not there, had better things to do. The third is, of course, that Phil is Witness A.

Leighton Finch lives in a bungalow behind the A127, and when I call around at six o'clock he is at home. He answers the door in his work clothes of heavy trousers, boots and a polo shirt, and he is holding a beer. He looks at me curiously as if he cannot place me.

'I'm Daniel. Daniel Connell. Frankie's boy.'

Leighton is small and wiry. He smiles in recognition, puts out his hand. 'Knew I'd seen you before. Can I do for you?'

'I'm representing Connor Blake.'

Leighton Finch is lifting his beer to his mouth but he stops and looks at me in shock. Got you.

'Oh yeah?' he says eventually, and there is hostility and suspicion in his voice.

'You were there that night.'

'So?'

'Didn't see anything?'

'That's right. What d'you want to know for? Said all this to the Old Bill.'

'Just following up. You were with Darren and Roy.'

'Yeah. Work drinks. Do it every month. Didn't see nothing, didn't hear nothing. None of us. End of. Leave it son.'

He is backing into his hallway, closing the door unconsciously, putting up a barrier between me and him. He is scared.

I look at him but he will not meet my eye. I can now only see half of his face through the gap left by the door.

'Phil with you?'

Leighton pushes the door and I have to put my hand out to stop it from closing. 'He was, right? You were all there.'

Leighton looks at me in exasperation but there is fear there too. 'He'd say the same as me.' He shoves the door and it closes, latches. 'He didn't fucking see nothing,' he says through the door.

Oh yes he fucking did, I think.

*

Fratelli's is a neighbourhood Italian that Maria and I have been to many times. When I arrive I am greeted by the owner, Paulo; he puts both hands to my cheeks and tells me that I am bad, that I have not been for a long time, and that I may well be responsible for putting him out of business.

Maria is already here and I am shown to her table. She smiles when she sees me but it is the smile of a colleague or acquaintance, something reserved in it.

'You look tired,' she says, and there is concern in her eyes. She is wearing a white shirt and her dark skin against its collar is beautiful. She has her hair up, which exposes her neck and makes her look vulnerable, as if she needs protecting.

'I'm okay,' I say. 'Maria—'

'Let's order,' Maria says. 'We'll order, then we'll talk.'

We look at the menu in silence and when Paulo comes across we both order. Paulo asks if we want wine and Maria says no and Paulo feigns shock, a pantomime act. But he sees that we are not laughing with him and he quietly takes our menus and makes himself scarce. Maria looks at me. This is it: I have nowhere to hide. I can no longer avoid her.

'I've been so angry,' she says.

'I'm sorry.'

'So angry, Daniel. I wanted to murder you.'

I do not answer.

'You didn't reply to my calls. How could you do that?'

'Maria, it's... I'm sorry,' I say again.

'Daniel.'

There are tears in her eyes and I find it hard to look at her.

'Then I thought, I know you. This isn't you. And being angry doesn't help.'

'You shouldn't be angry,' I say. 'Really.'

'So I thought, meet it with love. Try to understand. Try.' She smiles but it is not a happy smile. I nod, overwhelmed by the depths of Maria's compassion.

'So here we are,' she says. 'And it's over to you. Speak.'

I turn my empty glass by its stem. I feel a tightening of my skin, a feeling of horror and approaching panic, and I want to get away, to not have deal with this. I barely trust myself to speak.

'I can't,' I say, simply.

Maria's quiet smile fades, withers. 'No. No, Daniel.'

'I'm sorry.' It is all I can think of to say. 'I can't.'

'Is it me? Is there someone else? Just tell me, Daniel. Tell me. It'll be better than... Anything would be better than this.'

What can I say? I look up and she is crying softly, her hands clasped in front of her, her thumb rubbing at her first finger. She lifts her head and tears gently fall down her cheeks.

'Maria.'

She stands up and uses both hands to awkwardly smear away her tears. She looks down at me without malice, only sadness.

'Please,' I say.

'I do so love you,' Maria says, then turns and walks away.

I watch her and I cannot believe that I am letting her go, letting her walk away. How has it come to this? When she has gone I turn and there is a waitress standing there with our plates, one in each hand. She is smiling uncertainly and I look at her and I do not know what to say.

30

IT IS DAY five. One day left. I have been on the back foot for too long, have spent too much time on the defensive. It is not my natural game. Time to go on the offensive. There is a hammer on the passenger seat next to me, a crowbar propped in the footwell. Across the road from me is the bottom of Alex Blake's drive. I will run up there, a weapon in each hand. Steal up there in the night. Knock on the door. Force myself through and swing. However many come at me, swing, impact, forwards, keep momentum. Swing and scythe and punch and chop my way through muscle until I get to him. I am the one with the element of surprise. I am strong, I am motivated. Alex Blake is in there. One man or ten, I will find him. And then this, all this, will end. One way or another.

I have arrived here because I have realised that there are times when having a choice does not mean that you have a choice. If the two options on the table are equally unspeakable, then which way is there left to go?

That morning I had sat at my desk and looked at the name of Philip Tyson of 12 Hunter Drive, the man I suspected was Witness A. My choices were to give away his identity, or to sacrifice Maria, expose her to Connor Blake's monstrous entourage.

I listened to the ringing tone until it picked up and a voice said, 'Hello?' It was a small child's voice, a boy's – high and wavering and uncertain.

'Hello,' I said. I swallowed and when I next spoke, I did not recognise my voice. 'Is your dad in?'

'Yeah.'

I paused. 'Could I speak to him?'

A clunking sound and then fast running feet and the little boy's distant voice shouting, 'Daddy!'

I waited on the line and tried not to think about what I was doing: planning to put the life of a child's father in jeopardy.

'Hello?'

'Mr Tyson?'

'Speaking.'

'Philip Tyson?'

'Yes.' The voice was patient and slow.

'My name is Joseph and I am a liaison officer with the police.'

'Yes?' This said sharply, not without anxiety.

'Just a courtesy call to see how you are, how you're coping.'

'Fine.'

'We appreciate what you're doing.'

'Yes,' he said. 'Is there a problem?'

'No,' I said. 'No, not at all.'

'Nobody knows?'

'Nobody,' I said.

'Okay. Just a courtesy call.'

'That's right.'

'Right.'

I did not have anything more to say and I was aware that the more I said the more suspicious he was likely to become. I needed to end this call.

'We'll keep in touch. Thanks for your time.'

'No problem.'

I hung up and leaned back in my chair, rubbed my eyes with the pads of my fingers. I had the proof I needed. I had no doubt that Philip Tyson was Witness A. What I had thought was impossible I had achieved. And though it was an achievement that might save Maria from Blake's threats, it gave me no pleasure, none at all. I had spoken to the man. He had children. I had to choose between him and Maria. Like I said: sometimes a choice really isn't a choice at all. At least, not one that I could make.

There is suicide by cop; this then could be suicide by gangster. I have left a letter for Maria on my kitchen table. It explains what I am doing and why. I hope that she never has to read it. It is getting dark outside but it is not dark enough, and I cannot keep sitting here outside Blake's house. I have some hours left. Enough time to visit a friendly face before the war.

I park in Gabe's drive and knock on his door. Petroski answers, pulling it open a crack so that nobody passing can see his ravaged face, even though Gabe's gravel drive is twenty foot long and the street outside is empty in the cold still air.

'Daniel.'

'Hi. Gabe around?'

'Yeah. Not sure.'

'Not sure?'

Petroski hesitates and I feel irritated, being made to wait on my best friend's porch where I have stood thousands of times before, been welcomed in by Gabe, by his parents; a house that for years felt as much my home as anywhere else I had to go.

'He's...' Petroski starts but does not say anything more, seems unsure.

'He's what?' I say.

'He's not doing so well,' says Petroski.

'How about you let me in,' I say, and push open the door.

Petroski takes a step back and says quickly, 'Yeah, sorry, Daniel, I just—'

I ignore him. Inside Gabe's house it is quiet and dark, a spooky mansion occupied by a recluse and his freakish manservant. I stand in the hall not knowing where to go, what to do.

Petroski joins me and whispers, 'In there.' I am not sure why he is whispering.

Gabe is sitting at his dining table wearing cut-off running bottoms. He has taken off his prosthetic limb and I can see the pink pig's knuckle of his knee stump. He looks up as I come in and nods with little interest

302

as if I am a maid bringing in tea. On the table is his normal prosthetic, a complicated steel device that looks harvested from a redundant robot. Next to it is a newer one surrounded by opened packaging and it looks freshly unwrapped, unworn.

'You all right?'

'Never better,' he says and turns away from me, picks up the new prosthetic. It is shiny and a lot less complex than his normal leg; the shaft looks drilled from a single piece of aluminium, almost sculpted, a work of functional art.

'New leg?' I say and immediately realise how clumsy it sounds. Gabe raises an eyebrow but does not reply. He picks it up and turns it in his hands. He looks tired and he has not shaved, something I cannot recall ever seeing before. This is not the right time; I should not have come.

'Listen, Gabe, you took it to those soldiers,' I say. 'You saved my life.'

Gabe smiles, does not look up, keeps turning the leg, examining it from all angles. Although the light is dim, the leg catches it, reflecting mistily. 'Got you abducted, came that close to getting killed. Ambushed by a bunch of half-arsed psychos.'

'You couldn't have known the major—'

'Took you to find out about him,' says Gabe. 'You do the hard work, I almost get us killed.'

'You got us out of there.'

'Lucky. Shouldn't have been in that position. Would never have happened before.'

'You're being too tough.'

'You know most of 7 Platoon is over at Petroski's house? Got it under surveillance. Have done since last night. How I know we're safe here. They're all over there.'

I do not ask Gabe how he knows. I think of how tired he is, the shadows under Petroski's eyes, imagine them crawling through long grass at night, reconnoitring 7 Platoon's position. This problem of theirs is not going away any more than mine is.

Gabe sighs, shakes his head, says quietly more to himself than to me, 'Useless. Stupid.'

'Gabe,' I start, but he holds the leg up, waves it at me.

'This? I'm part of a programme,' he says. 'I get to try the newest prosthetics. State of the art, apparently.' He holds it horizontal in both hands. 'Like it?'

I do not reply, sure that whatever I say will be wrong.

'Sod it, you're here. Help me get it on.' He picks up a neoprene sleeve with a closed end and pulls it over his stump, getting his thumbs inside to work it over his knee, up his thigh. The sleeve has a thick pin at the end. He stands up and hands me the prosthetic leg.

'Stick a trainer on it,' he says.

I unlace a Nike trainer that is on the table, put it over the foot at the end of the prosthetic leg and lace it up. As Gabe watches me I am reminded of fathers helping their children in shoe stores, and it is an uncomfortable feeling. I have never considered Gabe as somebody who needed help before.

'Stand it up,' says Gabe.

I kneel and hold the leg vertical and Gabe lowers his knee covered with the sleeve. I hold the pin at the end of the sleeve and guide it into a hole at the top of the prosthetic leg. It makes a solid dry click as Gabe puts his weight onto it.

'In?'

'Guess so.' I let go and Gabe takes a careful step, arms out as if he is walking along a rope bridge. He takes another and another, and then puts all his weight on the new prosthetic. It slips and his leg gives out underneath him, and he goes down suddenly like a three a.m. drunk misjudging a kerb, lands heavily on his side.

'*Fuck*,' Gabe says, and hits the floor with his fist, and again. It may be the most emotion that I have ever seen Gabe show.

'You okay?'

Gabe is on his hands and knees and he cannot get up, cannot get the new leg to obey or get purchase on his polished floor. He gives up, turns, leans back on his hands and his face is so anguished that for a second I have the horrifying thought that he might cry. Men like Gabe cannot cry.

I had not come to Gabe to ask for his help, but I had wanted to feed off his strength, use his unflinching character to shore mine up. This is not what I needed. I hope that this is not the last image I have of Gabe, helpless and anguished. I reach out a hand to him but he just looks at it, then at me, and shakes his head.

'If you wouldn't mind, Danny,' he says, 'would you just fuck off and leave me alone?'

I nod and turn and walk away from Gabe where he is sitting on the floor. Outside in the hall I pass Petroski, who looks at me questioningly.

'Keep an eye on him,' I say, then open Gabe's door and leave. I take a deep breath of the cold air and head to my car. Whatever needs to be done, I'll do it on my own.

I drive past the Blakes' place, slow, turn, drive past it again. It is still too early. I need zero dark thirty, I believe that is what they call it, although in previous times perhaps it was simply called the witching hour. I drive away, pick up A roads which take me into the heart of the flat country, the sun behind me long since given up the ghost. Events are nearing an end and I do not know how many more sunrises I will see. I have an end-of-the-world feeling of unseen catastrophe and recklessness.

I take a left off the two-lane road and then a right at a T-junction, find myself on a long straight road under massive pylons that stretch to a vast substation I cannot hear but imagine fizzing dangerously in the gloom. I take another left. The road is funnelled by hedges, twisting, and the occasional gate revealing desolate fields waiting for a spring that still has not arrived.

I see headlights in my rear-view and when the road widens out, a big four-by-four rushes past me and disappears around the next bend. Its hectic passage scares dark birds into the air and it is now murky enough that I cannot tell what colour they are; they are only black against the darkening sky.

The road bends and I cannot see around the corner, and when it straightens there is a black Range Rover, perhaps the one that just overtook me, parked across the road, its headlights on and shining into the blackness of a hedge. I have to brake sharply and I come to a stop ten metres away, my beams shining into the Range Rover's windows. I can see a man in the seat nearest me, the driver, put an arm up to shield his face against the glare, and then his door opens and he steps out. He walks towards my car with his arm still in front of his face. I cannot see his head at all.

I do not wait for him to reach my car. I turn off the ignition and open the door and step out. He stops and we are only a few metres apart. Our breath makes big clouds of steam in the air. He puts his arm down and I see his face. Carl – Alex Blake's muscle. The man I had hit.

'Put the hammer down,' he says.

'Why?'

'Mr Blake just wants a word.'

'Oh?' The hammer's handle is rubber and fits my palm. I can sense the heaviness of its head.

'Drop it,' says Carl. 'Ain't going to need it. Make yourself look silly.'

There are only two of them anyway. I put the hammer back in my car, throw it gently onto the passenger seat.

'Give me your keys. I'll get this moved.'

I look at him curiously. The way he has asked me to do this is almost polite.

'He's waiting,' Carl says. 'Don't be keeping him waiting.'

Perhaps it is the solicitousness of his tone but I take my keys from my pocket and hand them to him, then pass him and walk towards the Range Rover. The door the other side from me opens and Alex Blake gets out and walks through the headlight beams. He is as good-looking as I remember, and while he is older and not as perfectly handsome as Connor Blake, the resemblance is strong. He is wearing only a polo shirt despite the cold and I recognise the gold watch on his wrist.

'What you doing parked outside my place?'

I do not reply. Alex Blake looks at me and I wonder whether this is my chance, whether I can take this man now, put an end to all this. But Blake smiles as if he knows what I am thinking and he shakes his head slightly and turns, walks away.

'This way,' he says. 'Walk with me.'

I follow after him and we walk down the quiet lane. I have heard that there are men who can walk into a room and cause silence merely by their presence, by the power they radiate. Alex Blake is so contained and assured that, as I walk behind him, the idea of attacking him seems suddenly inconceivable; he carries a silent authority that makes me feel young, weak and in his thrall. It is nothing I have ever experienced before. As we walk there is no sound, not even birdsong, as if his presence is so forceful that it even subdues nature.

'You're Connor's lawyer,' he says.

'Not out of choice,' I say.

'Not my concern,' says Blake. 'Between you two.'

'What do you want?'

'I'll ask again,' says Blake. 'What you doing parked outside my place?'

'You didn't think I'd come for you?' I say. But even as I say it, I realise how empty this sounds, no more than the impotent posturing of a wilful child.

'Been finding out about you,' says Blake. 'You're no mug. So listen.' He turns to face me. 'Look me in the eyes, son. That way we'll understand each other.'

I look into Alex Blake's eyes. I cannot read any emotion in them except perhaps a trace of boredom, as if these earthly dealings are beneath him.

'My son,' he says, 'is a fucking lost cause. Worse than that. He's sick, out of control, and he's no child of mine. What you've got going on with him, I don't want a fucking bar of. You hear me? Nod.'

I nod slowly. I am still looking directly into his eyes and despite being outdoors, I have a feeling of enclosed intimacy, of capture.

'He's got his people. Fuck knows where he finds them. Whatever they do, got nothing to do with me anymore. Clear?'

'Clear.'

'You and him, you work it out together. I don't want his problems at my door. Getting me attention I don't need.' He takes a deep breath, looks away, looks back. 'Do what you have to do. Won't get no comeback from me. Understand?'

I nod again.

'You and him, between you two. And you – you fucking stay away from my place.'

'No comeback?' I say.

'None. Do what you have to do. He might be my son but I'm finished with him. He's better off where he is.'

'You're throwing him to the sharks.'

Alex Blake looks me up and down. I regret what I have just said; regret my presumption.

'Son,' he says, 'you ain't no fucking shark.'

Blake leaves me standing there and after a few moments Carl comes to me and gives me my keys. He looks at me but he does not say anything, then walks back to the Range Rover, climbs in next to Alex Blake and they drive away. When they have gone it is still and quiet, and things suddenly feel very different.

31

I AM ON court coaching juniors when I notice that Maria's group are still waiting at the clubhouse and part of me is glad that she is not there, that I do not have to confront her today. The juniors are warming up, hitting rallies and volleys before they play doubles. It is cold and they are in running bottoms and hooded tops. None of them look entirely happy to be here. The numbers are down today, only the children of the pushiest parents coerced into making the effort. I tell them to warm up their serves and then push through the wire door of the court, walk around the corner into the clubhouse. George is behind the bar doing the crossword and he looks up as I walk in.

'No Maria?' I say.

'Wouldn't you be the one to know?' says George with a sly smile.

'Her group's waiting,' I say.

'She hasn't called.'

I take out my mobile and hit her number and I notice that my hands are shaking and it is not from the cold. I listen to the ring tone, hear it go to voicemail. I hang up.

'No?' says George.

'She'll turn up,' I say. 'Give her five minutes.'

'You all right?' George has known me for years, put an arm across my shoulders more times than I can remember, even now that I am taller than him. He has always looked out for me.

'Yeah,' I say, although I do not feel it. I have a sensation of floating; my hands feel big and clumsy, and are tingling. 'Let me know if you hear anything.' I walk out of the club-house and back onto the court where the juniors are still practising their serves and I have never felt more fright-ened in my life.

I had woken up unwillingly, knowing what day it was and what needed to be decided. Day six, the final day – the day I was expected to deliver the name and address of Witness A to Connor Blake. I had the number he had given me in prison. All I needed to do was pick up my phone, dial the number, give whoever answered a name, an address. Nothing more. The work of seconds. The betrayal of every-thing I stood for and held dear.

I thought about Alex Blake, of what he had said to me; how he was not a threat. Instead I was up against a man behind bars and his people who I did not know, could not find. They were like smoke, stealing into houses, whispering threats; I could not fight something that I could not see. I was left with only one solution, one way out – give them Witness A.

I listened to the news, made coffee, put off making a deci-sion. It could wait. Wait until later. I had all day. It could wait.

The juniors are halfway through their first sets and George has taken Maria's group onto the courts the other side of the clubhouse. I have tried her mobile five times and she has not answered. It is okay, I tell myself. She is okay. She doesn't want to see me. Not after the other night. She is staying away. It is okay. I say things to the juniors, encourage them after a good point, suggest a change to their technique – tell them to finish the shot with their racket over their shoulder, keep their weight going forward.

She is probably at home, watching her mobile ring. She has seen that it is me and does not want to pick up. I am probably bothering her. I should stop calling, stop over-reacting. A boy called Kieran hits a cross-court backhand volley for a winner and I shout across to him, give him the thumbs up. It is okay. She is okay.

George is claiming that the young children he just coached were too much for a man of his age, that they were too good and he would never walk again, he was finished. The children are giggling and jostling each other as he tells them this; George has a natural way with kids that has always seemed magical to me. He winks as I pass him on the way to the clubhouse and I force the ghost of a smile back at him. I am holding a basket full of balls and put them in the office of the clubhouse.

Now there is nothing more to do. The juniors have gone. The courts are empty under the blank cold sky. I have a sudden feeling of fear so sudden and debilitating that I have to put a hand to the wall to steady myself. It is not okay. How can it be okay? Maria would never miss a session of tennis. It cannot be okay. She cannot be okay.

'You sure you're all right?' says George. He is standing in the doorway to the little office and is frowning. My vision seems dark. I close my eyes, nod.

'Fine.'

'No word from Maria?'

'Nothing.'

'She wants a hiding, making me take those kids.'

'You did okay.'

'Two new knees; this rate I'll be wanting another pair.'

I nod but do not answer. I walk past George and head to my car. I have nothing to do and nowhere to go. I look at my phone but there is no missed call from Maria, no text asking me to leave her alone, to please give her time. There is nothing. She cannot be okay because if she was, she would be here. She might not be. I have nowhere to go and nothing to do and all I can think is that she is not okay but that does not mean that she is dead.

There is no answer when I buzz Maria's apartment. I stand outside and look up at her windows but they reflect white sky and nothing more. Maria's mother lives not far away but I do not wish to frighten her, so instead I call her to ask if she has seen Maria.

'Not today. Is there a problem, Daniel?'

'No. Course not.'

'Were you meant to see her?'

'No. Just can't get hold of her.'

'Want me to give her a message?'

'No. Yeah. Just to call me.'

'But there's no problem?'

'No problem.'

I have nowhere to go so I get in my car and drive to my house. I pass people carrying shopping and see a man having an argument on his mobile outside a bar. I wish that I was like them and that I did not have this terrible fear. That this terrible thing was not happening. She could still be okay. But I know that she is not.

My house is empty and cold and I put the TV on for company, reassurance, but then I turn it off. I pick up the paper that Blake gave me, the paper with the number on it. I am frightened of what will happen if I call it. I will have to give the name and address. I will have to ask about Maria. If I call the number it means that I think she has been taken. That Blake has got to her. If I call, I make it real.

I key the number into my phone. I look at it. I do not want to hit the green button, do not want to make this real. I hit it and listen to the call connect, hear it ring. I look at a leather armchair as it rings. It is old and scuffed. I should get it recovered. There is no answer. The call cuts off. My house is very quiet. So very quiet.

By the time it is dark I have accepted that all I can do now is wait for a phone call or a knock on the door, wait for somebody who will probably be wearing a uniform to let me know what has happened. I have watched my furniture sink into gloom, have watched people pass by the front of my house – children, parents, young lovers, old couples – talking, laughing. I have seen the lights in the street outside switch on, watched their yellow light brighten as the day around them dies. I have listened to the creaks of my house, shifting minutely, indifferently. For hours I have wondered what might have happened to Maria, wondered what I might have done differently. I was going to call, give them the name of Witness A. I had meant to call. I was going to call after I had coached tennis. I still have a day. This should not be happening. What could I have done differently?

I imagine Maria's look of amused scorn, imagine her telling me that there was nothing I could have done, to not be a dope. I think of the trust she put in me, a trust that no other person has ever managed. I think of the affection she had for me, her lack of fear and judgement. I did not deserve her, never deserved her. She's been killed and it is my fault. She should have had nothing to do with me. I think of her winning money at the dogs. Twisting on a bed. Laughing at me, head back, her perfect teeth. Laughing, always laughing.

My mobile rings, an impossible sound in the quiet darkness. The screen illuminates, throwing a supernatural blue light into the room. I look at the number but I do not recognise it. This is the call. This is what I have been waiting for. I answer.

316

'Yes?'

'Daniel Connell?'

'Yes.'

'Do you know a Maria de Souza?'

32

MARIA HAD BEEN dumped out of a white van which stopped only briefly outside Queen's Hospital before driving away. It was found later by police, burned out. She was naked when she was left outside the entrance, and unconscious.

When I arrive at the hospital she has still not regained consciousness and I am not allowed to see her, have to wait in a large room lit by neon tubing and lined with green plastic seats which cant forward so that the only way to sit is with my elbows on my knees, my head in my hands. Hushed voices around me, the desperate murmur of the frightened and uninformed. A doctor comes to find me after I have been sitting for two hours and explains to me that Maria has suffered significant trauma to her head, that she is in a coma and that at this stage it is impossible to give a prognosis. He speaks quickly and nervously, pushed his glasses up the bridge of his nose, from which they quickly slide again. I thank him and ask if I can see her. He hesitates briefly, pushes his glasses up his nose and then tells me to follow him.

Maria is lying in a room with no other beds. She looks as if she is asleep, peaceful, although she has a bandage wrapped around her head and a tube coming out from the back of her left hand. There are machines quietly doing what they need to do next to her. I do not get close, stop at the foot of her bed and look at her. The doctor is beside me and is clearly uncomfortable, trying to think of something to say to break my foreboding silence.

'She is your wife?'

'No.'

'Ah.' He taps his chin with a pen.

'Will she be all right?'

He shrugs. 'It is the brain, Mr...'

'Connell.'

'Mr Connell. No way to say. One way or the other.'

'It won't—' I begin but am interrupted by a knock at the door. I turn and I can see Sergeant Hicklin through the window to the side of the door. He looks at me and beckons, curling all the fingers of one hand.

'Police?' says the doctor.

'It's me they want,' I say. 'Take care of her, will you?'

'We'll do everything we can.'

I walk to the door and open it. Hicklin looks at me with an expression that is part disappointment, part pity. He rubs his moustache with his hand, then uses it to point down the corridor.

'Shall we?'

Hicklin tells me that Maria had not only been naked. When she was found outside the main entrance, the hospital staff had not been sure what was on her skin. It was only when she had been placed on a stretcher and curtained into a cubicle that the nurse examining her saw that all over her body were dotted lines marked in thick black ink. They were over her face, described arcs around her ribs, along muscles, across her stomach, her buttocks. They were, Hicklin tells me, the kind of marks plastic surgeons make on skin before beginning to cut. He tells me this looking down at his notepad and reading out what he had written there, without inflection or apparent judgement.

But when Hicklin looks up he seemed at a loss of what to say, of what to think about the information that he has just given me, of what had been done to Maria. I wonder whether she had been unconscious when they drew on her, drew all over her naked skin.

'But there wasn't...?'

'No. Nothing like that. Which is something, I guess.'

I rub my hand over my forehead, my eyes, pull down at my skin so hard that it stings. The room we are in is part of the hospital, reserved for the police, for conducting interviews. It is brightly lit, has a table and four chairs, and no windows. It could be a nurse's staff room.

'You haven't got many friends on the force,' Hicklin says.

I nod. 'Doesn't surprise me.'

'After Baldwin... They've been waiting for something like this.'

I shrug.

'Reason I got here first,' says Hicklin. 'Before they can get at you.'

'Think they'd set me up?'

'First thing they'd try to do,' says Hicklin. 'You wouldn't see the outside of a prison cell for months.'

'You're taking charge?'

'I'm picking this one up,' he says. 'See that some kind of justice gets done.'

'Want me to thank you?'

'What I want, Mr Connell, is for you to tell me what's going on.'

'No idea.'

'First that friend of yours, McBride, starts shooting up the place. Next, your girlfriend. She is your girlfriend?'

I do not reply.

Hicklin sighs. 'You've got no reason to trust us. But' – he breathes loudly through his nose – 'I think you're in trouble. You're representing Connor Blake, right?'

'What's this got to do—' I begin, but Hicklin interrupts.

'Men like you don't represent men like him. Men like him are the very worst.'

'And what kind of man do you think I am?'

'You?' Hicklin leans back in his chair, strokes his moustache again. 'Good, with a very bloody thick layer of arsehole.'

I cannot think of anything to say in response to this.

Hicklin sits forward again. 'Now, I don't know if what your friend's involved with, and what you're involved with, if they're connected. But something's going on. And it's happening on my manor. I'm not arresting you. But you've got Blake on one side; you've got my lot on the other. Your options, Mr Connell, are getting very thin. Very thin indeed.'

Hicklin threatens me then tries to reason with me, assures me that he will take care of things, that whatever is happening he can guarantee my safety, Maria's safety, Gabe's safety. But as much as I like and trust Hicklin, I know the extent of his powers; know that they are not far-reaching enough, nowhere near. I refuse to comment on my relationship with Connor Blake; invoke client confidentiality, hide behind my status as a lawyer, however hypocritical that might be. Eventually Hicklin gives up. He tells me not to leave town, tells me he'll be in touch. Tells me that I am free to go.

'Can I see Maria?'

'You can. And Mr Connell? I wish her all the best.'

I thank Hicklin and watch him amble away down the corridor. I believe that he is a good man and that I can trust him. But whatever is about to happen, I do not want the police anywhere near.

Maria's mother is in Maria's room when I finish with Sergeant Hicklin, sitting on a chair and rubbing Maria's wrist with her thumb, holding her hand carefully so that she does not disturb the needle in its back. She embraces me when I come in and I try to yield to it, but my back is stiff and my muscles tense and she must feel as if she is hugging a tree. Maria is still unconscious and Maria's mother deserves some time with her – deserves it far more than I do. I do not kiss Maria, do not touch her. For some reason I imagine that it might bring her bad luck, might jeopardise her recovery. I leave her with her mother and head for the car park.

I turn my mobile phone back on when I get outside. After it has illuminated it tells me that I have a new message. I open it and do not recognise the number straight away. But then I do. I had called it earlier but nobody had answered. The message is short but tells me all that I need to know. It says, simply: *Too late.*

'Marks where they were going to cut,' says Gabe.

'What Hicklin told me.'

'You know who did this, right?'

'I know.'

'This Blake guy.'

'His people.'

'Dan, I'm sorry. She'll be okay.'

'Yeah. Will she?' I look at Gabe and I can see compassion there in his pale eyes.

He nods slowly. 'Yes, Danny. She will.'

We are in Gabe's kitchen and I have not yet had a drink of the Scotch that Gabe has poured for me. I want to be sober in case there is any news, any call from the hospital. I think of Maria's skin, marked up as if by some deranged surgeon, her waiting in fear for whatever ordeal of unimaginable pain awaited. I think of Magnus, faceless men behind him. Of Alex Blake and his disgust at the men Connor Blake surrounded himself with. Of Connor Blake's boast of what he could do to Maria. There is so much I could have done. That this is all my fault I do not question. That Maria is lying in a hospital bed because of me is a fact I have to face. Like a sudden attack of nausea, my self-disgust and helplessness rushes through me. I close my eyes and I cannot help it – my throat swells and my eyes tingle as I begin to cry. I am ashamed that Gabe is here to witness this but my shame is distant and unimportant. I cannot stop. Nothing I do, nothing I have ever done, has resulted in anything but hurt. I do not know why, do not know what I have done to deserve all this. But my self-pity only disgusts me further as I think of Maria and what she has been put through. The thought of her causes my stomach to clench in terror. I cannot think about her dying. Under neon lighting. In that bed, alone, surrounded by machines. Please God, do not let her die because of me.

Gabe puts his hand on my shoulder and leaves it there, does not say anything. My silent sobs ebb away, leaving nothing but me, empty and pitiful at this table. Gabe lifts his hand, pushes the Scotch closer to me. I drink. Fuck it. There is nothing to say. She should have known. Should have known that no good would come from being with me.

33

BLAKE CALLS EARLY the next morning, awakening me from a sleep populated with shadowy figures I dare not look at. Even as I grope for my phone I have the residual impression of being trapped by thick low branches and entangled by thorns in some dark and ancient forest. When he speaks, it seems as if he is speaking to me from within my dream, his voice emanating from that ghastly place.

'Daniel.'

'Yes.'

'What did I tell you, Daniel?'

'You said six days.'

'Gave you six days.'

'No. Five. You... It was only five.'

'Oh, Daniel.' Blake laughs, a short sound, followed by a rich chuckle that he is barely in control of. 'Daniel. Seems we've got our wires crossed. You didn't count the day you came to see me, did you?' He laughs again and I imagine him in his cell, speaking into his contraband mobile, shaking his head in delight at our miscommunication. He thinks that it is funny, that what he has done to Maria is a fine joke.

'Anyway, doesn't matter. Took your sweet time, lost patience. Way it goes.'

'Fuck you,' I say.

'No, Daniel. We're not finished. I still need that name.'

'After what you did?'

'What I did? No, Daniel. I've barely started.'

'Nearly killed her.'

'Magnus tells me she put up quite a fight. Had to be subdued. To be honest, I think he's still pissed off. About you breaking his leg. Took it out on her.'

I do not say anything. I am on Gabe's sofa and my head hurts from the Scotch I drank. I look at my watch. It is still early: too early to visit Maria.

'You there?'

'I'm here.'

'We're not done.'

'Goodbye.'

'No, Daniel. Don't—'

I cut Blake off and hang up. I sit up on the sofa, rub my hair with my hands, scratch until it hurts. Gabe's house is quiet. I walk into his kitchen. There is nobody there. Then I remember Gabe telling me something about going to Petroski's place, checking on what was going on, seeing if it was still being staked out by the foot soldiers of Global Armour. I put on coffee and find some painkillers. There is an hour to wait until visiting time at the hospital. Nobody has called and I guess that means that Maria has not died, but also that she has not woken up. I think of her lost in that same dark forest that I have just woken from, alone and distressed and trapped. I sit at Gabe's kitchen table and drink my coffee, waiting until it is time to see her again.

My father suffered a heart attack the previous year and when he was in hospital I had barely visited him, left the doctors and nurses to do what they needed to do. But now with Maria I feel a need to question everything that is being done to her. Why is that tube in her hand? What have they put in that clear bag? Why has that machine made that sound?

I speak to the doctor before I go in to see her and he tells me that there are indications that she will soon come out of her coma, but that I must be aware that there could be associated problems. I ask him what problems and he pushes his glasses up on his nose, hesitates, and says that there could be a change in behaviour, that she might experience confusion, and that in the majority of cases there is some form of memory loss, though whether long- or short-term it is impossible to say.

Now I am sitting in a chair at the end of her bed and watching in silence as she sleeps. I have not touched her, have not stroked her hand or kissed her forehead. I have not even spoken, said her name aloud, although I have heard that speaking to people in comas can have beneficial results. The hospital beyond the door of Maria's room is in full swing, coping with the drunks and the damaged and the detritus of last night's drinking, but here in her room it is quiet and I can hear the gentle reassuring hum of the machine monitoring her breathing and brain activity.

I think of our time together, of what we have done and the things she has said to me. She once told me that it did not matter what we had been; what was important was what we wanted to become, even if it was something that we never achieved. She had told me this after I had spoken to her of my past, of the things that had been done to me by my father, of what I had occasionally done to other people. I had shaken my head at what she told me but she had held my chin and pulled it down, pushed it up, pulled it down, then had gravely intoned: *Yes, Maria, you are right*, until I had smiled and even half believed her. But I do not believe her any longer.

Maria screws her face up as if protecting herself from a blinding light and then she opens her eyes, blinks once, twice, three times. She squints and looks above her, to her left and right, down at the bed she is lying on, the sheets that cover her. She frowns and looks fearful, confused. I am holding my breath and have not moved.

She looks at me sat at the end of the bed and smiles uncertainly. 'Hello.'

I am about to speak but stop. I look at her and she is so beautiful and I am so happy that she is alive, so relieved. It feels like a miracle, something I never expected or deserved.

'Hello, Maria,' I finally say.

She frowns again, tilts her head on her pillow, and says, 'Who are you?'

I stand up and look down at her. It seems incredible that we were ever together, that she ever felt anything for me. Why did she? I think of Blake and what he is capable of, think of Vick and Ryan and their children, of all the enemies I have made and all the ones I have yet to make. I think about my blighted genes and the violence I drag around with me like the ghost of a drowned man drags the chains that weighted him to the lake bottom. I think of my history and although I try, I cannot see a future.

I look into Maria's eyes, which are so trusting and open and lovely. I swallow and close my eyes and say to her: 'Nobody.'

I find the doctor and tell him that Maria is awake, that she has some memory loss, that she did not recognise me. I ask him not to mention me to her, ask him to tell her mother the same thing. He looks confused but nods.

I leave the hospital. We had split up. It was over before this happened to her. There was no us. I would tell her mother this, would empty my house of Maria's things. She would never know the truth and would get on with her life, and that life would be better, immeasurably better, than if she had remained with me.

Outside, a wind has picked up and it blows paper and discarded Styrofoam cups across the concrete in front of the hospital entrance. To one side is a grassed area where there are benches provided for patients who wish to drink coffee, smoke and briefly escape the oppressive sterility of the wards. An old man is sitting on one of the benches and a younger woman, perhaps his daughter, is sitting next to him. She has an arm across his shoulders and he looks ahead vacantly, disbelievingly, and I wonder what fate has recently befallen him. How quickly we can lose people. How quickly those who mean everything to us can tumble from our lives.

34

WE ARE LYING on our fronts in a hollow of grass, which is damp and very cold. It is dark and the wind is blowing hard, making eerie sounds above us and around us. The moon is up and we can see for miles, any features in the landscape showing black against the silvered ground. I am on the left, Gabe is in the middle, with Petroski on the right. We have been here for hours now and I am grateful that Gabe gave me his spare goose-down parka to wear. It cannot be far above zero. My hands are cold on the metal I am holding.

Gabe has warned me that I must not raise my head, certainly must not kneel or stand. If I want to piss, he tells me, I should roll away from him and do it on the ground lying on my side. Petroski and Gabe laugh at my expression, as if I am a green recruit on my first patrol in enemy terrain. I shiver and move my legs, which are stiff and so numb that I can barely feel them. I wonder how much longer we will have to wait. Wonder if anything at all will happen tonight.

We parked four miles away, walked some of the way here, covered the remaining kilometre at a crawl. It was still light when we set off but it has now been dark for hours. I look at my watch. It is two in the morning. I look at Gabe, who is as intent as the moment we first took up position here. I cannot see Petroski the other side of him but do not doubt that he is equally alert. They have told me that they have done this many times, spent days lying in the same place, in the same position. No big deal. Just wait. Nothing else to do.

Out here there is no sound but the wind and the distant suck of the sea, and no light but the moon. We could be the last people on earth. But I know that we are not, know that there are other men close by. What we are waiting for are headlights. We have not seen another car for hours now. The next time we see headlights will be it. Of that I am quite sure. If we see headlights.

I put my head down, try to control my shivering. I hope it will not be much longer. I hope that it will happen. Although exactly what will happen is anybody's guess.

This was Gabe's plan, although, as he pointed out to me, if he had proposed a course of action this sketchy and unpredictable in the army, he would have been laughed at, demoted, court-martialled or shot. But we had nothing to lose. We had already lost too much. The worst that could happen already has. Fuck it. Roll the dice.

I had driven to Gabe's from the hospital. I could not face going back to my place where Maria kept clothes, a toothbrush, where there were towels that she had bought and books she had read and cups, plates, glasses that she had used. She had filled my house with her presence and it would still be there, would linger for I did not know how long. I hoped that it would not be too long.

As usual we had sat in his kitchen and I had told him everything, told him what had happened at the hospital. Told him I had no other choice than to walk away, that I only wanted to protect Maria, nothing more. Gabe had lifted an eyebrow and I could tell that he was not convinced but he did not comment, instead moved on to the situation at hand.

'So, this Blake. He still wants it? A name and address?'

'He's not going to stop. What's he got to lose?'

'Maria?'

'He'll get to her.'

Gabe nodded but it was not a nod of acceptance, instead one of calculation. Gabe had known Maria for as long as I had and I knew that he liked her, loved her, even. What had been done to her was something that he could not accept any more than I.

'Still camped out at Petroski's place?' I said.

'Huh?' Gabe shook himself from his thoughts. 'Yeah. Yeah, they're still there.'

'Got a plan?'

'Not yet. We'll get there.'

We sat in silence. There was a tension between us, an unspoken agreement that things had gone far enough and that they needed to end, that we needed to stop them by whatever means.

'His dad, this Alex Blake. We don't need to worry about him?'

'What he said.'

'Which is good, right?'

'Going up against him? Would've been suicide.'

'So it's this guy in prison, him and his people.'

'And you've seen what they can do.'

Gabe nodded, drank from his cup of coffee. He set it down, looked up above him, lost in thought. He nodded again, slowly.

'It's just a name, Danny. A name and an address. Bollocks to this. Enough's enough. Let's just give it to them.'

I picked up my mobile from where it lay on the table between me and Gabe, then found the number in my call log – the number Blake had given me in prison, that he had told me to call when I had the name and address of Witness A.

I called it, listened to it ring and heard a voice say, 'Hello? Daniel?' It was a high voice and I had recognised it immediately. I gave him the name, gave him the address, repeated it twice. Asked him if he had it.

'Good, Daniel. Knew you'd come round.'

'Goodbye, Magnus.'

Like Gabe had said, it was just a name. Just an address. But it was not the address of Philip Tyson, 12 Hunter Drive that I gave Magnus. It was the address of ex-sergeant James Petroski, currently resident of a dilapidated farmhouse on the edge of Essex, which was at that moment under the surveillance of at least six tired, hungry, battle-hardened and exceptionally frustrated killers.

We had no way of knowing what the outcome would be. We were dealing in pure chaos theory. But as Gabe had said with a flippancy that I could not share, if Connor Blake's entourage did not manage to curb their instincts to act like a bunch of violent and arrogant dickheads, the likelihood was that they were going to get shot, and quickly.

Gabe and Petroski had spent the previous two nights reconnoitring 7 Platoon's position, which was a long wheel-base Land Rover parked on slightly higher ground two kilometres away from Petroski's home. They had crawled to within four hundred metres and seen six men, although they did not know how often they were relieved, did not know how many there would be tonight. That Global Armour were committing so many resources to keeping track of Petroski betrayed their desperation: how much they wanted to get hold of him, how much they feared the information he had given us. What Petroski knew could ruin Global Armour. They would not stop until they had him.

From our position, Petroski's house is dead ahead, three kilometres away. The soldiers of 7 Platoon are two kilometres to the left of Petroski's house from where we are lying, making them over four kilometres in distance. Gabe told me that we should be safe, that they wouldn't be looking for us, but that they certainly had night vision and if they saw us, we were probably dead. He had paused, shaken his head. No. We were certainly dead.

Underneath this moon, our clothing and nerves torn by the moaning wind, I feel an unimaginable distance away from home, from lights and sound and civilisation. I feel as if I am trusting in magic out here in the desolate countryside, which might as well have last been walked by ancient spirits, so isolated it seems.

On the way here Gabe had seen a dead fox by the side of the road and he had stopped the car, got out and picked it up. As he put it in the boot he had told me that this was a good omen. Omens, signs, magic: it feels that this is all that I can believe in right now.

I think back to all that has happened, all that I have done and seen over the past weeks. I think of Vick and her children, of the bird in her bedroom, the fire in her house, and the fear she felt in a house she feared possessed by malevolent spirits. Everything I did, I did for the right reasons; I do believe this. Walking away from Maria, sparing her the knowledge that she fell in love with a man who could bring her nothing but fear and violence – I have tried to do good. But if I am honest, out here in the dark it feels hard to know what good is; if something that simple and defined even exists. I am hoping that good will triumph in this cold, flat and indifferent landscape, that it will prevail over the evil I have so recently witnessed. I hope that I am on the side of angels. But the truth is that I no longer know.

I am looking at Petroski's house through a telescopic night sight which Gabe told me came from Israel and cost so much that the British Army didn't supply them to their troops, that he'd had to buy his himself. Through the sight everything looks green and grainy, as if I am watching a show on an antiquated television. Gabe has two and he is watching through his. Petroski has a pair of binoculars that do not look remarkable to me, but when Gabe saw them he whistled. He offered to swap his sight for Petroski's binoculars and Petroski just laughed, said no chance, one eye or not.

'Cold,' I say.

'This the coldest you've done recon?' says Gabe to Petroski.

'Joking, aren't you?' says Petroski. 'Up in those mountains, in Afghanistan, must have been ten under, fifteen.'

'Hear that?' says Gabe to me. 'Stop your whinging.'

'Just saying.'

'Not even raining.'

'Rain's the worst,' says Petroski.

'Yep,' says Gabe. 'Give me snow.'

'Every time.'

'Once lay in a stream for thirty hours,' says Gabe.

'Cold?'

'Glacial.'

This sounds unlikely to me. 'That would have killed you.'

Gabe laughs. 'Damn. Got me.'

'Okay,' says Petroski. There is a slight lightening in the sky the far side of Petroski's house.

'That's a car,' says Gabe.

'Big engine,' says Petroski, although I cannot hear anything except the keening wind.

'Don't look through the sight,' says Gabe.

I put it down and in the distance I can see where the land meets sky, see its black mass. The sky above it is getting brighter and brighter and then a light appears, a long way away but heading towards us.

'Think it's them?' I ask.

337

'Chances are,' says Gabe. 'Not the centre of the world, this place.'

The light gets closer and soon I can hear the car's engine and recognise the light for headlights. Although the land is flat, the headlights occasionally disappear from view as the car is hidden by the brow of a dip in the road, only to reappear seconds later. There is only one car. There cannot be enough people in that car to inconvenience the soldiers of 7 Platoon. The people in that car have no idea what is about to befall them.

The car kills its lights a kilometre away from Petroski's house and I pick up the night sight and look through it. It takes me some seconds to locate the car and then I see it, a boxy shape travelling slowly along the lighter green of the road. It looks like a Range Rover. It comes to within a hundred metres of Petroski's house and stops. Nothing happens for a minute.

Then: 'Movement,' says Gabe. '7 Platoon.'

I swing my night sight left and see the bright white shapes of men moving fast from their position towards Petroski's house. I count four, then another behind them. Five men, with at least one left behind to drive the Land Rover. They are still over a kilometre and a half away. It will take them some minutes to reach Petroski's house. I look back at the Range Rover containing Blake's men. Two doors open and two men get out. They close the doors and walk along the road to Petroski's house.

Watching through the sight, these events seem unreal. What is about to happen cannot be real. These are actual men, Connor Blake's men, yet I have never met them. They have always operated in the shadows. This is the first time I have seen them and they are mere shades, wraiths, mysteries. My heart is beating hard against the cold ground and I feel the guilty thrill of the voyeur, getting my kicks vicariously.

I pan left and see that the men of 7 Platoon have covered a lot of ground and are closing in on Petroski's farmhouse fast. Blake's men are almost there. They walk onto his drive, split up. One goes to a window. The other to the front door. From this distance I cannot see them in detail but the way they are each dangling an arm makes me think that they are holding guns.

The man at the door kicks it open and both men rush in. I can no longer see them so I once again pan left and see that 7 Platoon are only five hundred metres away, less. Blake's men's Range Rover is the other side of the house from them. When they are within two hundred metres they slow and run in a crouch. Closer still, just a hundred metres away and they fan out, two heading for the front of the house, one to the back, one to each side. They approach the house very slowly.

'They'll get to the walls,' says Gabe, 'then wait.'

'Check windows. Give it a couple, then go in hard through the front door,' says Petroski.

'Two'll wait outside. One at the front, one at the back. Mop them up if they try to run.'

'Those two idiots inside,' says Petroski. 'Should have stayed at home.'

The soldiers are doing what Gabe and Petroski described, crouching low against the walls of the house. The two at each side join the two in front of the house. Three of them scrabble along the ground to the front door, one keeps watch. It is open from where it has been kicked in and this causes them to pause for a few seconds, wondering why this picture does not seem quite right. Then they stand up, one on one side of the door, two on the other. Then one by one the three men run in.

There is a long pause during which I hold my breath. It is silent in the house. The two soldiers outside are waiting. I cannot imagine what is happening inside. Terror visited on unwitting men in a confined space. Death appearing out of blackness. It must be pure horror. Then there is a flash in one of the windows and almost instantly the pop of small explosions.

'Pistol,' whispers Gabe.

'What kind?' I say.

'Hell would I know?' says Gabe.

There is another sound, soft, like a two-stroke engine muted by the distance, a Vespa puttering away over the flat expanse.

'Submachine gun,' says Petroski.

'That'll be the end of your boys,' says Gabe.

I see another flash in a window, and another, the sound of the explosions reaching us fractionally later. Then there is silence.

'Uh-oh,' says Petroski. 'Check the car.'

I pan across and see three men getting out of the Range

Rover and heading for the house. I guess the soldiers left behind with the Land Rover must be in radio contact with the soldiers at the house, because almost immediately one of the men at the house peels away and heads in the direction of the three men.

'Why didn't they just leave?' says Petroski.

'They don't have a clue,' says Gabe. 'Not the first idea.'

I can see the soldier approaching Blake's men as they run towards the house, oblivious. The soldier stops, crouching. The men keep running, still unaware. I cannot help but notice that one of them is small, barely larger than a child, and limping heavily. Then they all fall down and that gentle purr reaches us again. The soldier approaches them and goes to each of them, kneels, checks. None of us say anything. I feel nauseous, revolted. What we have just witnessed was so efficient and so effortless that it seems unjust, nothing any spectator can take any satisfaction in. A cruel, cold and entirely one-sided display of overwhelming and murderous force.

'Let's go,' says Petroski.

We crawl away in the opposite direction to Petroski's house. My legs are stiff and I have difficulty making them do what I want. I imagine that Gabe must be finding it even harder. We crawl until we are hidden by the rise of the land and then we stand and walk as fast as we can back in the direction of Gabe's car. We need to move fast. We need to move very fast.

35

GABE'S CAR IS on its side in the middle of the road and I am standing next to it. It is lying lengthways across the road, blocking it completely. It is nearly as tall as I am.

Gabe and Petroski are nowhere to be seen. I can see approaching headlights in the distance. They will be here very soon. There will be one car, a Land Rover, and in it will be the ex-soldiers of 7 Platoon, getting as far away from the scene of the massacre as they can. I cannot see the car but I guess that they are travelling up an incline as I can see the beams of their headlights momentarily search the night sky. I can hear their engine. After what I have just witnessed, I do not want to meet these men. They kill with the contemptuous ease of young gods. The night is still and the moon is baleful. I am scared. I would rather be anywhere else than here, right now. I am in over my head, way over my head.

The wind gusts and dies, then gusts again, making the sound of the approaching car's engine fluctuate so that one moment I think it is nearly upon me, the next it sounds distant again. I do not know how long I have. I stand where I am. I am going nowhere.

Now the car is no more than five hundred metres away. It immediately slows down when they see me. I am picked out in the beams of the Land Rover like I am an actor on stage, the car on its side behind me the backdrop. It keeps approaching slowly and I imagine the soldiers in the vehicle calculating, evaluating, wondering what the chances are of meeting an overturned car on this isolated road, at this time, after what has just happened behind them. They will want to get away. They will want to get past me. They have weapons, they have firepower and manpower to spare. I am alone. They will keep coming, get as close as they dare. I hope that that will be close enough.

They are so near that I can make out the distinctive shape of the Land Rover. I can see the circles of the headlights and when I look away they leave spots in front of my eyes. They cannot get much closer.

There is a flat crack, which is so incredibly loud that I expect it to tear the air open, rend a hole in the sky. Light flares beneath the Land Rover and it jumps into the air, all four tyres leaving the ground. The explosion must have gone off towards the rear of the car because its back wheels lift higher and it comes down on its front bumper, like a bucking horse kicking up its hind legs. The shock wave hits me, heats my skin and blows through my hair like the exhaust of a fighter jet. My ears ring. I take a step back. The back of the Land Rover is on fire. I wonder if anybody inside can still be alive.

*

I do not think I have ever seen Gabe lower than when he was sitting on the floor of his dining room, beating the polished boards in anger and shame and humiliation. Leaving him then I worried that he might never come back, that I would never again see the Gabe I used to know.

But what was done to Maria has lit something inside him, reawakened his sleeping animal. The aura he used to wear when he was in uniform is back. Looking at him over the past twenty-four hours I can imagine the officer who led men into battle, who set an example so impressive that they would follow him anywhere, and willingly. He exudes the air of a man who is motivated and capable and utterly ruthless.

He told me that no officer would deal with IEDs on a day-to-day basis without learning about the threat they carried in detail. He told me that he had lost count of the number he had taken apart, examined their workings, what they contained, how they were triggered. He said that making one was a piece of piss. Look at the sort of people in Afghanistan who laid them – medievalists with an instruction manual. If they could do it, so could he.

Normally, Gabe said, a decent IED would be triggered by a mobile phone from a safe distance. But we did not have the time for this so what he and Petroski laid out on the road was little more than four grenades hidden inside the dead fox that Gabe had collected along the way and a roll of wire, which they unravelled twenty metres off the side of the road and behind a low stone wall. There was only one road in and out of where Petroski lived; nowhere else to go but the sea. We knew they'd be passing. It was just a question of making sure we didn't miss.

Rolling Gabe's car onto its side took all three of us and even then it was not easy. We had to jack it up first, put our shoulders into it. But it was, Gabe and Petroski assured me, a good decoy. The Land Rover would slow, keep approaching, would come to a stop less than thirty metres away. They sited the IED fifty metres away. In the event, they got it exactly right.

Two birds with one stone, Gabe had said. First we get 7 Platoon to do our dirty work for us. Then we take care of 7 Platoon. Leave them with an inoperative vehicle loaded with automatic weapons less than a mile from the scene of a full-blown massacre. See how that reflects on the image of Global Armour: their employees running around the Essex countryside assassinating prominent members of the underworld. Gabe had smiled, laughed. Good luck with that.

Gabe and Petroski are out from behind the wall and at the Land Rover almost before it has properly settled back on its ruined suspension. They have guns in their hands. They get one of the rear doors open and haul out the unconscious or semi-conscious soldiers, pull them to the ground. Petroski points his gun at them while Gabe takes weapons from them. They work quickly and efficiently and at no point do any of the soldiers have a chance to fight back, even if they were in a condition to. I watch them work by the light of the fire burning in the back of the Land Rover.

I have to admit that it is an impressive sight. They have done this before; no movements are wasted and they work in efficient partnership.

The front door of the Land Rover is pushed open and Petroski points his gun at the figure emerging. The man puts his hands up and I see that it is Banyan, the man I saw at the tennis court and at our night at the edge of the cliff. He stands against the side of the Land Rover, does not move.

Gabe finishes taking the weapons from the men on the ground. He walks towards Banyan. When he is nearly to him he lifts his arm up so that it is parallel to the ground. He is holding a gun. His gun is only inches away from Banyan's forehead. I can see Gabe's face and he looks entirely remorseless. He means to shoot this man. He wants to shoot this man. He wants nothing more. This is the man who killed Lance Corporal Creek, the man Gabe felt he should have protected. I know Gabe. Know that he values the principle of revenge. This, shooting Banyan, would in his eyes even the score, deliver justice.

Petroski walks up to Gabe. His face is caught by the fire from the Land Rover. His shiny skin reflects the flames, which throws the ridges of his dreadful scar tissue into sharp relief, ravaged skin and shadow. In the orange flickering glare of the fire he looks like a creature from a lurid B movie: a sickly imagined monster.

Very gently Petroski places his hand in front of the barrel of Gabe's gun. I can see him speaking but I cannot hear what he says. He is speaking softly and I cannot imagine

346

what he is saying but know that the words he chooses will be kind and reasoned. I have rarely met a man so good and generous. He leaves his hand in front of Gabe's gun and eventually Gabe nods and lowers it, takes it away from Banyan's forehead and turns and walks away.

We right Gabe's car, watching for movements from the injured men, and drive away from the destroyed Land Rover and the six ex-soldiers of 7 Platoon. As Gabe drives, Petroski calls it in, speaks to a police officer and tells him that he has heard shooting, gives them his address although he does not tell them his name or that he lives there. They will be there in minutes. They will bring a helicopter. I do not rate 7 Platoon's chances of getting away very highly, experienced soldiers or not. Though what the police will make of the scene when they get there I cannot imagine. Five dead bodies at the hands of men who have never seen or heard of them before, who have no motive or explanation for what just happened. It will take some unravelling.

36

ON THE WAY back to Gabe's we meet a stream of police patrol cars, their blue strobing lights illuminating the edges of fields and branches of trees as they barrel past us. Overhead we hear the drone of a police chopper, see its searchlight probing the ground. We do not say a lot in the car. What we have just seen was too monstrous, too sudden, too final. We caused it and it happened, but none of us imagined it would work out so well, so terribly perfectly. At least five men dead, as a result of my phone call. How are these things even possible?

I do not go inside when we get to Gabe's. It will be dawn soon and I need to get some sleep. The three of us shake hands, almost guiltily, aware that we have been through something this night that we will try never to speak of again. Perhaps Gabe and Petroski feel the same way as I do: that we have done something we believe was right, but have at the same time committed grave wrongs. Then I think of Gabe and his time in the army, the ruthlessness that runs through him like a seam of hard mineral, and I doubt it. He will sleep like a baby.

Back at my place Maria's presence is everywhere so I sleep in my spare room, which is bare and cold. Although I think I won't, I fall asleep before it becomes light.

The first thing I do when I wake is call Maria's mother, who tells me that Maria is well although still disoriented and confused. I tell her to let me know if there is anything I can do, that I am sorry that Maria and I, what we had, had not worked out. I make coffee, then put a call through to Jack on the local paper. I take a drink of coffee as it rings, blink, try to force some energy into my body after three hours' sleep.

'Danny. How you doing?'

'I'm good, Jack. Listen, I owe you a story. Got a pen?'

'Yep.'

'Last night, about ten miles north of Bradwell.'

'The shootings?'

'This is in confidence, right?'

'Lips sealed, hope to die, et cetera.'

'The police will have found the shooters. Look into them. Connections with Global Armour. British mercenaries operating on domestic soil, carrying out executions. Might be a story in it.'

'Sounds like something I could sell. You're sure about this?'

'Very.'

'Can I ask where you got your information from?'

'You can ask, Jack. Won't help you.'

'Fair enough. Thanks for this, Dan.'

'No problem. Just leave me out of the story.'

'Never met you in my life.'

It has been days, weeks even, since I have done any proper work for any of my existing clients – if, that is, any of them still exist. After I have spoken to Jack I get in my car and head to my office. I pick up the post, check messages, see that Aatif is being definitively denied the right to remain in the UK. But before I even have time to sit down there is a knock at my door. I walk out into my entryway and through the glass door I can see Sergeant Hicklin. I do my best to hide my irritation at seeing him, open the door.

'Sergeant.'

'Mr Connell. You look tired.'

'Got a lot of work.'

'Really?' He takes a look about my shabby entrance, the scuffed floor tiles and bare bulb hanging from the water-damaged ceiling. 'Pays well, does it?'

I do not reply to this, stifle a smile at his guileless taunt. 'Want to come in?'

'Brief word. If I may.'

I walk through to my office, shove a hand at the chair in front of my desk as I pass it, sit down behind my desk. Hicklin settles himself, crosses his legs, ankle on knee.

'So,' I say.

'So.' Hicklin nods slowly, as if collecting his thoughts, remembering why he is here and what he wants. 'You hear about the shootings?'

'Shootings?'

'Right. Five men dead. All connected, in some way, to the Blakes.'

'Really.' I try to sound interested, surprised, remind myself that Connor Blake is my client and that this is relevant to me. 'That's something.'

'Something,' Hicklin repeats to himself. 'Yes, I suppose it is. It really is something.'

'Does it, however,' I say, 'affect my client in any way?'

'I suspect he will have known them.'

'What do you want me to do? Go visit him, rub his back, tell him I'm sorry about his friends?'

'No, Mr Connell. No. You misunderstand me. I want to know what you know about it.'

'About...?'

'You suddenly begin representing Connor Blake. Your girlfriend is attacked, put into a coma. And less than forty-eight hours later, five of Blake's men are found full of bullets. Doesn't sound odd to you?'

'Sounds circumstantial,' I say.

Hicklin nods. 'Your friend, Mr McBride. He was in the army. You know we arrested soldiers nearby?'

'Sounds like you've got a mess on your hands.'

'You know, Mr Connell, I'm beginning to revise my opinion about you.'

'Oh?'

'That layer of arsehole. It's a lot thicker than I thought.'

I do not want to make an enemy of Sergeant Hicklin. He

is the only ally I have on the force, the only policeman I can trust. I hold up my hands, show him my palms.

'Sergeant, I'm sorry, but I don't know what you're getting at. As far as I am aware, Connor Blake had nothing to do with what happened to Maria. I am still representing him. What happened last night has nothing to do with me. Purely coincidental.'

Hicklin nods, stands up. 'How is she, anyway? Your girl-friend.'

'She's awake. No permanent damage. And Sergeant? She's not my girlfriend.'

At Ryan's funeral I stand at the back and do not intro-duce myself to anybody, arrive late so that Vick does not see me. The funeral is held in a church built of local flint and the turnout is sparse. There are perhaps forty people in the church, which is small and gloomy. Ryan took his own life and I wonder if that is why so few people have turned up, reluctant to pay their respects to a man who committed an act against God. The minister speaks about Ryan's time in the army and his new career as a prison warden. He skirts the subject of his suicide, fudges the issue of whether or not he is bound for hell, says simply that he hopes that wherever Ryan is now, he is at peace. I sense that the minister does not hold out a great deal of hope for this scenario.

I can see Vick on the front pew and her children Ollie and Gwynn are next to her, with Ms Armstrong the social worker sitting the other side of them. I guess that she is the responsible adult assigned to accompany the children from where, I know, they are still being held in care. Ms Armstrong wears her usual African headdress, although today it is a sombre navy blue with a lighter blue pattern on it. I wonder how terrible it must be for Vick to be sitting before the coffin of the man she loved, sitting next to her children she is not allowed to look after. Connor Blake has torn a ruinous path through all of our lives in the last few weeks.

As I stand at the back listening to the minister, I console myself with the thought that I have now taken a measure of vengeance. Although – and I acknowledge that I should not be having these thoughts in a place of God – nowhere near enough.

I arrive at Vick's after the last guests have left her house, after her children have been taken back to the care home. When I get there she is clearing up paper cups and plates, wrapping up uneaten food, still wearing her dark skirt and jacket. She looks tired but when she sees that it is me she smiles and flattens her hair, asks me to come inside.

'I saw you at the funeral,' she says.

'Yeah. Showed my face.'

'Thank you, Daniel.'

'I saw Ollie and Gwynn. What's the situation?'

'The situation.' She sighs, nods me into the living room. 'Let's sit down.'

I walk through and sit in an armchair. Vick sits in the sofa facing me, her coffee table between us.

'The situation, Dan, is that it's still a mystery. Ollie and Gwynn, they say I never touched them. Ms Armstrong, I think she believes us. But still, we don't know what happened.'

'I know,' I say.

For a moment Vick does not react, as if she has not heard what I said. Then she looks at me slowly, says, 'You know?'

'I know everything,' I say. 'Time you did too.'

With Connor Blake's people taken care of and his father disowning him, lifting any protection, I cannot see how much of a threat he can now pose to Vick or her children. I tell her about Connor Blake, what he did to Karl Reece, tell her that he was held in the same prison that Ryan had worked in. I tell her how he had got to Ryan, had got his people to move Vick's furniture, hurt her children, terrorise them to ensure Ryan's compliance. How Connor Blake had placed Ryan in a situation so dreadful, so impossible to navigate out of, that he had taken his own life to spare hers and their children's.

'How do you know?' said Vick. 'How do you know all this?'

'Soon as he didn't have Ryan any more, he needed somebody else. Somebody else to blackmail, to get him out of prison by any means necessary. Me.'

As I tell Vick about what Connor Blake did to me, about the photographs and the drugs and the attack on Maria, she looks at me in horror and utter dismay. I go through it as quickly as I can and I can see her trying to keep up, trying to make sense of what I am telling her. But perhaps these events can never make complete sense, caused as they were by a man whose morality is so at odds with society's that he might as well come from another planet.

'Oh Dan. Oh Dan, I'm so sorry.'

'Not your fault,' I say.

'If I hadn't come to you...'

'You couldn't have known. How could we have known?'

'She be okay? Maria?'

'Think so. Hope so.'

Vick is quiet for a moment, her legs tucked underneath her on the sofa, thinking about what I have told her.

'Ryan... I thought...'

'He was a good man,' I say. 'He did his best for you, for the kids.'

Vick nods, puts her hands together and bends her head in an attitude of prayer. I do not say anything and when she lifts her head there are tears on her cheeks.

'So... I can tell Ms Armstrong this? Tell her this is what happened?'

'You can tell her,' I say. 'But we don't have any proof. To her it's just a story.'

'Will you come with me?'

'Yes. I'll come. But Vick, understand, we don't have any evidence.'

'No.' Vick is quiet again, running everything that I have told her through her mind, grappling with it. She looks at me. 'This man. Connor Blake. What's going to happen to him? He can't get away with it. Can he? He... He killed

Ryan. And what he did to my children...' Her voice rises as she recounts what Blake has done, how he has destroyed her family.

I hold out my hands, pat the air to calm her down. 'Don't worry,' I say. 'You don't need to worry. I'll take care of Blake.'

37

THAT BLAKE IS in prison has always been the problem. Inside he is safe, untouchable. I cannot get at him. He can taunt me, threaten me, cause harm to the people I love, and I can do nothing but sit opposite him and look into his smug, triumphant eyes. Outside he would not last a minute alone with me. But there he is, locked up under constant scrutiny from the guards.

I have arranged a meeting, told him that I have what he wants and that it is time to call a stop to this thing, get it done. I am going to see him in prison one last time. There will not be a next time, I know this. One way or another.

I pass through the security procedures of Galley Wood and I remember my feeling of near panic when I was here with cocaine hidden in my mouth. They do not X-ray my briefcase and for that I am grateful. I cannot wait to see Blake, feel the pulse-hurrying apprehension I do when warming up before a match. I feel good. Confident. I am looking forward to this, know that I am going in the strong favourite, the form man. For the first time since I met Blake, I can back myself.

The white-haired guard lets me into our meeting room and I sit alone for two or three minutes while he goes to fetch Blake. I look around the room. This is the fourth time that I have been here. I will not miss it, its drab brick and metal furniture and air of gathering oppression as if the steel doors are only just holding back the misery and hatred of the hundreds of inmates beyond. I open my briefcase. I want to be ready.

The door opens and Blake is led in, the guard holding him by the inside of the elbow. Blake is in cuffs and his eye that was black is now green and brown, and he has none of the insolent assurance of the last time that we met.

'You can take the cuffs off,' I say.

Blake looks at me, down at his wrists, off balance. 'You what?'

'Just get them off,' I say.

'Sure?' says the guard.

'Yes.'

He shrugs and unlocks the cuffs, unsnaps them, hooks them to his belt. 'You need me, bang on the door.'

'Thanks.'

'And you,' he says, pointing at Blake, 'you behave yourself.'

The guard leaves, closes the door behind him. It is just me and Blake.

I point to his chair. 'Sit.'

'Don't tell me what to do,' he says. 'D'you think you are?'

'Just sit down,' I say.

He looks tired and unsure, and he clearly knows about Magnus. I imagine that Liam was also among the number out at Petroski's. He cannot be feeling as secure as usual.

'Heard about your friends,' I say. 'Shame.'

'What d'you know about it?'

I shrug but I cannot keep the delight out of my eyes. 'Poor Magnus.'

'You want to watch what you say.'

'Oh?'

'What we did to your girlfriend, that's just the start. A taster.'

Blake's words have never sounded so empty. His attempt at bravado is as convincing as a drunk challenging a doorman.

'I've got the address,' I say, offhand. 'The name of your witness.'

Blake sits forward. His eyes widen. 'You got it?'

'Wasn't easy.'

'But you got it?'

'I got it.'

Blake nods rapidly. 'Go on then.'

'Question is, what're you going to do with it?'

'Fuck's it to you? Just give it to me.'

'Liam, Magnus, your crew – they're all dead. There's nobody left.'

Blake smiles and for the first time this visit he shows that smug self-confidence, exudes the air of the forever enti- tled. 'Nobody left? Fucking please, Daniel. My father, he's... You think there are limits? There aren't any limits.'

'Yes,' I say. 'Your dad. Met him the other night. Had an interesting conversation.'

'He wouldn't even notice you,' says Blake. 'He'd make you disappear' – he snaps his fingers – 'like that. Gone.'

'He told me you were dead to him. Told me he didn't have a son, said you were sick, doesn't want a bar of you.'

'Bollocks.' Blake is smiling and looks entirely confident, at ease.

'True,' I say. 'When'd you last speak to him?'

'We don't,' he says. 'In here. He's a businessman, keeps clear of all this. Doesn't get involved.'

'How does it feel?' I say. 'To be alone?'

'I ain't alone.'

'All alone. There's nobody left. In fact,' I say, taking some papers out of my briefcase, 'I'm all you've got.'

'You want to stop right there,' says Blake. 'Don't make an enemy of me.'

'Too late for that,' I say. I take a pen out of the inside pocket of my jacket, pass it to Blake.

'What's this?' he says.

'I'm giving you a choice,' I say. 'Sign here: release me as your lawyer. Just give me your signature.'

Blake looks at me as if I have told a joke that he cannot quite understand, is trying to puzzle it out. 'What?'

'Sign here and we're done.'

'You said a choice.'

'I did. If you don't sign, I'll beat you to a fucking pulp, right here. It's a choice. Your choice.'

'Please,' says Blake. 'Here? You're in prison, keep telling

you. Ain't nothing you can do. Nothing nothing nothing. You must be fucking stupid.'

I shrug, give the pen on the table between us an encouraging nudge. 'Your choice.'

'You know, Magnus told me she was like a fucking wildcat. Said she struggled so much it was like holding down an animal, scratching, spitting.' Blake leans forward, puts his elbows on the table, rubs his hand over his mouth. 'He never did get the chance to cut her. Can't tell you how much he was looking forward to it.'

'Last chance.'

'Give me that address.'

'Not going to happen. In a million years.'

'I'll see to it. You won't recognise her, won't believe it used to be a person.'

I reach back into my briefcase. In the lining I have hidden a weapon, what I have heard they call in prison a shiv. I made it the night before by embedding a razor blade into the handle of a toothbrush. I melted the plastic over my stove and stuck the blade in, let it harden around it. I hid the weapon in the lining at the back of my briefcase, taped it to the bottom with the blade next to the hinges. I had not known if it would pass an X-ray but in the event it had not mattered.

'Fuck is that?'

Blake has not shown any remorse. He has taken only pleasure in what was done to Maria, to Vick, Ryan, their children. I gave him his choice but he did not take it and now it is my turn.

I hold the handle and I cut a line into my cheek, from below my eye down to my mouth. It does not hurt, only feels a little cold.

'You like to look inside people, isn't that right?' I say to Blake. 'Like to cut them. Like this?' I can feel warmth on my face now. I am bleeding. I did not cut very deeply but the blade was sharp. Blake's mouth is slightly open and he appears transfixed by my wound.

'I've heard of the things you've done,' I say. 'The people you've hurt. Here.' I toss the shiv onto the table. He had not picked up the pen. I wondered what he would do with this. 'Want a try?'

Without a second's hesitation Blake picks up the weapon, looks at the blade, which is slightly discoloured by blood.

'You do. You really do, you sick little nightmare.'

I can see Blake's hand tighten on the blade's handle and I think of all the people he has hurt, the people he has frightened and bullied and mutilated and killed. I think of Maria in hospital and everything that we could have had together, the future we might have shared had it not been ruined by this smug and entitled monstrosity.

Blake stands up with the blade in his hand and that is enough for me. I come around the table and hold his wrist with one hand, put my other hand over his mouth. I can only see his eyes but they look surprised, astonished. I wonder if he has ever had to fight for his life before or whether he has always had people to do it for him. I force him back against the wall. The back of his head makes a sharp impact on the bricks and his eyes close in pain.

'For all of the people you've hurt,' I say. I take my hand away from his mouth and punch him in the cheek and this time his head bounces off the brick and his knees give. I step back and punch him in the temple, hard, and he goes down on the ground. He is still holding the blade. I kneel down next to him and peel his fingers off the handle, take it off him. I hold it to his face, up to his eye, press it just underneath, press a little harder.

'How many times have you done this to somebody?' I say. 'How many?'

Blake does not say anything but I can hear his breathing. It is fast and uneven.

'Shall I?' I say, and press the blade still harder. It is touching the bottom of his eyeball and he blinks quickly but he dare not shake his head.

'You would,' I say. 'You have done. Tell me why I shouldn't?'

Since my very first encounter with Connor Blake I have never seen him anything but composed, never seen anything in his eyes but assurance and disdain. Now I can see fear. He does not know what is happening, how this has occurred; he has no idea what I am going to do or what I am capable of. He is alone and vulnerable and I suspect that it is a feeling he has never experienced before. This is all I wanted. Just this. To make him understand what it is like, what he has made other people feel so often. Just fear, nothing more.

'Please,' he says.

That is enough for me. I stand up and walk to the door and bang on it, hard and fast, a reasonable impression of a frenzied panic. The white-haired guard opens up in a hurry and he sees my face dripping with blood and he rushes in, calls out for help. Blake is still on the floor. The guard looks at me in confusion.

'He came at me with a knife,' I say. 'Didn't have a choice.'

I stand by the door as one, two, and finally a third guard arrive in the room. They must be nearly as sick of Connor Blake's odious presence as I am. Certainly the way they subdue him is at the very end of the reasonable force spectrum. The first thing that the white-haired guard does is stamp on Blake's nose as he lies on the ground. There is a wet crunch like tearing lettuce and I imagine that those good looks of his might just have been ruined forever.

I watch for a while, back against the wall and arms folded, take it all in, enjoy the spectacle. Then one of the guards remembers who I am, realises that I should not be witnessing this, any of this. But as he walks me out I tell him not to worry, tell him that it's okay, really, I understand. Tell him the bastard had it coming.

38

THE OLDER GUY is disputing yet another call and I am losing patience; he is hitting the ball too hard and it is going long, but he questions every time we call it out. We are deep into the third set and still I do not know which way it is going to go. It may only be club tennis but this match has as much needle as a Tour final.

'Want your eyes testing,' he says.

'Need to practise your ground strokes,' I say. 'Learn where the baseline is.'

'Wanker,' the man says, but he turns as he says it so that it is not to my face, an act that marks him out as a coward in my book.

I am at the net and Gabe is serving. I turn around and wink at him. He grins back, bounces the ball at his feet. The older guy is at the net, his partner receiving serve, a rangy thirty-year-old with a truly sublime service action.

Gabe tosses up the ball and hits his serve. Because of his leg he cannot get the leap he used to and relies on putting action on his serve to keep us in the point. He is serving into the backhand court and hits a top spin that jumps up and to the right on impact, pulling the rangy guy out wide. But he is tall and fast and he wraps his backhand around it, pulls it cross-court too wide for me to intercept and too wide for Gabe to chase down. In truth it is a punishing and unreturnable shot. There is nothing to do but watch it land in the tramlines halfway up the court.

'Shot,' says Gabe.

'Have some of it,' says the older guy, an entirely unnecessary comment, which causes Gabe to stop in his walk to the other side of the court, stand and dead-eye him.

Gabe is now serving to the older guy and we are thirty–forty down, facing break point to go three–five down in the final set. This serve matters. I hope that Gabe does not lose his composure, let the older guy's taunts go to his head.

He bounces the ball, tosses it up and mistimes the contact point and the ball slaps the net cord and falls back into court our side. He turns, walks to the back of the court, talks to himself.

I walk back to him. 'Don't worry. Just get it over and in. Don't give him the satisfaction.'

I walk back to the net. Gabe bounces the ball again, throws it higher. He arches his back and I can tell that he is not playing safe, second serve or not – he is putting everything into this one. He brings his racket back behind his shoulders then whips it through, makes sound contact and the ball hits the T-line in the centre of the court dead on, the action he puts on it taking it away from the older guy, who in any case hasn't moved, is just watching as the ball blurs past.

He points at the spot the ball landed as if to question whether it was in but his partner shakes his head. It was probably the serve of the day. To challenge it would be a crime.

'Deuce,' says Gabe.

I turn around. 'We've got this one,' I tell him.

Gabe is playing better than I have seen in weeks, months; possibly the best he has played since he lost his leg. I suspect that he is still on a high after what happened with 7 Platoon. He has proved himself against the best that the British Army can throw his way and he has come out emphatically on top.

The ex-soldiers of 7 Platoon who were found near Petroski's house that night were picked up, charged with murder and are now awaiting trial. There will be no issue of witness intimidation for them: they were found with the murder weapons, their fingerprints all over them. They are going down, and for a long time.

But of course this was never Gabe's primary mission. He was always after justice for what they did to Lance Corporal Creek, the killing that Gabe believes he had the power to stop yet did not, the killing for which he feels culpable. But Petroski's affidavit has been enough to reopen the inquest into his death and this, along with the more recent killings involving the ex-members of 7 Platoon, should be enough. Justice, Gabe is certain, will be served.

Perhaps it is too much to expect happy endings to any story. Major Strauss had managed to keep his distance from the actions of 7 Platoon. As far as Gabe knew, he was in the clear, untouched by what happened at Petroski's house. But the story of Global Armour had broken in the nationals and as an organisation they were dead in the water: nobody would use them, their reputation ruined, chances of winning any kind of contract blown irrevocably. Strauss may have got away with it, but he was left with nothing.

Gabe serves out our game and we are four–all in the final set. It is the rangy guy's serve and so far in this match we have not broken him. His serve is too consistent, too well directed, and about twenty miles an hour too fast.

Gabe stays at the net when he is not serving and it is up to me to return. The rangy guy's first serve is an ace down the middle, the second into the body and onto me so quickly that I do not have time to make room and hit a shot, take it directly in front of me and can only fend it into the net. But I guess right for the next serve, make room and hit a forehand down the line, lace it down the tramlines and the older guy at the net can only watch it pass. I have a look at a second serve for the next point and return it fast cross-court. We rally three, four shots and then I hit a forehand with both feet off the ground, which comes off my racket sweet and hard, bouncing inches from the baseline and is good, far too good to be returned.

Thirty all and we are in with a shout. I push the next serve up the middle of the court and the older guy intercepts, hits it straight at Gabe who can only get his racket in the way of it. He gets lucky as it loops over the volleyer's head and into open court, bounces twice before the rangy guy can chase it down.

We win the game on the next point. I get hold of the rangy guy's serve and cream a return right at the older guy at the net, bad etiquette though it may be. It hits him in the gut and he goes down on one knee. I hold my racket up, apologise with a scandalous lack of sincerity. He just looks at me, shakes his head in disgust. Gabe has to turn away from the net so that our opponents do not see him laugh. There are moments in life that feel so good that we never want them to end.

We change ends and I stop at the net, take a drink. It is up to me to serve for the match and the pressure is on. But I feel as confident as I did before visiting Blake; I still have a lot of aggression left to unleash.

Connor Blake's brief reign of terror came to an official end yesterday when Vick and I met with Ms Armstrong and laid out what had been happening, the real explanation for what had been done to Vick's children. She had heard us out, told us to wait in her office, and left for thirty, forty minutes. When she had eventually come back she had asked us to follow her and we had been shown into the same room where Vick had met her children that first time after they were taken from her. Ms Armstrong had again left us but this time for only minutes, coming back with Ollie and Gwynn with her. She told Vick that she had sorted out the paperwork, that she was free to take her children home and that she was sorry, so very sorry, for all that she had been made to go through.

Outside we embraced and I watched them leave, the children chattering happily and Ollie constantly questioning whether they were really going home, really, for good, did she promise? Vick nodded, wiped away a tear, told him she promised, she really did. She turned and smiled at me and whispered, *Thank you*. And that was the last I saw of her.

For Connor Blake, things did not turn out so happily. A week ago, while he was on kitchen duty in prison, another inmate approached him with a pan of boiling water and threw it in his face. The inmate had poured sugar into the water, mixed it in so that the simmering liquid stuck to Blake's skin and continued to burn for some minutes. This I heard on the Essex grapevine; stories this lurid travel fast.

I do not want to believe that a father would order such an act to be carried out on his own son; do not want to believe that monsters like that can live among us. But I have looked into Alex Blake's eyes and, if I am honest with myself, it would not surprise me.

Connor Blake now has a face that people would rather not look at; would wish they could forget once they had. I remember his brilliant blue eyes, his strong jaw, those features so regular they seemed bequeathed by God. But perhaps the face he has now better suits the cruel and worthless soul that always lay beneath those astonishing looks. I can feel no pity for what has happened to him.

My serve is not as elegant as the rangy guy's but it has more bulk behind it and a great deal more residual anger, both recent and seeded in my distant history. I hit an ace with my first serve; my second is out wide and Gabe easily puts away the volley from the indifferent return. At thirty-love up I hit a serve so vicious that the older guy does not have time to play a shot, can only fend it away and out of play. I am feeling so loose and relaxed that match point feels like a formality. I bounce the ball, toss it up and hit it out wide. The rangy guy can only get a rim on it and that is it. We have won.

I feel the usual split-second of unreality, the ping of doubt – did I do that? Then we are shaking hands at the net and Gabe has his arm over my shoulder and there is nothing to do but walk off the court and buy our opponents a beer, if they still have the stomach for one. As we walk back to the clubhouse, George and five other members who have been watching applaud us and I feel as elated and heroic as if I had just won Roland Garros.

Before I met Maria I had lived on my own for years, but the months I spent with her have broken the habit. Now it is evening and I have nothing to do, nobody to speak with, share what has happened, seek reassurance that what I have done over the past weeks has been, on the whole, good and right. I turn on the TV but turn it back off after a couple of minutes, bored with its banality. The truth is that, outside of the tennis court, I can see little point in this life I have. I go to my kitchen and eye a bottle of wine, which will, at least, take the edge off these thoughts. But even as I open it I know that this is not the answer. I have no idea what the answer is, would not know where to begin.

I pour a glass but before I can drink I hear my doorbell ring. I walk to it and open it. Standing on my porch is Maria. She looks pale but still beautiful, and very, very angry.

'Maria.'

'So you know who I am?'

'Of course.'

'You, Daniel Connell, are some kind of bastard. You know that?'

She is trembling but it is not as cold as it has been today and I can only think that it is rage that is making her shake. She points a finger at me, jabs it into my chest, hard.

'Think I would never remember? You coward. Getting rid of me like that, just, you...' She shakes her head, runs out of words, awed by what she believes is my cynicism.

'Maria, it's not, it's nothing like that. It wasn't.'

'No? Spare me, Daniel.'

'Maria...'

But I stop because Maria is now crying, tears rolling down her cheeks although her face has lost none of its fury.

'Please, Maria. Please, come in, let me explain.'

'Explain what? I was in hospital and I needed you and you just, you just walked away, Daniel. You lied to me and you abandoned me.'

'I had to.'

'Please.'

'Maria, please come in. Please, come inside.'

Maria pulls her hands down her face, clears her tears. She passes me, walks into my house that once felt as much hers as mine. I head into the kitchen and she follows me.

'Sit down. I need to tell you everything. Everything that happened.'

'Not a little late?'

'Hear me out. Just, please. Hear me out.'

Maria sits down at my table, looks up at me. I take a breath, wonder where to start. Wonder how I can make sense of this for her, for us. I think back to the moment Vick walked into my office in tears, her sodden handkerchief, her unimaginable grief and confusion.

'This,' Maria says, 'had better be good.'

ACKNOWLEDGEMENTS

My thanks as ever go to my agent Tina and my tough-yet-fair editor, Sara. Thanks also to Maddie, Louise, Anna and everybody at Corvus for their support. Special mentions to Anthony Connell for his expert legal advice, and MH for his inside knowledge on the murky world of private security. The book could not have been written without you.